Angel's Flight

A MERCY ALLCUTT MYSTERY

ANGEL'S FLIGHT

ALICE DUNCAN

FIVE STAR
A part of Gale, Cengage Learning
MYSTERY

GALE
CENGAGE Learning

Detroit • New York • Sa͏ ͏le, Maine • London

GALE
CENGAGE Learning

Set in 11 pt. Plantin.
Printed on permanent paper.

LIBRARY OF CONGRESS CATALOGING-IN-PUBLICATION DATA

Duncan, Alice, 1945–
    Angel's flight : a Mercy Allcutt mystery / Alice Duncan. — 1st ed.
        p. cm.
    ISBN-13: 978-1-59414-783-8 (alk. paper)
    ISBN-10: 1-59414-783-3 (alk. paper)
    1. Secretaries—Fiction. 2. Murder—Investigation—Fiction. 3. Private investigators—California—Los Angeles—Fiction. 4. Los Angeles (Calif.)—Fiction. 5. Large type books. I. Title.
PS3554.U463394A54 2009
813'.6—dc22   2009010520

First Edition. First Printing: July 2009.
Published in 2009 in conjunction with Tekno Books and Ed Gorman.

Printed in the United States of America
1 2 3 4 5 6 7 13 12 11 10 09

For Anni and Robin, the best
daughters any mother ever had.

Thanks ever so much to Alice Gaines, who gave me the
perfect reason for the murder!

CHAPTER ONE

When I opened my sister Chloe's front door that fine Monday morning in August, I was looking forward to the start of another interesting workweek. I'd only had my job for a little over a month, and I absolutely loved it.

My name is Mercedes Louise Allcutt, and I am the first female person in my entire family who has ever dared step forth into the world and obtain a real job of real work. That probably doesn't sound like a big deal to lots of people, but, believe me, I'd struggled mightily and bucked not only family tradition, but stern denunciation from my mother and father and assorted aunts, uncles and cousins to become part of the worker proletariat. I'd done it because I needed to gain experience in order to write the novels I had burning within my bosom, but which had been stifled for the entire twenty-one years of my life. Trust me, you can't write significant novels when you're trapped in an ivory tower.

Very well, I know most people would probably love to trade places with me. *I* wanted experience.

That, however, is off the subject. On that particular Monday morning, I was eagerly anticipating a brisk walk of two blocks from Chloe's house on Bunker Hill in Los Angeles to the tiny, almost vertical railroad called Angel's Flight that would take me from the land of milk and honey (Chloe's neighborhood) to the so-called "real" world, where my job lay. I put the word *real* in quotation marks because we're talking about Los Angeles here, where the economy is based on fantasy. My job, however, was very real.

I worked for Mr. Ernest Templeton, P.I. In case you don't know what the initials P.I. stand for (I didn't until Ernie told me), they stand for private investigator. I was his assistant.

Oh, all right, that's an exaggeration. Actually, I was his secretary, but I aspired to the position of P.I.'s assistant, and I was learning fast and trying my very best to become completely indispensable to Ernie. At that point in time, if you were to ask Ernie, I hadn't done it yet. Nevertheless, I kept trying.

My plans suffered an almost paralyzing, not to say catastrophic, check when, flinging the door open (quite a feat, since it was a very solid, very heavy, carved oak door), I came face to face with my own personal mother. My mother, who was supposed to be in Boston, queening it over her exalted social set. My mother, who considered it her duty to squelch any hint of individuality in any of her children. My mother, who scared the socks off me.

"Mother!" shrieked I, horrified.

"Mercedes Louise Allcutt, you cut your hair!" said she, similarly afflicted.

Staggering backward across Chloe's gorgeously tiled front entryway, I patted the bobbed hair peeking out from under my tasteful hat almost hysterically. My *mother!* Could anything be worse than this?

The answer to that question is a resounding *no*. Well, unless you're talking about death or dismemberment. Mrs. Albert Monteith Allcutt, affectionately known to her friends as Honoria, and to her two daughters as The Wrath of God, was the absolutely last person on the face of the earth whom I wanted to see at that moment in time, unless you count a couple of loathsome murderers I'd encountered in the past few weeks.

The commotion brought Chloe to the front door, holding my

adorable French poodle puppy Buttercup, so named because she was sort of an apricot color. She was being held by Chloe in order to prevent her from following me to work. Chloe isn't an early riser as a rule, but that morning she'd staggered out of bed a few minutes before I was to leave the house in order to get ready for a doctor's appointment. She hadn't said anything to me yet, but I suspected my sister and her husband Harvey Nash, who did something important in the motion pictures although I'm not sure what, were going to have a baby. I was terribly excited about it. I think Chloe was, too, although she tried not to show it. I guess it was fashionable to affect an attitude of ennui about things like that.

When Mother saw Chloe, her attention veered to her. It's cowardly, I know, but I was glad of it. Mother is an extremely formidable woman, and she frightens me positively to death.

"Clovilla Allcutt Nash, what are you doing dressed in that scandalous outfit?" Mother cried, perhaps even more aghast at Chloe's pretty-but-short, silk Chinese breakfast coat than my pretty-but-now-short hair. Mother is the only person in the universe who calls Chloe Clovilla, which is her real name, but who'd want it? Certainly not Chloe, and I didn't blame her. I didn't like my own name a whole lot, but at least it wasn't Clovilla. "And what is that animal in your arms? Is that a *dog?*" She said the word "dog" as if it smelled bad. Buttercup, a very sensitive pooch, hid her nose in Chloe's armpit. Smart dog.

Since Mother's attention had swerved away from me, I did something utterly despicable, and that I will probably regret for the rest of my days. I sneaked past my mother and got ready to bolt. Poor Chloe, who had been kindness itself in allowing me to move in with her and Harvey when I left Boston, didn't deserve my desertion. But I was honestly rattled.

Mother heaved an exasperated sigh and said, "Well, don't just *stand* there Clovilla and Mercedes Louise. Surely you have a servant who can carry in my bags and pay the cab."

Chloe said, "Uh . . ."

And I, coward that I am, said, "I have to get to my job!" And I scrammed out of there as if I'd been shot from a gun, practically running down the long walkway from Chloe's massive front door to the black wrought-iron gate surrounding her and Harvey's property atop Bunker Hill.

Chloe called after me, *"Mercy!"* I know she wanted to call me another name or two, but didn't dare, what with Mother standing right there and all.

Mother bellowed, "Your *job?*" You'd have thought I'd just told her I was going to strip naked and dance down Beacon Hill in tap shoes, waving pom-poms.

Once I got out the gate, I tottered the two blocks to Angel's Flight in something of a blind panic, paid the engineer my nickel, and shook in my sensible shoes all the way to Broadway, from whence I walked to my place of employment, the Figueroa Building, on Seventh and Hill. Even in my agitated state, I was pleased to see that the old building looked much spiffier than it had when I'd first become employed there. The brass plaque declaring its name had been polished until it shone, and Mr. Emerald Buck, the new custodian who had been hired after the old one turned out to be . . . um . . . unsuitable kept the sidewalk swept and the lobby spic and span.

My shocking experience must have still showed on my face, because when I entered the building, Lulu LaBelle, the receptionist at the Figueroa Building, a job she intended to keep only until she was discovered by a motion-picture magnate and became a movie star, looked up from the blood-red fingernails she'd been filing and said, " 'Lo, Mercy. What's wrong?"

"N-nothing," I said, lying through my teeth and heading to the elevator, a self-serve number without a permanent operator.

My *mother* had come to Los Angeles. My *mother*. And Chloe's mother, too, although that notion didn't bother me as much as knowing that, as much as Mother would deplore Chloe's wardrobe and shingled hair, still more would she disapprove of me, her younger daughter and the only child in the family who had ever dared to question her authority.

With shaking fingers, I unlocked the door to my office workplace and stepped inside. I paused in the doorway, gazing around, telling myself that having a job was nothing to be ashamed of. In fact, it was something I ought to be proud of. I'd taken typewriting and shorthand classes (Pitman method) at the Boston Young Women's Christian Association, and was a whiz at both. *I* wasn't a shameless leech on society. *I* didn't use my privileged birth and position in society to grind widows and orphans under my boot heels. Never mind that I didn't wear boots. *I* was a member of the working class, as of a month ago last Thursday, and I was proud of myself.

So why, when I sank into my chair and removed my little brown hat and placed it in my drawer along with my little brown handbag, did my heart feel as if a funeral procession was rumbling through it, playing a dismal dirge?

My *mother!* Good God, what next?

As if answering my unspoken question, the telephone at my elbow jangled. I eyed it warily, suspecting who was at the other end of the wire. Taking a deep breath and bracing myself, I unhooked the receiver from the candlestick and spoke firmly, "Mr. Templeton's office. Miss Allcutt speaking."

"Traitor!"

It was as I'd feared. The voice that had spat the word was my sister Chloe's, tense and low, probably because Chloe was trying to hide from our mother.

"You ran out on me!"

I shut my eyes, feeling guiltier even than I had when I'd de-

13

fied our parents and moved west. "I'm sorry, Chloe. It was a cowardly thing to do."

"It sure was. Darn it, Mercy, what am I supposed to do now?"

Not having a clue, I said, "Um . . . find her a bedroom?" Something occurred to me. "Did she say why she's visiting? And why she didn't warn us?"

There was a pause at the other end of the wire. I got the impression Chloe was glancing around to make sure Mother wasn't near enough to overhear what she aimed to tell me. Then she said, "Oh, Mercy, it's awful. She's left Father!"

I felt my eyes widen. "She did *what?*" I couldn't recall another time when our mother had left our father behind when she traveled, except during the summer when she went to Cape Cod and Father only visited on weekends.

"Don't screech at me."

"Sorry."

"She left Father."

"Without telling him about it?"

"Of *course* she didn't tell him!"

I shook my head, trying to understand. "Well then, why didn't she tell you she was going to visit?"

"She didn't leave him *that* way," Chloe whispered harshly. "I mean, she *left* him. As in separation. Divorce. That sort of thing."

I'm pretty sure my mouth fell open. I'm surprised I didn't drop the telephone receiver. I couldn't believe it. People in my family didn't leave other people in my family. It wasn't done. It had never been done before that I knew of. And . . . Mother? Leaving Father? It wasn't possible. Managing to get my jaw working again, I stammered, "Um . . . I think you must have misunderstood her, Chloe. She couldn't have done anything so outrageous."

"You tell her that," said Chloe bitterly. "I tried, and she didn't buy it."

"Good heavens."

"You might say that."

"Where is she now?"

"Mrs. Biddle is showing her to the Green Room."

"Ah." Mrs. Biddle was Chloe and Harvey's housekeeper, and the Green Room in their house was the one reserved for royalty—or movie stars, which was as close to royalty as anything got in Los Angeles, except for when an exiled Russian grand duke paid a call a year or so ago. I wasn't in Los Angeles then, so I didn't get to meet him. Anyhow, it made sense that Mother would be deposited in the Green Room. "Um . . . did she say why she left Father?" I still believed Chloe must have been mistaken about that part. Perhaps she missed the end of the sentence, the one that mentioned she'd left him to go on a little holiday to visit her daughters in California or something.

"Evidently she discovered he was having an affair."

This time my mouth fell open so far, my chin almost hit my desk. So much for my pleasant-little-holiday theory. "He was *what?*" I regret to say I screeched again.

"Ow. Stop doing that."

"Sorry." My mind reeled. My head whirled. My stomach cramped. My thoughts scattered like so much chaff in the wind. "But . . . but . . ."

"That's what she told me."

"With whom?"

"What do you mean, 'with whom'? Do you mean who did he have the affair with?"

I liked my grammatical construction better than Chloe's, but I didn't believe it was the time or place to call her on it. "Yes."

"His secretary."

His secretary. A woman in a position much as mine. "I . . . I can't take it in." And my incredulity wasn't entirely due to the fact that no son or daughter relishes discovering his or her

15

father has feet of clay, either. I couldn't wrap my brain around the notion that some young woman, perhaps as young as I, was actually . . .

Ew. I decided not to think about it.

"I can't either, but I don't have a job to run away to." Again, Chloe sounded rather bitter. I could hardly fault her. I was even gladder than I'd already been that I had my job.

"True. Oh, Chloe, what are we going to do? How long is she going to stay here?"

"I don't know." Chloe's voice took on an edge of despair. "Forever?"

"Oh, Lord." My own voice had sunk to a whisper.

"I've got to go now. She's coming back."

Poor Chloe. I whispered, "I'm really sorry, Chloe. Good luck."

Chloe said something that sounded a good deal like a snort and replaced the receiver. I did so on my end, too, and sank my head into my cupped hands. Head and hands were propped up by my elbows, which were resting on my shiny desk—shiny because I polished it each and every week with LOOK UP Furniture Wax. I took the maintenance of my job's accouterments seriously.

Elbows, hands, and head were still propped as before when the outer door to the office opened and Ernie Templeton strolled in, tallish, handsome in a rugged sort of way, eternally casual, and looking as rumpled as ever. He stopped short when I lifted my head, dropped my hands, and tried to appear efficient.

"What's the matter with you?" he demanded.

"Nothing."

"Nothing, my left hind leg. Something's wrong. What is it?" He snatched the hat from his head and marched up to my desk. I must have looked as shocked and demoralized as I felt because I detected honest concern on Ernie's face. He was generally a nonchalant, kidding-around sort of person, so this expression surprised me.

I sighed deeply. "My mother has come to visit."

He squinted at me. "Well, that's a great thing, isn't it?"

I eyed him sternly. "You don't know my mother."

A crack of laughter rent the air, and Ernie's expression of concern vanished. "Aha! You mean stuffy old Boston's come to nasty old Los Angeles, home of the playboy and playgirl? Boy, I bet Mama'll make you mind your Ps and Qs."

I resented that. Ernie had pegged me for someone from the upper echelons of our supposedly classless society the moment he'd first set eyes on me. He'd assumed that, given my background, which he'd divined by some means known only to investigatory professionals I suppose, that I was an easterner, that I'd never held a job, that I "came from money," as he would have it, and that I was a dilettante who would soon tire of having to do a real job of real work, none of which assumptions were correct. Oh, very well, they were all correct except the last one.

I *wanted* to work, curse it! I *wanted* to be useful! I didn't want to fritter away my time being nothing more than a decoration in some wealthy Bostonian's mansion on Beacon Hill. I'd already done that for twenty-one years. Well, I'm not sure how decorative I was, but I certainly hadn't ever done anything worthwhile. I'd been as useless as your average appendix.

Until I'd secured this position as Ernie's secretary and started earning a living. Why, I'd helped rescue an abandoned child, capture a murderer, thwart a blackmailer, and liberate a kidnapped poodle during my first two weeks on the job! Not the poodle I now owned, but the one that had inspired me to buy Buttercup. Who had cost more than I earn in a week.

I buried my head in my hands again and might well have uttered a moan, although I don't remember.

"Hey, kiddo, I was only joking. Why are you upset about your mother visiting?" Ernie pulled out one of the chairs in front of my desk and sat on it.

"Well, for one thing, she didn't know I'd cut my hair."

He goggled slightly. "Your hair?"

I glared at him for a second before reburying my head in my hands. "Yes."

"Yeah? She was . . . uh . . . unsettled by the knowledge? I mean, is cutting one's hair a sin or something in your family?"

Peering at him through my fingers, suspecting him of sarcasm, I muttered, "You have *no* idea."

"Sorry, kiddo."

I heaved a deep and heartfelt sigh. "Oh, Ernie, she's . . . she's . . ." She was a battleaxe, but I couldn't say that aloud. I settled for, "She really, *really* disapproves of my having a job."

"Well, hell, so do I," said my irritating employer with a shrug.

I glared at him. "That's not fair, Ernest Templeton, and you know it. I'm a good secretary!"

He gave me one of his cocky grins. "You'll do. But did your mother come all the way from Boston to scold you for having a job? That's seems kind of excessive to me."

This time I know I groaned because I couldn't repress it. "She didn't know I had a job until this morning when she showed up at Chloe's front door just as I was leaving."

His eyebrows arched like soaring larks. "You didn't tell her?"

I shook my head. "I knew she'd disapprove. She's always disapproved of me."

"She has?"

"Yes."

"She disapproves of *you?*"

I didn't particularly care for his tone of voice, but I merely gave him another, "Yes."

"What's to disapprove of?"

I gave him a smallish glare. "I'm the only person in the entire world who's ever defied her."

Ernie's eyebrows lifted into an arch of incredulity, and his lips quivered as if he were suppressing a grin.

"It's the truth, darn it, Ernie Templeton! Don't you dare laugh at me! My mother considers that my holding a job as your secretary is only slightly less mortifying than if I'd gone to work for one of her society friends as a housemaid. And it doesn't matter that she doesn't know I'm a secretary yet." Which made me think of something else, and I took up what was becoming my normal pose of the day with my head in my hands. "And when she finds out, she'll be furious, because she claims my father is having an affair with his *own* secretary." I'm pretty sure I whimpered.

Ernie's expression sobered. "Wow, I'm sorry, kiddo."

"It's all right." My voice belied the words.

The phone rang again, and Ernie rose from his chair, patted me on the back and sauntered to his office, where he flung his hat at the hat rack in the corner, slipped out of his suit coat— since already the August morning weather hovered around the ninety-degree mark—sat behind his desk, propped his feet up, and flapped open the morning edition of the *Los Angeles Times*. Mind you, I couldn't see him doing any of those things, but I knew from experience that this was the way Ernest Templeton, P.I., started his workday.

"Mr. Templeton's office. Miss Allcutt speaking." My voice lacked conviction, even though I'd spoken nothing but the truth.

"Mercy, it's me again."

Chloe generally chose her words more carefully than that, but, again, I wasn't going to point out her grammatical lapse this morning. " 'Lo, Chloe."

"Listen. Mother is going to go with me to the doctor's office." I heard her suck in a deep breath on the other end of the wire, and my heart gave a hard spasm in anticipation.

I knew what was coming.

I was right.

"Then she insists on seeing where you work. We should be there about ten-thirty or so."

I think I whimpered again.

"So spiff up the place, okay? And tell Mr. Templeton to brace himself."

"Thanks, Chloe," I whispered and hung up the receiver.

I don't know how long I sat there, staring at the pretty picture of Angel's Flight that I'd bought from a street artist in Pershing Square and hung on the office wall, but it was long enough for Ernie to notice.

"Who was that?" he called from behind his newspaper.

"Chloe."

"Your sister?"

"Yes."

"What'd she want?"

I heaved a sigh loud enough to have been heard by all my relatives in Boston. "She and Mother are going to visit me so that Mother can see where I work."

"Well, that's nice."

"No, it isn't."

"Hey, Mercy, snap out of it. She can't be all that bad."

Showed how much he knew about anything. I said, "Huh," something I'd never have done as little as six weeks earlier. Ernie chuckled, and I considered throwing something at him, but I didn't want to get fired. Especially not when my mother was going to visit my place of employment.

But moping would accomplish nothing and if it was possible, which I sincerely doubted since it's very difficult to penetrate closed minds, I aimed to make my mother admit that I was not only rightly and properly, not to mention gainfully, employed at a job I liked, but that my working conditions sparkled.

Therefore, I opened another desk drawer, grabbed the dust cloth I kept in there, and began dusting for all I was worth.

I'd just climbed down from the chair I'd pushed over to the wall behind my desk so I could straighten the two pretty flower pictures I'd hung a few weeks ago when the office door opened. Aha! A client! For a moment I was happy I wasn't stuck on the chair when the client arrived until I recognized Francis Easthope, one of the world's most handsome men, a great pal of Chloe's, and a man who had done an enormous favor for me once upon a time. Mr. Easthope worked as a costumier for Harvey at the studio, and he knew everything there was to know about ladies' fashions. He was also a sweetie pie.

"Mr. Easthope! How good to see you."

"Good morning, Miss Allcutt." He was always impeccably polite. He removed his hat now, and bowed slightly.

Did I detect a hint of nervousness in his mien? By gum, I think I did. Instantly, I adopted my soothing-secretary attitude in spite of my dust cloth, which I hastily tucked in my desk drawer. "What can we do for you, Mr. Easthope? Won't you sit down?" I gestured to the chair beside my desk. Usually I seated clients in one of the chairs in front of my desk, but I liked Mr. Easthope a lot.

He sat with a sigh. "Thank you." Placing his hat on his lap and leaning his stick against my desk, he appeared pensive for a moment, as if he didn't relish having to divulge his reason for calling. I gave him my most sympathetic smile, and he sighed again. "I need Mr. Templeton's help," he said at last. Then, with a quick, apprehensive glance at me, he added, "And yours."

"Certainly," said I, glad he'd acknowledged my usefulness, even belatedly. After all, he knew everything about the previous cases in which I'd been involved, so he understood how helpful I could be. "What can we do for you?"

Ernie poked his head out of his office and frowned slightly

when he spotted Mr. Easthope, who turned and glanced at him. After lifting an eyebrow in surprise, Ernie said, "Mr. Easthope," in a neutral voice.

"Good morning, Mr. Templeton."

For some reason, Ernie had always been a little touchy where Francis Easthope was concerned. Perhaps he resented Mr. Easthope's degree of handsomeness, although that didn't sound quite like the Ernie Templeton I knew. Anyhow, I didn't understand it, but I aimed to quash any petulance on his part before it leaked into the conversation. "Mr. Easthope is here for our help, Mr. Templeton." I always called him *Mr. Templeton* when we had clients.

"Yeah?" Ernie seemed minimally interested.

"Indeed." I gave him a good frown to show him he needed to shape up and treat Mr. Easthope as a gentleman and a client ought to be treated.

I have to admit that the differences between the two men couldn't have been much more marked. Francis Easthope was dressed in the very height of fashion, in a summer-weight tan suit and hat, crisp bronze-colored four-in-hand necktie, highly polished shoes and a lion-headed walking stick. Ernie had come to the office clad in a cheap seersucker suit, limp tie and the same old brown shoes and hat he always wore. Of course, Francis Easthope worked in the pictures and made a lot of money and Ernie . . . didn't. Either one of those things.

"Yeah?" He gave every appearance of not being overly delighted when he said, "Why don't you come into my office, Mr. Easthope? You can tell me all about it."

Drat. I'd been hoping he'd tell *me* all about it. Oh, well.

Mr. Easthope rose from his chair and said, "Thank you." Turning to me, he said, "And thank you, too, Miss Allcutt."

I have a feeling my smile was wan.

My dispirited condition didn't last very long, thank heaven.

Before I could do more than begin fretting about my mother's looming visit, Ernie's office door opened and his head popped out again. I looked up, ever hopeful.

My hopes were dashed almost at once. Ernie stepped back and Mr. Easthope came through the door, looking unhappy. Ernie stood at his back, rolling his eyes. Well, pooh.

"I'm sure sorry, Mr. Easthope," said Ernie, sounding not at all sorry. "But that just doesn't sound as if it's in my line."

"That's all right," said Mr. Easthope sadly. "I feared as much." And he walked farther into my office as Ernie shut his door and, I presume, went back to perusing the *Times*.

Mr. Easthope sighed heavily, and my heart was stirred. "Do you think there's anything I might do for you, Mr. Easthope?" I asked, not expecting much in the way of excitement to ensue.

He gazed soulfully at me long enough for my heart to take to fluttering like a hummingbird. He was a *very* handsome man. "Well . . . would you mind listening to my tale of woe? Perhaps you might be able to offer an insight or two."

Would I *mind?* Would I mind seeing King Tut's Tomb? I would not! "Heavens, no. I'd love to hear your problem. And I promise I won't tell another person. We're the soul of discretion at Templeton's." At least I was, and I was pretty sure Ernie was, too, or he'd have gone out of business long ago. Smiling at him, I said, "I'll even take notes."

"Thank you."

"Thank *you*." I grabbed my lined, green stenographer's pad and a pencil as Mr. Easthope resumed the chair beside my desk. Then I smiled at him as if he were offering me reprieve from doom and destruction instead of merely my mother. Did I say *merely?* I didn't mean it. There's nothing mere about my mother. Both her stature and her personality are imposing.

I poised my pencil—I always kept several sharpened pencils at the ready—over my pad. "All right. Fire away."

23

With a sigh, Mr. Easthope turned to me and, with a small, strained smile, commenced to do as I had asked of him.

"It's my mother," he said, his voice and visage both grim.

Chapter Two

Shocked at hearing words that echoed my own exact thoughts, I looked up from my pad and stared at him, my mouth agape. "Oh, I know *just* what you mean!" I hadn't meant to speak, and I felt my cheeks get hot as I returned my gaze to my pad and dutifully wrote his words thereon.

Mr. Easthope blinked at me and said, "I beg your pardon?"

"Sorry," I said. "I've just been having a mother problem of my own."

"I see," said Mr. Easthope, who clearly didn't.

I resolved to keep my mouth shut during the remainder of his narrative.

"Um . . ." Mr. Easthope paused for a moment, my comment evidently having scattered his thoughts, then forged onward. "As I said, it's my mother. She's come under the spell of some dreadful spiritualists, and I fear they're taking her for a ride. She's already spent hundreds of dollars on them. I don't begrudge her some entertainment, but I'm worried that her interest in spiritualism is getting out of hand. What's more, I'm sure the two people who are conducting the so-called séances she keeps having are dirty crooks. I can't help but get the feeling they're making careful notes detailing the décor and layout of my place and plan to do something in the line of theft before they bleed Mother dry and move on to greener pastures."

"My goodness," I said, breaking my vow of silence almost as soon as I made it. I'd make a lousy nun.

"Goodness doesn't enter into the picture," said Mr. Easthope with uncustomary acidity. "What's worse is they're doing their dirty work in my house and at my expense. So it will be my possessions they pilfer, if they end up pilfering anything." Mr. Easthope sighed heavily. "My mother lives with me, you see, Miss Allcutt. And it's not that I don't love her and can't afford to support her, but . . ."

She *lived* with him? Good heavens, the poor man! "Oh, dear," I said, and left it at that, proving that occasionally I can hold my tongue.

"I had hoped that Mr. Templeton—and you, of course," he said in what I knew to be an afterthought, "might attend one or more of these séances, so you could investigate this pair and determine if they really are crooks—well, crooks who are determined to do more than dupe gullible elderly women. I'm afraid I can't make myself believe in their spiritualistic mumbo-jumbo."

"Understandable," I muttered under my breath, since I, too, was a skeptic.

Another sigh escaped from Mr. Easthope's lips, which were, I must say, beautifully molded and went very well with the rest of him. In actual fact, I do believe he was the most handsome man I'd ever seen, and that includes several men who act in the motion pictures and who have been guests at Chloe and Harvey's table.

"I know spiritualism is all the rage these days, but I do wish my mother hadn't fallen under these people's spell."

Aptly put, I thought. I said, "Hmm," and kept my head bent over my pad.

"And I honestly do fear that these people are worse than average. They give me quite a queasy feeling in my tummy."

A queasy feeling in his tummy? I glanced up from my note-pad and had the fleeting and no-doubt unreasonable wish that

Mr. Easthope's spoken words were as elegant as his outward appearance. Oh, well. Nobody's perfect. "Um . . ." I paused, trying to think of something eloquent—or at least pertinent—to say. Then I had a thought. "What are these people's names?" That was pertinent, wasn't it?

"They call themselves the d'Agostinos." He spelled it for me. "Supposedly they're Anthony and Angelique d'Agostino. It's probably a phony name."

"Why do you think it's phony?"

Mr. Easthope hesitated for a moment. He sounded a trifle petulant when he said, "Oh, it's just too perfect. They waft around the house, pale as death, looking like spirits themselves, all dressed in black, and they both talk as if they're communing with spirits even when they're asking for poached eggs for breakfast." He scowled gloriously when he concluded, "I tell you, Miss Allcutt, I'm just sick of them."

"I can certainly understand that."

"And they have a ghoul who does all their fetch-and-carry work for them."

A ghoul? I was about to ask what he meant, but he spoke again and I didn't.

"I don't know what his name is. He lurks in corners and never speaks, just lurks. What's more he looks like how I picture that servant Igor in *Frankenstein.*"

That did sound ghoulish. "I read that book. The fellow sounds creepy."

"He is. I was hoping Mr. Templeton could help me, but he says exposing spiritualists isn't in his line."

It was then I had my brainstorm. "Perhaps *I* can help!"

Mr. Easthope's eyebrows soared into his hairline. Before he could express any doubts, I rushed to explain.

"Why don't *I* attend a séance or two at your house and do some snooping on my own? Ernie—Mr. Templeton, I mean—

has taught me heaps about the investigative process, and I bet I could ferret out any criminal tendencies on the part of these so-called spiritualists."

I held my breath, praying Mr. Easthope would accept my offer, and not merely because the case sounded interesting. If he allowed me to snoop, it would mean I'd have to be at his house quite often. And *that* would mean I wouldn't be at Chloe's house, which, of course, would mean I wouldn't be around my mother as much as I feared I'd be if he didn't accept my offer. If you know what I mean.

"Well . . ." He chewed his lip.

"I wouldn't charge anything, of course," I hastened to add, hoping to sweeten the deal. Not that Mr. Easthope was hurting for money, but people in every income bracket like a good deal when they can get it.

"Um . . . I'm not sure that's a good idea. I mean I'd hate to get you involved in anything that might be the least bit unsavory."

"Unsavory?" I scoffed, since I couldn't think of anything unsavory about exposing a couple of crooks who conned old ladies out of their sons' money. I mean all I had to do was discover their bag of tricks and call the cops, right? Or maybe the police wouldn't even get involved if Mr. Easthope didn't want them to be. At any rate, that would mean *they* were the unsavory ones, not I. "Don't be silly, Mr. Easthope. There won't be any risk of that involved. Even if they discover me snooping, what can they do to me?"

"But these people might be real criminals, Miss Allcutt."

"Exactly. Which is why you need me." I beamed at him, hoping he was as impressed by my logic as I was.

"Well, why don't you let me think about it and I'll get back with you."

"Of course. Perhaps you might be able to find another private investigator who will take the case." I refrained from pointing out that this scenario was highly unlikely, given that most P.I.s were like Ernie. At least, I presumed they were.

Mr. Easthope heaved another big sigh. "I probably won't be able to do that."

I gave him a genuinely sympathetic smile and thought to myself that mothers could be *such* a problem and that it didn't seem fair, when I heard low voices outside in the hall and my heart clanked down into my shoes.

Speaking of mothers . . .

"Oh, dear, I think that's probably Chloe and . . ." My voice trailed off.

Mr. Easthope brightened slightly. "Oh, is Chloe paying you a call?"

"Yes. Along with . . ." I took a deep breath. ". . . our mother."

"Your mother? From Boston?"

I nodded.

"Oh." Mr. Easthope, who had heard about our mother from Chloe, seemed appropriately distressed. I appreciated him for it.

"Exactly."

Ernie's office door opened. "Mr. Easthope, will you come in here for a second?"

"Certainly," said Mr. Easthope, and he did. He seemed relieved, which was a sensible reaction to being spared a meeting with my mother.

Ernie's office door closed just as the doorknob on the outer office door turned. There was no help for it. I straightened my spine, took two deep breaths for courage, hugged my pencil and pad close to my bosom in an effort to look professional, and sat up straight, ready to face my doom. I mean my mother.

The first thing I noticed when the door opened and Chloe and Mother entered the office was that Chloe was much more conservatively clad this morning than was usual for her. She always dressed beautifully and in the very height of fashion—she could afford to do so, since Harvey made tons of money in the movies—but today she wore a soft green crepe suit with a hip-length unfitted jacket, a green confection of a hat and green shoes and handbag to match. I recall seeing the costume in her closet once when we were selecting a dress for me to wear to a speakeasy—and I prayed to heaven Mother never learned about *that* incident—but I'd never seen it on Chloe.

As for Mother, she wore one of her Boston outfits of navy blue bombazine, mannishly cut, with red trim that should have given the costume a sporty look but didn't, my mother's overall majesty of demeanor overawing even frivolous red trim. Her hat sat on her salt-and-pepper waves squarely and, while the rest of us in Los Angeles permitted ourselves to wilt slightly in the summer heat, Mother looked as if she had conquered even the weather. She stood straight and tall—she was taller than Chloe and me by a good deal, probably because she wouldn't allow any child of hers to outdo her in any way—and as free from perspiration as if she'd been standing in the middle of a Boston street in January.

Hoping to gull her into thinking her presence didn't distress me, I pasted on a broad smile. "Good morning, Mother. Welcome to the Figueroa Building." And, as boldly as if I weren't secretly quaking in my sensible, two-tone lace-up shoes, I walked up and kissed her on the cheek. In order to do so, I had to walk around my desk and then stand on tiptoes, due to the aforementioned height difference. Come to think of it, that might be one of the reasons she intimidated me so much. Probably not. I think it was her personality.

She stood still for the kiss, a demonstration of tolerance I hadn't expected. I'd anticipated that she'd light right in to me.

Chloe, bless her heart, decided to reveal the reason for this unusual forbearance on our parent's part. "Oh, Mercy, guess what?"

She had her hands clasped to her bosom, which was most unlike her, but I guess she was putting on a show for our mother, too.

"Have a seat," said I, waving the two of them to the chairs before my desk. I'd already decided I'd sooner face my mother this morning with a wide expanse of wood between us, and that if she were seated at my side in Mr. Easthope's chair, she'd be more apt to strike out at me than if she had to reach across the desk to do it. Not that Mother was one for physical violence. Shoot, she didn't need it. She could cow most people with a single glance. "And tell me what the doctor said."

Chloe pulled out a chair for Mother, who sat stiffly. Her face, since she'd entered the office, had not lost an iota of its expression of frozen disapproval. With a sigh, I sat, too, ever so grateful for my desk. "So what's up, Chloe?" I still smiled brightly, figuring I might as well.

"Harvey and I are going to have a baby!" Chloe blurted out.

I, for one, was glad she did that, because it diverted our mother's attention from her errant younger daughter to her errant older one. "Well, really!" she said to Chloe, her uppercrust Boston accent in full bloom. "Your move to Los Angeles has done nothing to improve your manners, young woman."

Mother didn't approve of people speaking openly about having babies and stuff like that. She thought this sort of thing ought to be whispered from woman to woman in the privacy of one of the women's homes. God alone knew how the men involved were supposed to get the news.

I thought that was a stupid and antiquated notion and figured it wouldn't do me any more harm to say so than to keep it to myself. "Why not?" I rose from my chair, skirted around my desk and threw my arms around my older sister. "Oh, Chloe,

I'm so happy for you!"

"Thank you, Mercy." Hugging me back, Chloe sounded a trifle misty. I guess, after having been in the company of our mother all morning, she needed a dose of good, honest friendship and sisterly love and a dollop of congratulations.

Mother's gloved hand knocked on my desk as if she were calling her wayward offspring to attention, thereby effectively breaking the hold my sister and I had on each other. Reluctantly we pulled apart. Lucky me, I got to sit behind my desk again.

"Really!" Mother said stiffly. "I've never seen such an unseemly display in public."

Feeling protected by the desk, I pointed out, "This isn't really public, Mother. It's my workplace, and I'm the only one who works in it since Mr. Templeton has his own office, and I'm very happy for Chloe and Harvey."

"Clovilla and Mr. Nash's news is best discussed in the home. What I want to know is how you, Mercedes Louise Allcutt, can have the audacity to work for hire. Why, Clovilla told me you were actually in a gunfight not two weeks ago! I've never heard of such a thing!"

If I'd had anything to do with it, she wouldn't have heard about it today, either. I thought about directing a dirty look at Chloe but didn't. After all, she'd been stuck with Mother all morning long and could be forgiven for saying a little too much. Anyhow, I deserved it after having run out on her.

"I wasn't *in* the gunfight, Mother," I said, aiming for a dignity that seemed pretty far away at the moment. "I was in Chinatown, doing my job, when gunfire erupted around me. It had nothing to do with me, and I wasn't hurt." I didn't consider the latter comment in the nature of a lie. I had been hurt, a little, but that was only because I'd scraped my knees when Ernie pushed me to the pavement. The bullets missed me entirely.

She chuffed out an irritated breath. "Stop equivocating this instant, Mercedes Louise. You know very well what I mean."

"But—"

"And what was this that Clovilla told me about you shoving a man down an elevator shaft?"

"Well, but he was going to murder me . . ." I wished I hadn't said that the second it was out of my mouth.

Have you ever heard it said that someone swelled with outrage? That's what Mother did then. "I," she said in as stiff and firm a voice as I'd ever heard her use, "am ashamed of you, Mercedes Louise Allcutt."

"But—" I said, and I tried to say more, but was again overborne.

"But—" Chloe said.

She tried to say more, too, but our mutual mother could trample the Queen of England, if there were one, under her Brahmin feet, never mind two such insignificant objects as her daughters. "Mercedes Louise Allcutt, you are a disgrace to the family."

"I am not!" I really resented that. I mean, me? *I* was a disgrace to the family? What about *her*? I hadn't run off and left any husbands behind in Boston! *I* wasn't the one who'd had an affair with my secretary! Knowing if I said either of those things, God would strike me dead on the spot, probably using Mother as His agent, and although I felt my cheeks heat and my mouth go dry, and also feeling such a dreadful pain in my chest that I wonder to this day how I survived, I only drew my breeding around me like a shield and continued speaking mildly. "I am a disgrace to no one, Mother. I am gainfully employed at a job I like, and am earning an honest living." Sort of. I saw no reason to mention the quarterly allowance that was paid to me through the bank in Boston, and that my mother couldn't touch if she decided to be vindictive and cut me off since it had been bequeathed to me by my great-aunt Agatha.

Very well, so I cheated a little bit. Still and all, I was fulfilling my goal in moving to the west coast, which was to get experience of the world. I was doing so with a vengeance in fact, and enjoying every minute of it.

"You're taking a job away from someone who needs it," my mother stated flatly.

I have to admit I'd never considered the matter from that perspective before. I didn't want to start thinking about it then, either. "Nonsense," I said bravely. "I am gaining experience that will serve me well for my entire lifetime." Recalling a newspaper headline I'd seen recently—I hadn't bothered to read the article because stuff like that bored me—I added, "The stock market might go bust one of these days, you know. These good times might not last forever."

As soon as I saw her eyebrows form that alarming V over her eyes, I knew I'd erred in talking so plainly. "Where in the world did you learn to speak in that pert way, using such abominable language, Mercedes Louise? *Bust,* indeed. Slang is as inappropriate on your lips as this so-called *job* of yours is to you."

Whoops. Before I could apologize, which I'd been on the verge of doing, thereby ruining my pretense of being an independent woman of the world, the door to Ernie's office opened. I silently blessed him as we all glanced doorward.

Ernie used good sense when he allowed Francis Easthope to exit the office before him. He might have done so even if Mother hadn't been presiding over the outer office, although he's not a slave to gentlemanly behavior. In any event, allowing Mr. Easthope to appear first defused the situation slightly. When Chloe saw him, she jumped to her feet and let out a joyful shriek. *"Francis!"*

Mother's posture became even straighter, if such a thing was possible, and her expression of outrage intensified. Perhaps I'd been hanging around Chinatown too much, because she reminded me of one of those statues of Buddha they sell there, although without the benevolent smile. She was actually more obelisk-like than Buddha-like, I guess.

Fortunately for all of us, Chloe was too ecstatic at discovering another friend present to pay any attention to our mutual parent. Utterly forsaking everything our mother had ever tried to teach her about proper deportment, Chloe threw her arms around Mr. Easthope, who smiled and patted her on the back, looking a trifle self-conscious. Not even Chloe was this demonstrative as a rule, but I believe anyone might have snapped from the strain under which she'd been operating for the past few hours.

After several seconds, during which I held my breath, Chloe broke from Mr. Easthope. Keeping his hand in hers, she turned to our mother. Her cheeks were pinker than I'd ever seen them, Chloe having perfected the pale-and-interesting look since moving to Los Angeles. I saw her swallow when she recognized Mother's aspect of righteous anger. Nevertheless, probably because she didn't know what else to do, she said, "Mother, please allow me to introduce you to one of Harvey's and my best friends, Mr. Francis Easthope. Francis is a costumier at Harvey's studio."

She still held his hand, but in spite of that Mr. Easthope executed a bow that would have done credit to one of Mother and Father's courtlier friends on the east coast.

"How do you do, Mrs. Allcutt? It's a pleasure to meet you."

I peeked at Mother to see if she'd thawed any after this dazzling display of gentlemanliness. She hadn't. She was unfailingly, if rather chillingly, polite, however, since that was the Boston way, and she said, "How do you do, Mr. Easthope?"

Then she looked pointedly at Ernie, and I realized I'd forgotten all about him in the excitement of the moment. Instantly I tried to cover my gaffe. "And Mother, please allow me to

Alice Duncan

introduce you to my employer, Mr. Ernest Templeton."

Ernie's bow was more ironic than gentlemanly. I got the feeling he was making sport with me, which I might have expected. Darn him anyhow! "Pleased to meet you, Mrs. Allcutt. Your daughter is quite the diligent worker."

At least he'd paid me a compliment. Mother sniffed haughtily. No surprise there. "Mr. Templeton," she said, speaking the words as if she'd been keeping them cold in the Frigidaire. "How do you do?"

"Swell, thanks."

Inwardly I groaned. My mother deplores slang. Any time it rears its head, she reacts like a queen being spat upon by a lowly subject. She did so now, closing her eyes for a moment in an expression of long-suffering agony that was totally false. She never suffered anything for long. If something troubled her, she stomped it flat.

Chloe nervously picked up the conversational ball and then fumbled it. "Francis, I just got the most wonderful news!" She heard Mother's censorious sniff and clamped her tongue between her teeth. Her cheeks turned a deeper pink.

"Indeed?" Mr. Easthope, who of course didn't have a notion in the world what was going on, kept smiling.

Chloe stood there, her mouth pursed, her blush deepening, and didn't know what to do or say. Neither did I.

With an aplomb of which I hadn't known him capable, Ernie stepped nobly into the breach. "May I offer my congratulations, Mrs. Nash? When is the bundle of joy expected?"

Even my mother looked nonplused for a second before her natural stateliness subsumed her expression of surprise.

Chloe blinked at him. "How . . . how did you—?" She looked at me.

I shook my head. "I didn't know until you told me."

"You mean you're . . . er . . . expecting?" Mr. Easthope picked up Chloe's hand, since she'd finally let his go, and pumped it heartily. "What happy news for you and Harvey. I'm so pleased for you both."

"But how did you figure it out?" I asked Ernie, irked by this display of uncanny knowingness on his part.

"I'm a private investigator, remember?" He tapped his noggin. "I'm good at my job."

If there was one thing guaranteed to set my mother off, it was an audacious wink like the one he tipped at me then. She stood and said, "Well, really!"

Ernie pretended to misunderstand her. "Oh, yes. It's true. I can tell." He tapped the side of his head once more. "I've got a sixth sense about this sort of thing."

Deciding I might as well go along with him, I said, "It's true, Mother. Mr. Templeton has developed his detecting skills with vigor and discipline over the years." The vigor part was true, anyway. "He's really good at this investigative stuff."

"We will discuss this position of yours later, Mercedes Louise. It's time Clovilla got home and rested. There's been too much of the wild life lived around here. It's a good thing I got here in time."

In time for what? I didn't ask, having learned years earlier that it's best not to question Mother when she was on her high horse—which was pretty much all the time.

"Come along, Clovilla," Mother said then, and turned a frowning countenance upon Ernie and Mr. Easthope. "Good day, gentlemen." She was using the word loosely when it came to Ernie. I caught the nuance of sarcasm in the word. My mother is a mistress of nuance.

"It was a great pleasure to meet you, Mrs. Allcutt," said Mr. Easthope, bowing elegantly over the hand she'd held out to him.

"Yeah," said Ernie, grabbing the hand as Mr. Easthope let it go. I have a feeling he didn't anticipate her extending it to him, so he usurped her prerogative. Clever devil, Ernie Templeton. "It's been great meeting you."

Mother harrumphed and turned toward the door. Then she paused. It took a second, but both men caught on to what they were supposed to do. Mr. Easthope beat Ernie to the door, but I don't think Ernie tried very hard. I know I wouldn't have if I'd been treated to a display of Bostonian hauteur by my mother. Mr. Easthope bowed again as the ladies left, Mother first.

"Come to dinner tonight, Francis," Chloe whispered at Mr. Easthope as she passed him. "Please." There was a definite note of desperation in the word.

"Delighted," said Mr. Easthope, lying manfully. He was a true friend.

"Thank you, Francis." Chloe cast a desperate glance at me over her shoulder.

I gave back a thinnish smile and waved a couple of fingers at her, hoping the expression on my face conveyed only my compassion and none of the ecstasy I felt at not having to accompany our mother back home again. Home being a relative term in this instance, since when Honoria Allcutt enters through one's front door, all of one's usual comforts exit through the back. Or the windows or chimney or chinks in the plaster if the back door was locked.

I sighed heavily when the door closed behind Chloe and Mother.

"Clovilla?" said Ernie, grinning.

"It's not her fault. No more than Mercedes Louise is my fault. People slap these perfectly heinous names on innocent infants without their knowledge or approval."

Chuckling, Ernie said, "True, true."

"I must be off now," said Mr. Easthope. "I can't thank you

enough for agreeing to help me out, Miss Allcutt."

"Happy to be of service," I said, straining to regain a modicum of my general workday vim.

Fortunately the door closed behind Mr. Easthope before Ernie ground out between his teeth, "What the devil did he mean by that? Help out? How are you going to help him out?"

I lifted my chin and hoped I conveyed a fraction of my mother's hauteur. "Since *you* won't help him, *I* will."

"Oh, brother."

"Don't you 'oh, brother' me, Ernie Templeton! Mr. Easthope is a friend of mine, and he has a problem. I believe in helping out my friends when they're in trouble."

"Yeah? Well, let me tell you what I think."

He didn't have a chance to do so, fortunately, because the outer office door opened, and Lulu LaBelle, of all people—she's generally confined to the lobby—peeked in. I looked from Ernie to the office door, surprised. "Lulu!"

She stared at me with huge blue eyes, generously decorated with eye shadow and surrounded by curled and mascaraed eyelashes. "Was that your *mother?*" she asked in an awed voice.

I nodded, feeling too unnerved by recent events to speak.

"Scary, huh?" said Ernie, grinning and forgetting his pique with me. I hoped it would last.

"Oh, my Gawd," drawled Lulu. "No wonder you looked so peaky when you came to work this morning."

Peaky didn't begin to describe my feelings, but I appreciated Lulu's sympathy, found a smile somewhere within heretofore unplumbed depths of my character, and presented it to her. I even managed to whisper, "Thanks."

"Say, did you guys know that my brother is here in town?" Lulu asked, stepping into the office and dropping her air of sympathetic understanding. "He came here all the way from Oklahoma."

The word *Oklahoma* snapped my mind away from my problems for a moment. "Oh, my, are you from Oklahoma?" I tried to recall things I'd read about Oklahoma but could only fix on the fact that it used to be called the Indian Territory, which sounded quite wild and woolly to me.

Lulu nodded. "I came here to L.A. a couple of years ago to get into the flickers." She tossed her platinum-blond, shingled locks. "Wilbert only got here yesterday. He's younger than me by a couple of years."

To the best of my knowledge, Lulu hasn't come any closer to the motion pictures than the local movie palace, but I've never probed deeply into her ambitions for fear of wounding her feelings. Not that she wasn't good-looking or anything, but it seemed to me that if one aspires to do something, it's probably best to pursue one's goal a little more actively than Lulu seemed to be pursuing hers. Mind you, I know nothing about the inner workings of the motion-picture industry since Harvey never talked about it, but working as a receptionist in the lobby of the Figueroa Building and hoping a picture magnate would stroll in one day and discover her seemed to be leaving a lot to chance, if you see what I mean.

"Your brother's name is Wilbert?"

"Yeah. Stupid name, if you ask me, but nobody did."

"I understand completely," said I, Mercedes Louise Allcutt, who has a sister named Clovilla.

Lulu parked her fanny on my desk, ignoring the chairs set out for the purpose. I didn't mind. Lulu and I were friends. Kind of.

"Hmm. Wilbert LaBelle. Interesting name." Ernie scratched his chin and leaned back against the doorframe. He appeared amused.

She waved a pointy-nailed hand in a careless gesture. "Oh, his last name isn't LaBelle. I just chose that last name for me. I thought LaBelle would look good on a marquee."

"Ah," I said, clarity dawning. "I see."

"Ah," said Ernie. "So do I."

"Our last name is Mullins." Lulu made a face not unlike the one Chloe makes when she admits to her name being Clovilla. And then Lulu got down to business. Not that I didn't believe her primary reason for visiting to be commiseration. I'd have done the same thing if she'd had a mother like mine who'd come to town. But she now revealed her underlying reason for paying us a call.

Pinning Ernie with an entreating smile, she said, "Say, Ernie, can you think of some kind of job Wilbert can get? I'd have set him up as the custodian here, but the management already hired Emerald Buck, and he's doing a good job so I don't think they'll fire him just to hire Wilbert. But he really needs a job. Can you think of anything?"

I thought that was a little bit pushy, but I'm neither Lulu nor Ernie. Perhaps people in Los Angeles do this sort of thing all the time—you know, ask each other if they have a line on employment opportunities. I'd never had to think about jobs until I moved to Los Angeles, and I didn't actually *have* to think about jobs then.

Rather than brushing her off as I almost expected him to do—you never knew what, if anything, Ernie would take seriously—Ernie tilted his head to one side and considered her question. "I can't think of anything offhand, but—"

Proving my mother was correct in assuming my move to Los Angeles had damaged my manners, I interrupted, having just been struck by a brilliant notion.

"I do!"

CHAPTER THREE

Ernie and Lulu looked at me, and I felt silly. However, that didn't prevent me from forging onward, ever onward. Shooting a quick glance at Ernie and deciding it didn't matter if he heard my idea or not, I said, "Maybe he can work at Mr. Easthope's place."

"Huh," said Ernie, wrinkling his nose. He didn't scoff at me, though.

"Who?" said Lulu, wrinkling her nose, too, although hers was a puzzled wrinkle and not a derisive one.

With the air of one who is attempting to clarify muddled logic, Ernie said, "Are you thinking of having Wilbert work as a plant in your buddy Easthope's establishment?"

Although I'd been picking up the vocabulary of my new profession speedily, I was still unsure of some of the expressions used by its perpetrators. "A plant?"

Before Ernie could explain, Lulu's interest spiked. "Easthope. Is that the name of that gorgeous guy who came in to see you this morning?"

I smiled. "Francis Easthope. Yes. He is rather good-looking, isn't he?"

Lulu clasped her hands to her bosom. "You betcha! What a doll! He's better looking than Valentino."

Ernie, looking displeased, muttered, "The guy's a faggot, for God's sake."

I didn't know what a faggot was, either, in popular parlance, but evidently Lulu did. Her hands fell away from her breast, and she said, "Oh, yeah? Well, ain't that just the way?" She appeared quite disappointed.

Since I didn't know what they were talking about, I frowned slightly at Ernie, taking "faggot" to mean something not quite right, and whatever it meant, I didn't think he should be talking about a client in that way. Not that Mr. Easthope was his client. Still and all, I didn't approve, and I decided to take command of the situation.

"Why don't you have your brother come up and see me tomorrow? I'll talk to Mr. Easthope this evening when he comes to dinner, and perhaps we can come up with a job for him."

"I sure will, Mercy. Thanks a lot." Slithering off my desk, Lulu gave Ernie a peck on the cheek, and I was shocked, although I didn't want to be since being shocked seemed entirely too priggish a reaction to a friendly gesture. I guess I still had a lot of early childhood training to overcome.

But that didn't matter. I'd thought of an excellent idea, and I aimed to carry it out that very evening.

Francis Easthope speared a piece of asparagus and said thoughtfully, "I've pondered a good deal about your suggestion this afternoon, Miss Allcutt, and I do believe you could be very helpful if you're still interested."

"Oh, I'm still interested," I assured him, peeking at my mother and suppressing a shudder.

"And I do believe your idea of having Mr. Mullins work for me so that he can snoop around is quite clever."

Ha! I knew I wouldn't be the only one to think so. To heck with Ernie Templeton.

Mr. Easthope's smile was a work of art. In fact, I wished I had a flair with a paintbrush. I'd have painted him myself. "As for the séances, are you sure you won't mind attending one or two? I don't think there's any danger involved."

Danger? I hadn't thought about danger. I'd only thought about getting Lulu's brother a job and maybe helping Mr. East-hope foil a couple of mean-spirited tricksters. Oh, very well, I also anticipated more time away from Chloe's house and, therefore, my mother. I guess I'm not a very dutiful daughter. "I certainly hope not." I laughed softly. "No, I'm sure there won't be any danger, unless one of the d'Agostinos unlooses a ghost on poor Wilbert Mullins or me."

Mr. Easthope, bless his ever-so-polite heart, smiled at this weak sally and forked up a piece of swordfish. The chow at Harvey and Chloe's house was always good, and this evening Mrs. Biddle had surpassed herself.

I was seated next to Mr. Easthope at the dinner table. My mother was lording it over all of us from the other side of the table, proving that position isn't everything, since Harvey sat at the table's head and Chloe at its foot, and they both appeared as children compared to our majestic mother. I think Mother disapproved of the Nashes hosting so casual a get-together, it having been conceived of on the spur of the moment and handled without months of planning and engraved invitations. Not to mention the fact that there was an uneven number of males and females—but this was Los Angeles, she'd come here of her own free will, and she'd just have to put up with it.

"Thank you so much. Lulu will be so pleased about her brother. She was worried that Mr. Mullins wouldn't be able to find work. He's from Oklahoma, you see."

Mr. Easthope arched an elegant eyebrow. "Oklahoma? Hmm."

"Yes. I don't think I've ever met anyone from Oklahoma before. Well, except for Lulu."

He smiled for some reason.

"Mercedes Louise," said Mother, making me jump. "Your manners have declined deplorably since you moved to this benighted city. It is terribly impolite to whisper at the dinner table."

Whoops. "I'm sorry, Mother. Mr. Easthope just agreed to do a good deed for a friend of mine, and I didn't think the rest of the diners would be interested." It was weak and I knew it. My mother didn't care for excuses.

"Nonsense. Conversations that cannot be shared with others should be carried out in private."

"I beg your pardon, Mrs. Allcutt," said Mr. Easthope, trying to save my skin. "Entirely my fault."

Mother shook her head in a manner that conveyed both pity and despair. "You are not at fault, Mr. Easthope. My daughter—" She said the word *daughter* as if she wished she didn't have to. "—has been taught manners but seems to have forgot them all. I don't know what's to become of her." She looked at me as if she wished she could think of a solution to the problem of me that involved something other than cold-blooded murder. Her expression riled me.

"Oh, for heaven's sake, Mother—"

I didn't get to finish my thought, which was probably a good thing, because Mr. Easthope spoke over my words. "Miss Allcutt is doing me a great service, Mrs. Allcutt. She is going to help me solve a puzzle in my life." He gave me one of his heart-stopping smiles. "I truly appreciate her efforts on my behalf."

I could feel myself blushing, curse it. "It's nothing, really," I muttered.

"Oh?" dropped from my mother's lips like a chunk of ice.

"It's not nothing," said Mr. Easthope heroically. "Miss Allcutt has been all kindness in her offer to help. You have two lovely and generous daughters, Mrs. Allcutt."

Mother said, "Hmm," in a way that conveyed her deep skepticism.

I seethed with impotent fury and longed to deliver unto my

mother a few home truths. Not that doing so would have done anything but confirm her low opinion of me. Talk about frustrating. Nevertheless, we didn't discuss the details of Wilbert Mullins's employment or the next séance taking place in Mr. Easthope's house until after dinner, when we were all gathered in the front room sipping port (or having tea, in the case of Mother, Chloe and me).

I tried to corner Mr. Easthope, but Mother wouldn't let me. Ergo, I had to more or less explain to the entire room the problem of Mr. Easthope's mother and my offer to help rid him of her phony spiritualists whether I wanted to or not. Smiling what I prayed looked like a confident smile, but which was as phony as a three-dollar bill, I said, "So you see, I believe there must be a way to discover the tricks being used by the d'Agostinos and rid Mrs. Easthope of their influence."

Mother looked as if she smelled something rotten. "Spiritualists?" She sniffed disapprovingly.

Mr. Easthope sighed. "Yes. I'm afraid they've quite taken hold of Mother's imagination."

"It's all nonsense, this notion that people can communicate with the deceased." Mother sipped tea. She never used cream or sugar in her tea, deeming both frivolous.

"I agree with you," said Mr. Easthope.

"Whatever could have induced your mother to seek advice from such a fraudulent source?"

Mr. Easthope sighed mournfully. "I fear she was awfully cut up when my father died, Mrs. Allcutt. I tried to assist her in every way, but a friend of hers, Mrs. Hartland, convinced her that she could communicate with my father through the d'Agostinos. She's been a victim to their charms ever since."

At the words *my father,* Mother stiffened as if somebody'd stuck her with a pin. I cringed, praying inwardly that she wouldn't begin telling Mr. Easthope her own problems with the father of her children. I should have known better. My mother would never reveal dirty family linen in public, although a hint of her annoyance with Father seeped into her next words.

"Why ever would a sensible woman wish to establish communication with a deceased husband?" Her voice was as waspish as I'd ever heard it.

"She loved him," Mr. Easthope said simply. "He was a fine man."

I got the feeling Mother was biting her tongue so as not to spew forth on the stupidity of women who sink so low as to love the men they marry. She sniffed, but said nothing, drowning her spite in another sip of tea.

"I think I understand why she did it," said Chloe, shocking me completely.

Mother turned regally, the only way she could turn given her personality and state of corseting, and pinned her older daughter with a glacial stare. Chloe turned pink.

Nevertheless, she lifted her little chin, took Harvey's hand, and clarified her shocking declaration. "If anything ever happened to Harvey, I might want to try to communicate with him from beyond the grave. I'd be completely devastated."

Harvey smiled indulgently and squeezed her hand.

"Being devastated," said mother in her chilly voice, "is no reason to behave in so foolish and wasteful a manner. Spiritualists are twaddle."

"Of course they are," said Mr. Easthope with a sigh that sounded as if it were being wrenched from his soul. "Unfortunately, I fear my mother doesn't possess your strength of character."

Chloe mumbled, "I don't, either."

I felt like asking, "Who does?" but didn't, which was the right thing to do.

Mother said, "Hmph."

A fairly stiff silence followed Mother's huff. I don't know why Mr. Easthope didn't up and leave at that point. After all, my mother had pretty much called his mother a fool, which she undoubtedly was, but it was impolite to say so; and Chloe had admitted to being weak-willed enough to attempt to get in touch with Harvey from beyond the grave, although there was no need to do that thank God; and everybody was sitting there, staring at the lovely Persian rug under their feet and not knowing what to say next.

Eventually Mr. Easthope cleared his throat and smiled at me. I jumped a little bit, but that's only because I hadn't expected it.

"Fortunately for me, your daughter has offered a couple of excellent ways to delve into the spiritualist problem and thwart the d'Agostinos' evil influence."

Dramatic, but well put.

Mother eyed first Chloe and then me. Her gaze rested upon me, blast it. She knew of old who the troublemaker in the family was. "I presume you mean Mercedes Louise."

Undaunted, which I consider gallant of him, Mr. Easthope continued to smile as he said, "Indeed I do. Not only has she offered to attend the next séance at my house, but she's offered for employment a young man of her acquaintance. He can serve as my houseboy while he investigates the d'Agostinos."

"Well," I said, suddenly remembering that I didn't know Wilbert Mullins from Adam, "I don't actually *know* him, exactly. But he's Lulu's brother—you know Lulu, the receptionist? Well, she's bringing him to work with her tomorrow, and you can pop by and interview him. Unless you want him to go to your home for the interview." I attempted a smile bright enough to match Mr. Easthope's, but I'm certain mine fell far short of the mark. "If you think he'll work out, you'll be giving him employment, and he'll be helping you rid your house of the spiritualists. He can be sort of like a pest exterminator."

Chloe giggled, but Mother didn't think my little joke worthy of so much as another huff. She stood, precipitating a flurry of masculine foot shuffling as Harvey and Mr. Easthope rose, too, being polite fellows. "I," she said magisterially, "am going to bed. I'm perfectly exhausted after that long train journey across the country." She pinned first me and then Chloe with a razor-like glance. "I will speak to you two again tomorrow."

Hallelujah, I'd be at work tomorrow! I didn't sing or anything, but just said, "Good night, Mother," in my most sugary tone.

Before I could breathe a sigh of relief, Mother's eyes thinned, she glanced at me once more, and she said, "Mercedes Louise, show me to my room."

My heart, which hadn't exactly been soaring at the thought of being at work while my mother was on a rampage and Chloe was her only victim but had come pretty close, fell with a sickening thump. I got up on shaky knees. "I thought Mrs. Biddle showed you to your room earlier."

Narrowing her eyes still more into an expression I recognized, Mother said, "I wish to speak with you. Now."

With a last glance at the other occupants of the room, feeling like a French aristocrat being hauled to the guillotine in a tumbrel, I followed my mother with dragging steps. I appreciated everyone's expressions of commiseration, although I knew they weren't going to help me through the perils awaiting me in the immediate future.

Mother and I didn't speak until we were inside the Green Room and I'd shut the door. I didn't want to shut it, but Mother gave me a look and I knew I'd better.

"Mercedes Louise Allcutt, you're a disgrace to the family. I want this *job* nonsense to cease at once."

Blunt, but not unexpected. I straightened and took a deep

breath. This wouldn't be the first time I'd defied my parents, but before this I'd generally done so either behind their backs or from a distance of a couple of thousand miles. This act of defiance to Mother's face was testing my courage a whole lot.

"My job is not nonsense, Mother, and I shan't leave it. And I don't believe I'm a disgrace to anyone. If more people in our family worked, perhaps they'd be more understanding of others who aren't as fortunate as they." So there. I stood straight, but my insides felt kind of like not-quite-set Jell-O gelatin.

Her glare got icier. "You're speaking to your mother, Mercedes Louise. How dare you use that tone with me?"

Feeling really resentful and really scared, I didn't back down. "Mother, I'm using no particular tone with you. I'm telling you the truth. We aren't living in Queen Victoria's reign anymore. Anyhow," I said, thinking of what I considered to be a salient point, "we aren't British. We're Americans. America is supposed to be a classless society." So there again.

"There is no such thing as a classless society," Mother said, eyeing me as if I were a bug in need of being stepped on. "Quality will always rise to the top. You are deliberately choosing to be less than your station in life demands of you."

"It seems to me that the quality of which you speak was already at the top when I was born. There's no earning it."

"You were born into a level of society that requires you to behave in a certain way, Mercedes Louise. You're deliberately misinterpreting my words."

"I don't believe I am at all, Mother. What you're saying is that because our family is fortunate and has more money than most, I shouldn't work for a living."

"There is no need for you to *work for a living,* young woman. Indeed, you were fortunate to have been born an Allcutt. Yet you insist upon defying us and behaving in a manner that's disrespectful of the family name."

"How do you figure that?" It was tough, but I put the lid on my temper. If I lost it, Mother would have gained a point or two. At least that's the way I saw it. "I'm earning my own living. How is that lowering myself from what you call my station in life or being disrespectful of the family name? If more women in our so-called *class* had to earn their keep and got jobs, they might understand what the world is really like."

"What is this world of which you speak, Mercedes Louise? Do you mean the world of crime and dirty dealings? Do you mean the world of bomb-throwing anarchists? The world of Irish day-laborers? The world of cooks and servants? Do you mean the world of that vulgar woman in the lobby of the building in which you *work?*"

"Lulu's not vulgar," said I nobly, even though she actually kind of was. Poor Lulu.

Mother only looked at me for a moment, as if divining my secret thoughts. Then she sniffed and said, "Why in the world should a well-bred young lady wish to see or understand the world of underbred, unintelligent, unmannerly hooligans?"

"That's not the world I mean!" I said, frustrated almost beyond bearing. "I mean the world of working-class people, who *aren't* vulgar. Not being rich doesn't mean you're vulgar, for heaven's sake. There are more of them than there of us, you know, and they're becoming mighty peeved at not getting what they deserve from life. It's not only anarchists who are straining at their bonds. Normal, law-abiding, everyday people are demanding more of a role in the leadership of this country, not to mention fair wages for their work."

"Labor unions," said Mother, as if the two words were filthier even than slime in the gutters.

Shoot, I hadn't even thought about labor unions until that moment. I didn't know beans about them, either, barring a couple of articles I'd read in newspapers, but I nodded, believing Mother had brought up a salient point. While my parents would never agree that it was so, I thought labor unions might be helpful to coal miners, railroad workers and so forth, although I couldn't imagine unions assisting secretaries since our jobs weren't generally dangerous.

Mother shook her helmet of neatly marcelled, pepper-and-salt hair. Not even a hair dared stray from its mooring on *her* head. Which means I caused more trouble than a hair, I guess.

"If you wish to compare yourself to criminal agitators or that person in the lobby of that building in which you *work*, or that miserable worm of a creature, Eugene Debs, so be it. I am ashamed to call you my daughter."

That stung, but I'd be hanged if I'd show her how much. Lifting my own little chin, much as Chloe had done earlier that evening, I said, "I'm sorry you feel that way, Mother. Perhaps one day, you will understand my wish to participate in what I consider to be the *real* America."

Naturally, I didn't mention the fact that I was determined to understand the "real" America because I wanted to write books about it. Mother would not merely fail to understand that particular longing, but would probably have me locked up in an insane asylum. There was no way in the entire world my mother would ever be brought to understand that what I was doing wasn't actively evil.

I went to bed that night feeling more abused and mistreated than usual. And I was defiantly glad that I wouldn't see my battleaxe of a mother before work the next day. In actual fact, I fumed half the night, wondering if I should get my own apartment. Other working women did it. Why not me?

The next day I woke up without the happy anticipation that had become customary for me during the past month. It didn't take me long to recall the reason for this uncharacteristic mood of gloom.

Mother. My *mother* had come to town.

CHAPTER FOUR

That same morning, however, a welcome diversion from thoughts of my mother entered the Figueroa Building in the person of a new tenant. This wasn't any old tenant, either, but an extremely handsome fellow named, according to the shiny brass plaque outside his office, James Quincy Carstairs, Esq.

To my mind, this points out the importance of general maintenance and upkeep. When Ernie Templeton first hired me, the Figueroa Building was a most unprepossessing building. The old maintenance man, Ned, did a very poor job of keeping it clean, swept and polished. Mr. Emerald Buck, the maintenance man who'd been hired after I pushed Ned down an elevator shaft—for good reason (it wasn't merely a whim on my part)—had the place looking like a bright new day. I doubt that Mr. Carstairs, a newly minted but increasingly bright coin in the lawyering business, would have bothered with the Figueroa Building had it retained the aura of dilapidation permeating it when I first started working there.

Mr. Carstairs had himself a perfect gem of a secretary, too. I discovered this when, along about two in the afternoon, I toddled down the hallway two offices, knocked lightly on Mr. Carstairs's door, and peeped in. A young woman whom I'd viewed from my office window carrying boxes looked up from organizing her desk and smiled brightly.

"May I help you?" she asked in a crisp, but friendly, voice. It was the perfect tone for a secretary to adopt in my humble opinion, and already I admired her.

She looked the perfect secretary, too. Her dark hair was modestly shingled and shone in the electrical lighting. She wore a sober, lightweight gray suit and dark-rimmed spectacles. Her brown eyes were quite pretty behind the glasses, but her overall attractiveness did not diminish her businesslike appearance. Anyone entering Mr. Carstairs's outer office would instantly know this was a professional woman working for a professional man. Indeed, she personified the image I strove to achieve. In fact, since I had no role models of my own to follow, working outside the home being anathema to my family, I wondered if perhaps I hadn't just found a model in this woman.

I walked up to her desk, extending my hand. "How do you do? I'm Mercy Allcutt, and I work in number three-oh-three, for Mr. Ernest Templeton. Mr. Templeton is a private investigator."

She shook my hand warmly. "It's so nice to meet you, Miss Allcutt. My name is Sylvia Dunstable."

We remained smiling at each other for a second or two, I on my feet, she on her chair, before she said, "Won't you be seated, Miss Allcutt? I'm happy to meet another tenant here."

"Thank you." I took the proffered seat, pausing only to remove from it a couple of files. I was terribly impressed. Ernie and I had a couple of files, too, and I kept them in pristine order, but I doubt they were as interesting as these. Even if they were, Miss Sylvia Dunstable had ever so many more of them to work with than did I. Ernie's business wasn't exactly booming. "I'm so glad the Figueroa Building seems to be attracting more people."

"Yes," she said. "I must admit I was rather surprised when Mr. Carstairs said we were moving in here, but the building is ever so much nicer than when I saw it last."

"Indeed it is. We strive to improve our image all the time."

She looked at me with lifted eyebrows, and I think I blushed.

"I mean the management is taking much better care of the business than it once did."

"I see. Well, the management seems to have done a smashing job so far. Mr. Carstairs was perfectly correct to move here. The rent is lower than it is in some more fashionable places, and it's certainly not what you might call fancy, but that's a good thing in my opinion, since Mr. Carstairs's clients prefer to maintain a degree of anonymity that can be difficult to achieve in some parts of the city."

"My, yes," I said, thinking it interesting that Ernie's clients weren't the only ones who didn't want the world nosing into their business. It crossed my mind that perhaps Ernie had selected this building for that same reason, but that notion only lasted a second. The low rent was what had attracted Ernie; I was certain of it.

We smiled at each other again.

"Your work must be so interesting," I said, hoping to hear all about the stars, which was silly, really, since I lived with Harvey Nash and saw picture people all the time. But when those picture folks were at Harvey's house, they just seemed normal. I guess I wanted to think that movie stars were different from the rest of us, even though I knew they weren't. I swear, Los Angeles has a lot to answer for. Imagine the whole world having its perception warped like that!

"It's not interesting very often," she said with a laugh.

I'd actually read about Mr. Carstairs in the newspaper a time or two. He seemed to be establishing himself as an attorney to the people in the motion-picture industry. I'd seen his name in connection with Mr. Thomas MacCready, a fellow who'd acted in a couple of cowboy pictures, and Miss Jacqueline Lloyd, a newish actress who had made quite a hit in the melodrama *Whispering Oaks*. I'd seen that one, and thought Miss Lloyd had been stunning as the orphaned Lillian, a maiden taken cruel advantage of by Mr. Wallace Reid, who had seduced and abandoned her. Well, his character had. I'm sure Mr. Reid is a gentleman of impeccable character. Chloe and I had seen the picture together and cried buckets through most of it.

But back to the matter at hand. "I'm so happy to have another secretary to talk to," I told Miss Dunstable eagerly. "I've only had my job for a little over a month, and I'm sure you can give me some valuable pointers on organization and so forth."

She blinked once or twice and said, "I'll be happy to help in any way I can, Miss Allcutt."

"That probably sounds . . . um, unusual," said I, noticing her puzzled expression. Little did she know. Since I didn't want to go into my family background and how useless I'd been in the world until Ernie'd hired me, I only said, "I'm so new at this secretarial business, you see. I've only had my job for a month or so. This is my first job, too."

"Ah. Yes. Well, I'll be happy to answer any questions you might have."

"Have you worked as a secretary long?"

"Several years."

She didn't look very old, but perhaps she'd started young. I didn't think it would be polite to ask her age. "Oh, I'm sure you know ever so much more about secretarial organization than I." I popped up from my chair, deciding I'd made enough of a fool of myself for one day. "I'm so glad you and Mr. Carstairs decided to move into our building. I won't keep you from your organizing. I'm sure you have a ton of work to do."

She sighed. "Yes. I really detest moving offices. There are so many files and things to put in order."

I'd said, "Yes," although I didn't know that from experience, when the door behind Miss Dunstable opened, and there stood Mr. James Quincy Carstairs in the flesh. It was pretty good-looking flesh, too. In fact, Mr. Carstairs could easily have passed for one of the movie actors he represented. He wasn't quite as tall as Ernie, but he, unlike my employer, was clad in a well-cut summer-weight tan suit. He wore his dark hair slicked back *a la* Rudolph Valentino, and had one of those little pencil-thin mustaches. To tell the truth, I'm not much of a fan of those types of mustaches, but they were becoming all the rage in the flickers, so I suppose any man who worked with actors as Mr. Carstairs did might want to wear one.

He'd opened his mouth to say something to Miss Dunstable when he spotted me. His mouth closed and then he smiled. He had the whitest, most perfect teeth I'd ever seen. "Well, well, well, what do we have here?" He took a step forward and looked as though he wanted to shake my hand.

As I'd had etiquette drummed into me since birth, I forestalled a lapse on his part (the lady is supposed always to initiate hand-shaking) by sticking my own hand out. "How do you do. I'm Mercy Allcutt, and I work down the hall for Mr. Ernest Templeton."

"Ah, so you work for Ernie, do you? James Carstairs here. And I presume you've met Miss Sylvia Dunstable, the most efficient secretary on the planet."

"Yes, we've just met." I glanced back at Miss Dunstable for a moment and returned my attention to him. "You know Mr. Templeton?"

He chuckled. "Everyone knows Ernie Templeton, Miss Allcutt."

Did Mr. Carstairs sound a little snide? I couldn't tell. "I didn't know that."

"He's quite well known in criminal circles." Seeing my shocked expression, Mr. Carstairs elucidated. "He used to be a policeman."

"Oh. Yes. I did know that." I guess Mr. Carstairs figured

Ernie's police background explained his odd comment. Not that it mattered, and I did have a job to do down the hall. "Well, I'd best be going. I'm so glad you've joined us here in the Figueroa Building."

"Pleased to meet you," said Miss Dunstable.

"*Very* pleased to meet you, Miss Allcutt," said Mr. Carstairs.

I almost floated back to my office. My elevated mood suffered a quick puncture when I opened the door and saw Ernie glowering at my empty desk.

"Where the devil have you been?"

Stiffening, offended, I said, "I went down the hall to welcome our new neighbors. In case it's escaped your notice, a new tenant has joined us here in the Figueroa Building."

Ernie said, "Huh. Yeah, I saw. Carstairs, of all people."

"He seems very nice," I said, regretting that I sounded slightly defensive.

Sneering, Ernie said, "He's slick. I'll give him that."

"If being well groomed is considered 'slick,' I suppose he is," said I, going to my desk chair and seating myself with something of a flounce.

"Just watch out for him, is all I have to say."

"And exactly what does that mean?" I asked.

"He's a devil with the ladies," said Ernie, twirling an imaginary mustache like the villain in an episode of *The Perils of Pauline*.

"Don't be ridiculous, Ernest Templeton. I'm sure Mr. Carstairs has absolutely no interest in me." Which was moderately depressing, actually. I mean, I'm not ugly or anything. In fact, I'm rather nice looking. However, I didn't doubt for a second that if a man could choose between, say, Jacqueline Lloyd and Mercedes Louise Allcutt, he'd select the former. Miss Lloyd, at least on screen, was perfectly stunning, which beat "nice looking" all hollow.

"Well, just watch out, is all I have to say."

I said, "Hmm," and pretended to be looking for something in my desk drawer.

It was Lulu LaBelle and her brother Wilbert Mullins who rescued me. I'd asked them to visit my office, and they were early for the appointment we'd set for two-thirty that day. I smiled at them both, though, considering them in the light of salvation from Ernie's too-penetrating gaze and snippy commentary.

" 'Lo, Ernie," said Lulu, taking one of the chairs in front of my desk.

"Afternoon, Lulu," said Ernie, friendly again. "This your brother?" He smiled at the nervous young man who'd accompanied Lulu and who now stood beside her chair fidgeting.

"Yes. Ernie Templeton, please say hello to my brother Wilbert Mullins."

The two men shook hands, Ernie at ease, as ever, Wilbert looking as though he might faint. I hoped he wouldn't act like a frightened rabbit when Mr. Easthope arrived. If Ernie scared him this much, how much more might he be affected by the smashingly handsome Mr. Francis Easthope?

I found out a second later when Mr. Easthope entered the office. Ernie nodded at him before retiring to his own office. Mr. Easthope stood at the door, smiling upon Lulu and Wilbert. For a second, it looked as if brother and sister both might swoon, but Wilbert, who had just seated himself, sprang to his feet once more and Lulu, putting a hand to her no-doubt palpitating bosom, only gazed soulfully at the vision of graceful masculinity lingering by the door.

Since this was my party, sort of, I got up, too, and made introductions. Mr. Easthope was suavity itself as he shook the hands of the Mullinses. Lulu recovered from her semi-swoon enough to say, "Pleased to meetcha." Wilbert nodded and gulped.

I waved to the chair beside my desk. "Please, Mr. Easthope, won't you be seated? I'm hoping that Mr. Mullins will be able to be of use to you, both in doing the duties of a houseboy and in helping rid your home of invaders." I smiled brightly.

"Ah, yes. Has Miss Allcutt told you about my problem, Mr. Mullins?" Mr. Easthope asked politely.

After gulping again, Wilbert said, "M'sister did, sir. She told me about them fakers taking in your mama."

Mr. Easthope's eyebrows rose slightly, and he seemed to be contemplating Wilbert's response. I wondered if Mr. Easthope was faintly disappointed, as I was, by the naive and ill-spoken Wilbert. However, as so many people have said before, beggars can't be choosers. Wilbert was here, available, and needed a job, and he might well be smarter than he appeared. He certainly wouldn't be the only bright person in the world who, through lack of opportunity, had failed to achieve a first-class education. At least that's what I'd read often enough.

Surreptitiously eyeing both brother and sister from the corner of my eye, I wasn't sure about that. It might well be that both Lulu and Wilbert had been given ample opportunities to learn grammar and had simply avoided doing so. I know good and well that I managed to avoid learning very much in the mathematics classes I'd been forced to endure when I was in school.

However, that is neither here nor there.

"Good," said Mr. Easthope. "I'm glad to hear it."

"I'll really try to help, sir," said Wilbert in a rush of words. "And I really need a job."

That sentence ended in something of an "Oomph," and I realized that Lulu had elbowed him in the side when I saw Wilbert rub his ribs. To prevent further violence, I said, "I think this will work out very well for all concerned. Don't you, Mr. Easthope?"

"Indeed I do."

Mr. Easthope then went on to tell Wilbert what he expected of him in terms of houseboy and spy duties and how much he intended to pay him. Wilbert, who still had a glazed look about him, might or might not have been listening. I have a feeling he was so desperate for work that he would have taken anything anybody offered him at that point in his life. Lulu looked happy about the pay arrangement, so I guess the wages were all right. From personal experience, I only knew what my own were. I hadn't a single clue how my pay stacked up against anybody else's, since I'd had no experience working until Ernie hired me, and I didn't know anyone else in the working classes to ask. I mean, you can't just waltz up to a secretarial stranger and ask her what she's making, now can you?

At last Mr. Easthope stood. Wilbert jumped to his feet, too, I guess believing he shouldn't remain seated if his employer was standing. To my mind, this proved he had decent instincts even if he appeared a trifle rough around the edges.

"I'm so glad we could meet and settle this matter, Wilbert," said Mr. Easthope. I guess that a fellow, after he's been hired on as a houseboy, no longer qualifies as a *mister.* "Would you like to come along with me now, or do you have to pack some things first?"

"Um . . . I guess I have to pack." Wilbert cast a desperate glance at Lulu, who nodded. He nodded, too, relieved. "Yeah. I'll pack some stuff and get to your place as soon as possible."

"Very well. You know the address."

"Uh-huh."

Mr. Easthope had given his address, that of a swanky bungalow on Alvarado Street, and I'd written it down in case Wilbert was too befuddled to do so.

"You can take the bus there, Will," said Lulu. "I've got the schedule."

"Okay," said Wilbert docilely.

"I'm very pleased to have you on my staff," said Mr. East-hope, shaking Wilbert's hand once more. He turned to me. "The next séance is set for tomorrow night, Miss Allcutt, scheduled to start at eight o'clock. Will that be all right with you?"

You bet, it will! "Yes," I said in a polite, dignified voice. "That will be fine. I'll be there at eight."

"Come a little early if you will. I'll introduce you to Mother and the . . . d'Agostinos." He spoke the spiritualists' name as if it was bitter on his tongue—which it probably was.

Oh, goody. That meant I'd get to leave Chloe's house even earlier than I'd anticipated. Hiding my glee with difficulty, I said, "That won't be any problem at all. I'm looking forward to it."

Heaving a large sigh, Mr. Easthope said, "I wish I were. I'd like to wring their necks."

I didn't fault him for that. "I understand. Perhaps, with my assistance and that of Wilbert here, we'll have this problem fixed before too long." I smiled at Wilbert, who nodded vigorously.

"You bet I'll do my best, sir," said he.

Giving us one of his spectacular smiles, Mr. Easthope said, "Thank you both very much. With two such enthusiastic assistants, perhaps my troubles are on their way to being solved." And he left the office as elegantly as he'd arrived.

Lulu, who evidently had been holding her breath for several seconds, let it out with a whoosh when the door closed behind Mr. Easthope. "Oh, boy, is he one honey!" She sagged in her chair and fanned her face with her meticulously groomed hands.

"He seems real nice," said Wilbert, sounding diffident.

"He's *very* nice," I assured him. "He's one of the best. And he's a great friend to my sister and me." I added myself there at the end to boost my own morale, which had flagged considerably since the advent of my mother into my life in California. Not that I didn't consider Mr. Easthope a friend, but I really hadn't known him all that long or that well. He was Chloe's bosom buddy.

"Well," said Lulu, getting up from her chair with what looked like a good deal of reluctance, "I gotta go back to work. Can't leave the lobby unattended, even though Mr. Buck said he didn't mind watching it for me for a few minutes."

"That was nice of him," I said, thinking Mr. Emerald Buck was a real gem, even as his name implied.

So Lulu and Wilbert left my office, and I glanced at the prettily decorated wall clock I'd bought and put up my very own self. It was a little past three, which meant I had less than two hours of perfect tranquility before I had to return to Chloe's house and endure another evening in my mother's company.

Unfortunately, the afternoon was sped along by the entry of James Quincy Carstairs, who tapped on the office door and entered about ten minutes after Lulu and Wilbert had fled. He peeked around the doorframe and spied me seated at my desk, wishing I had something to do. "Ah, Miss Allcutt." He stepped into the office.

"Good day again," I said, happy to see him, and not merely because he was a handsome man. The awful truth about Ernie's business was that . . . well, there wasn't much of it. I'd just been contemplating Miss Dunstable's files and wishing I had some of my own to organize.

"So this is Ernie's office, is it?" said Mr. Carstairs, looking around. "I must say it's nicer than I anticipated."

My reaction to this comment was mixed. One the one hand, I didn't think it spoke well of my employer. On the other hand, it *did* speak well of my decorative abilities. It was, after all, I who had put the rug on the floor, the pictures and the clock on the wall, and made sure the windows were washed, the brass plaque polished to a high shine, and the wooden furniture buffed until it gleamed.

"Mr. Templeton's business is quite lively," I said, lying through my teeth. My overall self was vaguely nettled by what it perceived to be Mr. Carstairs's unpleasant attitude toward Ernie, and it goaded me into the fib. I know there's no valid excuse for lying, but I'm weak in some areas of my character.

Mr. Carstairs's eyebrows lifted ironically. "Is it now? Well, I must say I'm happy to hear it. Ernie is a good fellow, and he was an honest copper, which was a nice change from the usual kind. Sometimes. At other times, his honesty was a little annoying when it got in the way of doing business."

Doing business in this case meant bribing the coppers so they wouldn't interfere with Mr. Carstairs's clients, no doubt. I vividly recall Mr. Easthope telling me about the botched investigation into the murder of Mr. William Desmond Taylor, and how Ernie had tried his best to keep it clean but had been foiled at every turning. In fact, it was the Taylor case that eventually led to Ernie's resignation from the police department. He was too disgusted by the shenanigans surrounding the case to remain in an organization for which he'd lost all respect.

That being the case, there was nothing at all vague about my state of nettled-ness now. I said coldly, "I think it's a shame that the police need to be dishonest for businesses to prosper in Los Angeles."

To my surprise, Mr. Carstairs beamed at me. "I figured that's what your opinion would be. God, I love naiveté."

That comment irked me, and I was about to say so when Ernie's door opened and Ernie himself stepped into the outer office. Spotting our visitor, he leaned against the door frame, crossed his arms over his chest and eyed Mr. Carstairs without favor. "Thought I heard voices out here. Figured it might be a client. You have a case for me, Carstairs?"

His voice was colder than I could recall ever hearing it.

"Not at the moment, but I might be able to throw some business your way one of these days."

If that wasn't a sneer on Mr. Carstairs's face, I don't know a sneer when I see one. My hackles rose instantly. "We're so busy, Mr. Carstairs, I doubt that Mr. Templeton would be able to take on your case." I gave both men a sweet smile. Ernie rolled his eyes, which I didn't think was very nice of him. After all, I was leaping to his defense, for pity's sake!

"Ah." Mr. Carstairs gave me a knowing smile, and I suppressed a strong urge to heave my pencil holder at him. "Well, then, I'll leave you to get at it. Don't want to interrupt your busy schedule."

"Thanks," said Ernie sarcastically.

"Good day to you, Mr. Carstairs," said I. Then I immediately started thumbing through my lined green secretarial pad. Fortunately, I'd been practicing my shorthand, so the pad was full of notes that I was pretty certain Mr. Carstairs couldn't read. He didn't need to know that I'd written "Now is the time for all good men to come to the aid of their party," and "The quick brown fox jumped over the lazy dogs" five hundred times in succession. For all *he* knew, my notes were taken in pursuit of a very important case.

When the door closed gently behind Mr. Carstairs, Ernie hooked a thumb in its direction. "You like that guy?"

After a second or two of thought, I said, "I'm not sure. I do like his secretary. She seems most efficient, and I'm hoping to gain some secretarial tips from her."

"What for?"

I looked at Ernie, feeling as blank as I'm sure I looked.

"Um . . . I beg your pardon?"

"We have no work. What's the point of being efficient? I should think you'd want to drag out your work so you don't get bored."

"I'm never bored," I assured him. It was the absolute truth, too, at least for the time being. True, when I ran out of things to prettify, I might succumb to ennui, but I could always bring a book to read during dull moments. "Anyhow, your kind of business waxes and wanes. We were really busy for a while there."

"Huh," said Ernie, and he turned and went back into his office.

Oh, dear. I hoped he wasn't going to decide he didn't need a secretary because there was so little work to do. Then and there I decided to do what I could do to drum up business.

I think I survived that evening with my mother only because I knew salvation was only a day away, in the form of the upcoming séance at Mr. Easthope's house. Poor Chloe appeared frazzled. She'd been sick that morning, which, I understand, is a common complaint among women who are expecting, a fact that makes me wonder why women bother having children at all, although I'd never admit that aloud.

Mother's presence during the day had certainly not contributed to Chloe's peace of mind, and I felt more than slightly guilty that I had a job to which I could escape. Mind you, I didn't feel guilty enough to stay home with her.

Anyhow, I had business to attend to before I went to the office that morning. After dinner the night before, I'd gone to my room, pleading work as an excuse. And, by gum, I *did* work, too. By the time I went to bed, I had composed a perfectly splendid advertisement to place in the *Los Angeles Times* Classified section under the heading "Services Rendered." My ad read:

Discreet, professional, confidential investigation services
Suite 303, Figueroa Building, 7ᵗʰ and Hill
Broadway 6-3062

All right, I know it doesn't look like much, but I was attempting to get in everything I wanted to say in as few words as possible. I'd decided not to use Ernie's name, since I ultimately determined his name didn't matter for the newspaper. It was enough to give a description of the services he could provide and a means of getting in touch with him (through me, of course, at the office). I was very pleased with the result and I hoped Ernie wouldn't mind since I'd also decided not to tell him about it, mainly because I suspected he'd object, although I don't know why he should. It seemed only logical that a person advertise his business. Perhaps he didn't want to spend the money for an advertisement, but that didn't bother me since I was using my own funds and had lots of them from which to draw. He probably wouldn't like that, either, being a man and stubborn and all, so I figured not telling him about it was my best option.

My business at the *Times* office didn't take too long, and I was only about five minutes late for work. Since Ernie never got to the office until long after I did, he'd never have to know about my errand that morning. Unless he read the posting in the *Times*. I wasn't sure how he'd feel about it. But there was no point worrying. After all, the advertisement would first appear in the next day's edition, so I had a day to prepare myself.

It turned out that I didn't have to prepare anything, because other events transpired that made so trivial a thing as an advertisement in the *Times* fade into insignificance.

CHAPTER FIVE

Mr. Easthope's bungalow on Alvarado Street was an extremely elegant abode and I liked it a lot. Unlike Chloe and Harvey's house, you didn't need to take Angel's Flight in order to get to the heart of the city from Alvarado Street. The heart of the city was right there, surrounding it.

I don't know what you think of when you hear the word *bungalow*, but my mind's eye had pictured a lowish building, small and cozy. Mr. Easthope's house was nothing like my mental picture. Set back from the street, it was one of several houses in a courtyard with a grassy strip separating two walkways leading to the houses. A pretty gazebo had been built at the far end of the grassy strip, and Mr. Easthope's place was the last house off the right-side walkway. Two stories, it was surrounded by riotously blooming flowerbeds which gave its otherwise formal visage a soft, approachable demeanor. It was truly a charming house, although I don't think I'd have called it a bungalow if anybody cared to ask me, which nobody did. Anyway, it was a great place.

Chloe had offered me the use of her little car, an open and sporty Roadster, in which she tootled herself around the city (Mother, naturally, didn't approve, believing women had no business driving and should always be chauffeured everywhere, and then only in closed conveyances), but I hadn't thus far in my sojourn to the west coast learned to drive very well. So I took Angel's Flight to Broadway, and from there I hailed a cab.

Mother didn't approve of *that*, either. I guess you were supposed to get a servant to hail a cab for you, too, if you were a female. Stupid rules.

Wilbert opened the door when I rang the bell, and we smiled at each other. "How are you doing, Wilbert? How's your job so far?"

"It's swell, Miss Allcutt. Mr. Easthope is a very nice gentleman, and his place is swell, too. I have a swell room all to myself, too."

From this I deduced that Wilbert enjoyed both his employment and a very small vocabulary. I was happy for him about the job situation. "I'm so glad to hear it."

"Yeah, it's swell. I really do thank you for arranging it for me."

"All I did was get the two of you together," I said modestly as Wilbert took my wrap and led me to Mr. Easthope's living room. To get there, we traveled a hallway with a perfectly spectacular Persian runner guiding our way. There were fabulous pictures on the walls, too, and a beautiful padded bench next to a charming table adorned with a crystal vase filled with roses. "Oh, my, I do like the way he's decorated his home."

"Yeah," said Wilbert, sounding wistful. "Isn't it swell?"

"Swell," said I. A feeling of joyful freedom, almost of abandonment, swept through me as I uttered the slang word, use of which was forbidden in my mother's home. While I believe Wilbert might be well served if he learned another adjective or two to convey his rapture with his employment and his surroundings, and while I believe one should be polite in company, I, as a budding novelist, do not approve of censorship, even though I was born and bred in Boston, home of the banned-book brigade.

As soon as we got to the living room, Wilbert straightened, took on a heretofore unnoticed by me air of dignity, and said in a voice an octave deeper than his normal speaking voice, "Miss Allcutt." Then he stepped aside and I entered the room.

I'd only had an opportunity to register the overall loveliness of the décor when Mr. Easthope leapt to his feet as if he'd been anticipating my arrival with some anxiety. The way he rushed over to greet me, and his obvious mien of relief, led me to believe that he was in a state of nerves, poor fellow. He took both of my hands in his.

"Miss Allcutt! I'm so very glad you could come this evening."

"How do you do, Mr. Easthope? I'm looking forward to the séance." If I'd ever learned how to do it, I'd have winked at him to demonstrate my complicity in his plan. Instead, I gave him a knowing smile.

With flattering eagerness, Mr. Easthope led me over to a grouping of people that included two older ladies as well as a man and a woman who could only, I deduced, be the spiritualists. I came to this conclusion after a glimpse of their clothing and air of studied mystery, and I was right. After introducing me to his mother, Rosemary, and one of her friends, Vivian Hartland, Mr. Easthope's manner cooled considerably when he turned to the man and the younger woman.

"And this is Miss d'Agostino," said he.

I held out a hand to the woman, who was, I hate to admit, perfectly lovely. She had alabaster skin, black hair and dark eyes, wore a drapey black gown on her slim form and, all in all, made me think of Gypsy queens and fairy-tale princesses. She extended a limp hand to me, and I shook it probably too heartily for her comfort. But, darn it, I don't like people who take advantage of gullible old ladies.

The man seated next to her had stood upon my entry into the room. He, too, was good-looking, tall, dark and elegant. With a pale face, extremely dark, penetrating eyes and thick black eyebrows, he looked rather like my mental image of a

Spanish grandee, not that I've ever seen a Spanish grandee. He bowed gracefully over my hand when Mr. Easthope introduced us and said, "Charmed to make your acquaintance," in an accent I didn't recognize. Was d'Agostino an Italian name? Would it matter, considering they'd undoubtedly plucked it out of the air?

However, I like to think I betrayed none of the uncomplimentary notions cluttering my head upon meeting the d'Agostinos, but merely smiled serenely and went back to chat with Mrs. Easthope. I was fascinated with her story, and really wanted to know how a couple of fakers could hoodwink an adult human female into believing in ghosts. She was delighted with my arrival.

"Francis has told me so much about you, Miss Allcutt," she said, sounding like a jolly little old lady, which is what she looked like, too. True, she was dressed very elegantly, in a dark burgundy-colored evening dress with a long, scalloped skirt and a string of perfectly matched pearls, but she still sounded and looked jolly, which wasn't what I'd expected. I'd anticipated a gray, washed-out, vague sort of woman who was in deep mourning for her late husband. Oh, well. I guess this points out that one shouldn't judge anyone or anything without sufficient data. I think Sherlock Holmes advocated that same principle.

I took her proffered hand. "It's a pleasure to meet you, Mrs. Easthope."

"Please, dear, sit down between us on the sofa." She patted the space separating herself and Mrs. Hartland, whose face was quite a bit sharper than that of Mrs. Easthope. In fact, she reminded me of a weasel I'd seen in the zoo back in Boston. "Francis introduced you to Mrs. Hartland, did he not?"

"Yes, indeed," I said, smiling at Mrs. Hartland, who smiled back. I wasn't sure I liked her smile, although if she was indeed a friend of Mrs. Easthope, she must be a nice woman.

"Vivian's son George was supposed to be here this evening, but he's ill tonight."

"I'm very sorry to hear it," said I.

"I was too," said Mrs. Hartland, sounding as if she counted her son's absence in the nature of a defection.

"It's very nice to meet you, though," I said, valiantly attempting to draw the woman's mind from her wayward son.

Mrs. Hartland sniffed, and I was trying to think of something else to say when Mrs. Easthope spoke again.

"There's more to Vivian than meets the eye," she said in a titillated whisper. "Miss Allcutt, did you know that Vivian Hartland is really Hedda Heartwood? Or the other way around, I suppose."

I'm pretty sure I gasped. "Good heavens, really?" I goggled at the ferrety woman. "*The* Hedda Heartwood?"

"None other," said Mrs. Hartland, smirking slightly. When she smirked her chin seemed to become pointier, which might be the reason I wasn't exactly drawn to her. A pointy chin wasn't her fault, of course.

And I certainly couldn't blame her for the smirk. Hedda Heartwood was the most famous gossip columnist in the motion-picture industry. I was now seated next to the woman who'd fed the American public choice tidbits about every star in Hollywood's firmament. She'd written about love affairs between Pola Negri and Rudolph Valentino, Douglas Fairbanks and Mary Pickford, John Gilbert and Greta Garbo, and Gilbert Roland and absolutely everyone. She knew *everybody*.

"My goodness!" I said, for once at a loss for words. I'd been bred to socialize, so this didn't often happen to me. After gulping once, I blurted out, "Why, you must have the most interesting life, Mrs. Hartland. Or do you prefer Heartwood?"

"Oh, my dear, just call me Viv," she said with what sounded like an honest laugh. Her laugh softened her features and made her appear more approachable and kindhearted. I presumed she must laugh a lot in pursuit of her career or nobody would want to talk to her. "As to the interesting-life comment, you'd be surprised by how boring most Los Angeles celebrities are."

"She's told me some astounding stories, my dear," said Mrs. Easthope in a lowered voice. Then she giggled. If I'd ever been asked to describe a person who might be duped by phony spiritualists, my description wouldn't have come within ten miles of Rosemary Easthope.

"Oh, but still," I persisted, "it must be fascinating to actually *know* some of the most famous people on earth."

"Of course, it is," admitted Mrs. Hartland. "Although some of them take themselves far too seriously."

I darned near asked to whom she referred, but caught myself in time. Instead, I said, "Really?"

"Really. Especially some of the newcomers. They get a motion picture or two under their belts and think they're stars." She sniffed meaningfully. "If you only knew where some of these people came from and their backgrounds, and—" She lowered her voice to a conspiratorial whisper. "—you'd be shocked and amazed."

Oh, boy, I *really* wanted to pursue that subject.

However, almost as if the moment had been staged, Wilbert appeared at the living room door and intoned, "Miss Jacqueline Lloyd and Mr. John Quincy Carstairs."

I glanced up instantly, catching the look of worshipful adoration on Wilbert's face as his gaze lingered upon Miss Lloyd for a second before he vanished. Then, just as he'd announced, in walked Miss Lloyd and Mr. Carstairs. *My* Mr. Carstairs. Or, that is to say, the Mr. Carstairs who'd just moved his office into the Figueroa Building.

It was only then that I noticed another occupant of the room, one who'd been there all along, I guess, but who seemed to blend in with his surroundings. He was a tall, thin man who resembled Mr. d'Agostino slightly. He stood apart from the rest of us at the fireplace, as if he were trying to disappear into the lovely carved-granite hearth. His eyes were hooded, and he gazed upon the assembled company as if he were assessing us for a human auction. I'd not been introduced to him, and he gave me the creeps. I presumed he was the ghoul Mr. Easthope had mentioned when he'd unburdened himself to me in Ernie's office.

I didn't have a chance to think about the odd man since Mr. Carstairs spied me at once, gently took Miss Lloyd's elbow, and steered her in my direction. His smile looked to be one of utter delight. "Miss Allcutt! It's such a pleasure to see you out of the office."

We shook hands. "I had no idea you'd be here, Mr. Carstairs."

"Indeed, the astonishment is mutual. But please," he said, "allow me to introduce you to Miss Jacqueline Lloyd. Jacqueline, this is Miss Allcutt. Miss Allcutt works right down the hall from my new office."

Miss Lloyd didn't display any overt sign that she was thrilled to meet me, but I made up for her coolness. I took the hand she extended and said, "It's such a pleasure to meet you, Miss Lloyd. I thought you were brilliant as Lillian in *Whispering Oaks*."

My gushing speech thawed her considerably. "Why, thank you, Miss Allcutt."

She eyed my companions on the sofa, and I could tell the moment she registered Mrs. Hartland's presence. It was plain that the two women had met each other before. It was also plain that Miss Lloyd was more interested in making a good impression on Mrs. Hartland than in continuing the conversation she'd begun with yours truly.

"Hedda, darling!" she cried, extending her arms.

Mrs. Hartland rose from the sofa to receive Miss Lloyd's embrace of greeting. "It's good to see you again, Jacqueline. Your career is taking off like a rocket."

The clinch didn't last long. Both women looked kind of stiff to me, but then, I'd have been stiff too if someone had embraced me like that. I wasn't yet accustomed to Los Angeles motion-picture manners, which included a whole lot of hugging and cheek-kissing.

"Please, dear," said Mrs. Hartland—I had a hard time thinking of her as Hedda Heartwood. She looked so innocuous. "Let me introduce you to my very good friend Mrs. Easthope, and Mr. and Miss d'Agostino. The d'Agostinos will be leading the séance this evening."

"So pleased," Miss Lloyd murmured graciously, shaking everybody's hands in turn. Then she introduced them to Mr. Carstairs.

You know how sometimes you can go to a party or some other kind of function, and everyone there is relaxed and happy and ready to have a good time? Well, Mr. Easthope's séance gathering wasn't like that. I felt a tension in the air that I'm pretty sure wasn't merely my imagination. There were awkward gaps in the conversation and then, when it seemed as if the silence would drag on into eternity, two or three people would speak at once, rushing into the blank space in desperation. That, naturally, precipitated a spate of "Oh, please excuse mes" and "I beg your pardons." However much I admired Mr. Easthope, his house and his overall kindliness and social grace, this particular evening's entertainment appeared destined for failure.

I did learn the name of the ghoul at the fireplace. His name, according to somebody, I forget whom, was Leonardo Fernandez, and he was, again according to the same someone, assistant to the d'Agostinos. From the very little bit of information I was able to gather, he was as taciturn as he looked and only attended these functions so that he could oversee the action during the séance—what little there was of it—and make sure nobody cheated and/or fell into a faint or a fit or anything like that. I hadn't realized the spiritualist business could be so dangerous. When I said this to my companion (I think it was Mrs. Easthope) she stared at me blankly. I don't think she possessed her son's quick mind.

Evidently Mr. Carstairs and Miss Lloyd were the last people expected to arrive, because the two spiritualists arose not very long thereafter, and a hush fell over the room's occupants. Not that conversation had exactly been scintillating before that.

In spite of the awkwardness of the general conversation, Mr. d'Agostino displayed no overt signs of displeasure when he rose like a wraith from his chair, raked his dark gaze over those of us in the living room and said, "Shall we retire to the dining room? The time is ripe."

I didn't ask for what. The spirits to show themselves, I guess.

It's probably time for an admission here. I know I said I suggested attending a séance for altruistic reasons. And I honestly *did* hope to assist Mr. Easthope in ridding his home of a blight. And it's also true that I most assuredly wanted to get out of Chloe's house as much as possible so that I wouldn't have to put up with my mother. But the absolute, unvarnished truth is that I'd always wanted to attend a séance and could hardly wait for the silly thing to start. Anyhow, what true, red-blooded, aspiring novelist *wouldn't* want to sit through a séance and learn how the things were conducted and try to figure out how crooked spiritualists ran the things?

Besides, who ever said it was a sin to enjoy one's work? Nobody I know. Well, unless you count my mother, who believed it was a sin to enjoy anything at all and positively wicked to work at a job, and who wants to live like that? Certainly not I.

Mr. Easthope escorted me into the dining room. The table

there appeared to me to be particularly appropriate for a séance, since it was almost round, and it looked as if someone, probably Wilbert, had removed a couple of leaves to make it small enough to seat the eight of us. There was an uneven number of males to females, a situation that would probably have made my mother faint, but I guess these inequitable seatings happen a lot during séances, the females of the species being generally more likely to experiment with spiritualist matters than the males perhaps. I mean that comment in no way to disparage my own sex. I think it's keen that women are open-minded about things. Even stupid things like spiritualism.

However that may be, Miss d'Agostino sat herself at the head of the table and Mr. d'Agostino took the foot. The rest of us spread around it in no particular order, although I made sure Mr. Easthope was on one side of me. His mother sat on my other side. Across from us sat Mr. Carstairs, Mrs. Hartland and Miss Lloyd, in that order. Miss Lloyd would hold hands with Mr. d'Agostino, and Mr. Carstairs would hold the hand of Miss d'Agostino.

"Most of you have experienced the process of communication with the Other Side before," said Mr. d'Agostino after we'd all sat down and shut up. "But for those of you uninitiated into the cabalistic arts, let me give a brief précis of what will transpire this evening."

He was a well-spoken young fellow. If I hadn't already pegged him for a fraud and a cheat, I might have found him attractive. Nobody said anything.

Mr. d'Agostino continued, "First of all, I must insist upon silence. No one must speak, and no one must move. Communication with the spirit world is a chancy business, and there is great danger to the medium through whom the control speaks."

The control? I didn't know what the man was talking about.

Therefore, and because I figured I was allowed a question or two as a rank beginner, I raised my hand—not without some trepidation. Mr. d'Agostino, with his dark eyes and lowering eyebrows, scared me a little bit. "Um . . . I beg your pardon?"

Those black eyes pinned me to my chair and I swallowed. Mr. d'Agostino said, "Yes?" in a not-very-friendly voice.

"What's a control?"

"Ah," said he, and he seemed to relax slightly. The corners of his lips even lifted a teensy bit. "You are truly a novice, eh, Miss Allcutt?"

I only nodded.

"The control in this case is the priestess Nefreziza-Afret. The priestess Nefreziza-Afret was a powerful figure in a cult that reigned in Egypt almost six thousand years ago. She came to Angelique one night in a mediumistic trance and is occasionally willing to communicate through her yet." He looked at me, his brows lowering over his deep-set eyes, as if asking me if I had any more stupid questions.

"Thank you," I said meekly.

Okay, here's the thing. Well, one of several things, actually. From what I'd learned in school, there weren't any priestesses in ancient Egypt, which, according to my teachers, didn't allow women to do anything but breed and wait on men. Right after King Tutankhamun's tomb was discovered, the entire world was flooded with information about ancient Egypt, and I, totally fascinated, devoured most of it, as did millions of other people. Evidently not everyone read the same material I did.

Another thing is that even if departed souls did hang out in our world for a little while before traipsing off to heaven (or wherever their particular souls went), why would the soul of a lady who died six thousand years ago still be lingering around this mortal plane now? And if it did, wouldn't there be millions, if not billions, of other souls flitting about and getting in its way? Why is it that every time you hear about a spiritualist medium getting in touch with the dead, nobody ever comes up with, say, the spirit of Jesse James? Or, God forbid, Jack the Ripper? Or even Joe Blow from down on the Boston docks? How come it's always some princess or ancient king or someone like that? And what about the language barrier? Does nobody but me sense an incongruity in being able to communicate with a six-thousand-year-old person when most folks can't even read the King James translation of the Bible without getting confused?

Oh, never mind. Perhaps I'm just being picky. However, I do believe that this nonsense about summoning only the spirits of dead exalted ones is merely one more aspect of the overall phoniness of the spiritualist business. My understanding, now that the control part was explained to me, was that the medium goes into a trance and then somebody's ghost takes over his or her body. Why's it always somebody of high rank? I think it would be keen if some entranced medium some day was invaded by the ghost of a milkmaid or a goose boy or a farmer or a person occupying a similar situation in life. Or death.

Anyway, I shut up once I knew what a control was, and Mr. d'Agostino continued with his instructions. He had a wonderful voice, deep and rich and, as I said before, softened by some kind of accent. It was probably a fake one, but it sounded nice.

"We will first take hands."

We followed his instructions.

"Then I must insist upon utter silence as Fernandez puts out the lights and Angelique calls upon the spirits. You understand," he said with solemn intensity, "that occasionally the spirits are not available to us."

I heard assorted murmurs of assent and saw five or six heads nod gravely, as if the people attached thereto actually believed this folderol. Nevertheless, I murmured and nodded, too. I might have been there to debunk the d'Agostinos, but I wasn't supposed to reveal my intentions to the crooks or dupes involved.

The lights went down and the séance began. I have to admit that sitting there in the dark holding hands with Mr. Easthope and Mrs. Easthope got kind of creepy after a few minutes—or perhaps it was only seconds—of almost total silence. There was an occasional rustle of a skirt, but that was about it. We were good little boys and girls.

Then, so gradually that I was scarcely aware of it, a faint noise began to rise from Miss d'Agostino's end of the table. I also was scarcely aware of the smoky light gradually coming up until I realized that I could make out her face. She swayed slightly in her chair. You couldn't see another single thing in that room. Only her beautiful, pale, ethereal face. I wondered where the light source was, but there wasn't much I could do in the way of investigation right then. The effect was most spooky. The d'Agostinos might well be fakes, but they were sure good ones.

Suddenly Miss d'Agostino slumped sideways in her chair, her head lolling and her dark hair falling over her face. A deep voice, wholly different from Miss d'Agostino's former speaking voice, issued from her mouth. "I am here," the voice said, and everyone at the table sighed.

What ensued then was total hogwash. It was presented in an extremely competent manner, however, and I admit to experiencing an eerie sensation or two. The d'Agostinos didn't go in for ectoplasm, for which I was grateful, and they also didn't present those silly emanations I've heard about. You know what I'm talking about: arms and trumpets and stuff like that flying through the air.

Messages from the late Mr. Easthope started coming through loud and clear, and I could tell that Mrs. Easthope derived great satisfaction therefrom. I had almost decided that the d'Agostinos weren't absolutely to be despised until I remembered the money angle and the fact that these two crooks were taking advantage of a bereaved woman's vulnerability. It was flat wrong to deceive a grieving widow in this way. How was she ever supposed to come to grips with her loss and get on with her life if she remained stuck in her grief and in believing that her husband could still communicate with her? The spiritualism trade was despicable, and that was that.

I don't know how long the séance lasted. It seemed like forever to me, and more than once I experienced an urge to scratch an itch or feel under the table in search of some kind of switch that might regulate the ghostly light illuminating Miss d'Agostino's face.

Eventually, however, the spirit of the priestess claimed she was tired and departed. Miss d'Agostino sank a little farther forward with a soulful sigh, and the room fell into utter blackness once more.

Then Mr. Fernandez turned on the lights, and we all looked at each other. Except for Mrs. Hartland, who appeared to have fallen asleep. I thought her reaction to the evening's shenanigans was rather amusing until Jacqueline Lloyd, her beautiful eyes fairly starting from their sockets, jumped to her feet, pressed her hands to her cheeks, let out an unearthly shriek, and fell to the floor in a gloriously theatrical swoon.

CHAPTER SIX

Naturally these antics drew everyone's attention to Miss Lloyd—except that of Mrs. Hartland, who remained slumped on the table. She looked as if she were napping to me, but Mr. Carstairs, who'd been holding her hand until then, looked at her and opened his mouth as if to say something, then suddenly thrust the hand aside, leaped from his chair and said, "Good God!"

Well, as you can imagine, everything was confused for a while. I am pleased to report that it was I, Mercedes Louise Allcutt, who demonstrated the most common sense in the bewilderment that ensued after Miss Lloyd's faint and Mr. Carstairs's startled exclamation.

While Mr. Carstairs was on his knees rubbing Miss Lloyd's hands between his and muttering broken syllables indicative of concern, and all the other people there looked at each other and muttered, I calmly walked over to Mrs. Hartland. There I bent over, pressed two fingers to what should have been the pulse in her neck, and didn't feel any. Then I picked up her hand, which was warm and floppy, pressed my fingers to where the pulse in her wrist should have been, and didn't feel any pulse there, either.

Only then did I drop the hand, leap backward, and utter a soft scream of my own. At least I didn't shriek loud enough to wake the dead—a mere expression, I assure you, since it didn't awaken any corpses present at that moment—and then faint like Miss Lloyd. I did emulate Miss Lloyd in that I clapped my hands to my cheeks. Then my gaze frantically sought that of Mr. Easthope, and I cried out—not hysterically, I assure you—"She's *dead!*"

Mr. Easthope stared at me as if he didn't know what to do about that.

Fortunately I did. Gathering my wits together with some difficulty—I hadn't encountered any dead bodies thus far in my career as a human being, although I'd come close to being one myself a few weeks previously—I sought Wilbert as the person most appropriate to do some telephoning and gestured him over. He came to my side, looking pale and shaky.

Mr. Easthope hurried up to me. "What should we do?" he said, wringing his hands.

"Call the police," I said, sounding much more confident than I felt. After all, the poor woman had probably died of a heart seizure or an apoplectic fit or something. Still and all, I didn't think it would be politic merely to call an undertaker. After all, she *did* have access to a whole lot of personal information about a plethora of celebrities, and she *had* died in a room full of people sitting in the dark during a séance. The circumstances sounded suspicious to me, although I couldn't have said why particularly.

"The police?" Mr. Easthope appeared both shocked and pained.

"And her son," I said, thinking I should have thought of her son before I thought of the police. I guess my employment had begun to affect my thinking processes.

"But why the police?"

"Um . . . and a doctor." There. That was the best suggestion of all.

"But why the police?" Mr. Easthope repeated, and his voice had taken on an edge.

Why, indeed?

"I really don't want any negative publicity to come out of this, Miss Allcutt. After all, such publicity might affect the studio."

"Yes, yes, I know," I said, thinking madly. Even I couldn't have said precisely why I wanted to involve the police. I suppose, under normal circumstances, a doctor and the family were the most logical people to call. Still . . .

Then it came to me. I took Mr. Easthope by the sleeve of his well-cut evening jacket and hauled him to the side of the room and away from the action. "Listen, Mr. Easthope, this looks fishy to me. You've got two crooked spiritualists, you've got Hedda Heartwood, the most famous and meddling Hollywood snooper in the picture business, and you've got a motion-picture starlet and a motion-picture lawyer, all together in one place for a séance, of all things. Something doesn't seem right. Now maybe Mrs. Hartland died of a heart attack or a fit of apoplexy or a similar affliction. I still think you need to call in a detective to check things out. That way, when nothing is found to be amiss, there won't be any wild rumors circulating in picture circles. That would surely hurt the studio, probably even more than if, by some odd chance, the poor woman had been . . . um . . . done away with by some person." I'd lived and breathed motion-picture gossip since I'd come to live with Chloe, and I knew how vicious rumors and tittle-tattle got started and spread, not unlike the influenza pandemic of a decade or so earlier.

Mr. Easthope said, "Well . . ."

I seemed to be having a spate of dazzling ideas around that time, because another one struck me then. "And I know just the person!"

Mr. Easthope blinked at me. "You do?"

"I do. Detective Phillip Bigelow. He's the most circumspect

detective I know. Well, besides Mr. Templeton." In truth, Phil Bigelow was the only detective I knew besides Ernie, but I felt no need to reveal that fact at the moment. "You should have Wilbert telephone the Los Angeles Police Department and ask specifically for Mr. Bigelow."

Mrs. Easthope began to scream then, and Mr. Easthope got pretty rattled. As he turned to give aid and comfort to his mother, he said in a distracted undertone, "Very well. But please, tell the man to be discreet!"

"I certainly will," I said, relieved to have been given permission to do what I'd aimed to do anyway. Hurrying back to Wilbert, I instructed him in a voice that brooked no argument to call the police. "And speak only to Detective Bigelow. Don't speak to anyone else." I had a troubling thought. "And if he's not there, get his home number and phone him there. Tell him I made you do it."

Wilbert saluted and dashed off to the telephone room. Gee, I don't recall seeing anyone ever salute my mother. I must either be really good at giving orders or have a formidable personality. The latter might not be such a sterling character trait if my aim in life was to be different from my mother, but I didn't have time just then to contemplate the matter.

And then I thought of something that truly frightened me.

If this wasn't a simple case of a heart seizure or stroke, and if someone had somehow done away with the gossipy Mrs. Hartland, the murderous someone had to be a person in Mr. Easthope's house at that very moment.

That being the case, I took it upon myself to request that no one leave the premises. I did so by lifting my arms and my voice and demanding everyone remain until the doctor arrived. I didn't mention the police.

"But why?" said Miss Lloyd, still looking faint and shaky.

Again my brain raced. "Because we need to know that poor

Mrs. Hartland didn't die from some kind of contagion." I was proud of that particular fib.

I didn't expect it to happen, but both Mr. Easthope and Mr. d'Agostino came to my aid.

"Yes," said Mr. Easthope, sounding about as faint and shaky as Miss Lloyd looked. "Please, everyone, gather in the living room. I'll have the cook prepare something to calm our nerves."

"Yes," said Mr. d'Agostino. While Mr. Easthope looked ill, he looked fierce. Either he didn't appreciate people dropping dead during his séances or he was doing a good job of acting like it. Probably both, actually. "This needs to be looked in to. This is not good."

For business, I presume he meant.

Twenty minutes later, Phil Bigelow, accompanied by a couple of outriders in the form of uniformed Los Angeles police officers, arrived at Mr. Easthope's home. Phil didn't look awfully pleased to see me there, but I think that was only Ernie's influence working on him. He and Ernie were really good friends, you see, and Ernie had impressed upon him before this that I was snoopy and shouldn't be allowed to get involved in investigations, even those that he'd rejected.

Too bad. I'd been involved in this one even before it became an investigation, and there wasn't a single thing either one of those anti-feminist men could do about it.

I was too glad to see Phil to berate him for his opinion of female detectives, however. As soon as he appeared in the doorway, I rushed over to him. Although it's embarrassing to admit, I felt a little teary there for a minute. The past half hour or so had been *very* stressful.

Believe it or not, people had even objected when I'd had Wilbert call a doctor.

"She's dead. She's beyond the need for a doctor," said Miss

Lloyd. Her statement was somewhat callous, I thought.

"The doctor needs to confirm death before a death certificate can be officially entered into the records of law," I told Miss Lloyd, proud of myself for being able to inform her of that fact, even though I'd only learned it myself within the past month during the course of my employment.

Miss Lloyd sighed heavily. She really did look kind of sick, and I'm sure she wanted to go home, but so did everyone else. Poor Mrs. Easthope was still in a state of pitiable agitation. It must have seemed as though death were dogging her. First her husband. Now her friend. I felt sorry for her and figured calling in the doctor might be good for her, too. Maybe he could give her a nerve pill or something. Mr. Easthope sat on the sofa, his arms around her, giving her all the consolation he could, considering he appeared pale and shaken too.

I couldn't imagine myself sitting on a couch and putting my arms around my own mother. Not only would she stiffen up like setting cement, but I'd feel like an idiot. For a brief moment, I felt a trace of envy for Mr. Easthope.

We had all gathered in the living room by that time, and Wilbert, rather wan and wobbly himself, had served a variety of beverages from hot tea to different kinds of liquors, although the liquors were disguised in teapots. It looked a little silly, really, to have six teapots sitting on the coffee table, but I'm sure the police were used to it. Prohibition might have been the law of the land for a number of years, but the law never had and never would stop anyone with enough money to circumvent it. My goodness, that sounds cynical. I guess Ernie was rubbing off on me.

Anyhow, I've digressed from my narrative. The police arrived, and I hurried over to them.

"Oh, Mr. Bigelow, I'm so glad to see you," I said in a low voice. "This has been a harrowing evening."

He frowned at me. I guess he figured that since Ernie wasn't there to do it, he should. "I'm not happy to see you, Miss All-cutt. What the devil happened here?"

Well! I no longer felt the least inclination to cry. Rather, I decided to be punctilious and businesslike. I'd show him I wasn't a hysterical female. "We were all attending a séance conducted by the d'Agostino siblings." I ignored his contemptuous snort. "Then, when the lights went on after the séance was over, Mrs. Hartland was slumped over the table. I thought she was sleeping, but she was . . . dead." I admit to a gulp at that point but believe I may be excused for it.

"A séance? For cripes' sake." Still scowling, he surveyed the room full of people. "Who are all these nuts anyway?"

In a furious whisper, I said, "They aren't *all* nuts. Including me. I'm only here because . . ." But I didn't want to go into that in front of everyone. I said softly, "There's a good reason I'm here, and it might actually tie into Mrs. Hartland's death, but I'll have to tell you about it later. Maybe tomorrow if you can come to Ernie's office."

It looked to me as though he was going to protest loud and long, but fortunately the doctor showed up at that point and Mr. Bigelow had to deal with him. Blasted man. He was very nearly as annoying as Ernie. I never would have thought it since, before that evening, he'd always seemed nice and polite.

Men. Unpredictable creatures.

Nevertheless, whatever Mr. Bigelow thought about séances and the people who attended them, the police worked efficiently and, as far as I could tell, with commendable rectitude. From the little Ernie had let slip about the Los Angeles Police Department before this time, the department was riddled with corruption. These fellows seemed legitimate enough—on the surface at least. I mean to say that I didn't notice anyone accepting or receiving a bribe or slipping an expensive bauble into a pocket.

Nor did I see anybody trying to persuade an officer to let him go before questioning. And no one offered any of the policemen a drink from one of the tainted teapots. Of course, all three men from the police department studiously ignored those teapots, but I don't really count that as corruption. Murder was much more important than people in private party who had suffered a severe shock being served with calming doses of liquor.

Did I say murder? I meant to say death.

Oh, very well, I didn't mean to say death. I said murder, and I meant murder. It just seemed too convenient that the most widely published of the burgeoning legion of gossip columnists, Miss Hedda Heartwood, should have died in a pitch-dark room during a séance. A *séance*, for heaven's sake!

"I know this is an inconvenience," Mr. Bigelow said to the assembled attendees. "But my men will be talking to you one at a time before you go home. They'll only be taking down your names and addresses and asking a very few simple questions. Purely routine, I assure you."

A likely story.

Mr. Bigelow went on, "While my men chat with you, I'm going to accompany Dr. Fitch to the body." He turned to whisper to the doctor, "Where is she?"

Instantly I said, "I'll show you!"

Before he could protest, I hastened ahead of him and the doctor and was out of the living room, down the hall, and at the door of the dining room in a wink. Mr. Bigelow's frown was magnificent to behold when he caught up with me, but I was impervious. Well, almost.

"Miss Allcutt—" he began, but I cut him off.

"Listen, Mr. Bigelow, there's a lot more going on here than you know about yet. I need to fill you in on some stuff."

He rolled his eyes, looking in that instant exactly like Ernie

Templeton, only a little older and considerably less rumpled. I think Mr. Bigelow had a wife to take care of him. Ernie was on his own.

"I'm serious!" I whispered, impassioned. "I don't think this is a simple death by heart attack. I think the woman might well have been bumped off on purpose."

"Bumped off?" His lip curled and his left eyebrow rose.

Furious, I said, "Yes!"

"Okay, okay. Let's see."

My first choice would have been to tell him all about the spiritualists, Mrs. Easthope's infatuation with same, and the circumstances surrounding Mrs. Hartland's death right there in the hall, but both Mr. Bigelow and the doctor strode past me and on into the dining room. I followed with some trepidation. Hanging out with dead bodies wasn't one of the things I had aimed to gain experience with when I came to Los Angeles to gain experience, if you know what I mean.

Standing as far away from the corpse as I could, I watched the doctor inspect it as I explained things to Mr. Bigelow. His face remained impassive during my narrative, which was pretty darned concise and coherent considering everything that had happened that evening.

"Anyhow," I concluded, "I wouldn't be surprised if someone did her in on purpose. I mean, consider the circumstances."

"The circumstances?"

"Yes! I mean, the d'Agostinos are crooks, for heaven's sake."

"Of course, they are, but they depend on people's gullibility. They don't want their victims dying on them."

He had a point there. I instantly thought of another one. "But what if she was going to change her will in their favor? What if she was going to leave everything to them? She must be a wealthy woman." I was proud of that, but only for about a tenth of a second.

"Was she?" Mr. Bigelow asked, puncturing my happy conjecture and sounding sarcastic.

"Um . . . I don't know."

"And why would the d'Agostinos want to kill her if she was going to leave all her money to them?"

"Blast it, *I* don't know! Maybe she'd already changed her will." Another thought slapped me upside the head. "Or maybe she was *going* to disinherit someone, and they bumped her off to prevent her from doing so. A relative or someone like that." I thought it was a moderately intelligent suggestion.

Mr. Bigelow clearly did not. "Were any of her supposedly disinherited relations here at the séance?"

"Um . . . I don't know."

"You said it was Mrs. Easthope who was smitten with the pair, not Mrs. Hartland."

I heaved a hearty sigh. "Yes. That's true." After fuming for another moment or so, I muttered, "I still think there's something really fishy about all this." I pondered for a heartbeat. "Anyway, what if she was spreading malicious gossip about someone and whoever it was decided to stop her permanently?"

"Was she?"

"Darn it, *I* don't know. But it's possible, isn't it? Or maybe she was being blackmailed by somebody."

"As a rule, Miss Allcutt," he said, sounding insufferably condescending, "people who are blackmailing other people prefer those other people to remain alive so as to keep making payments."

Fiddlesticks! "Well, maybe *she* was blackmailing somebody! I'm *sure* this is no simple heart attack. It's up to the police to investigate!"

He grunted, once again reminding me of Ernie, but darned if my suspicions weren't confirmed in the next instant. Well, at least one of them was.

Dr. Fitch was leaning over Mrs. Hartland's back. He'd lifted her hair and was squinting at her collar when he said in a distracted voice, "Detective, you should see this."

With a glare meant, I'm sure, to keep me in my place and across the room from the body, Mr. Bigelow walked over to the doctor. Since I grew up with an expert at keeping young women in their places, and Mr. Bigelow didn't even come close to my mother's expertise in the activity, I followed him—very softly, so he wouldn't hear me—across the thick Persian carpet.

"What is it?"

"Do you see this?" The doctor gestured at the back of Mrs. Hartland's dress.

I stood on tiptoes and peered over Mr. Bigelow's shoulder. Fortunately for me, he was bending over the body because he's much taller than I. I didn't see anything.

"Do I see what? I don't see anything."

"This," the doctor repeated, pointing.

"Ah. Yeah, I see it."

Finally I saw it, too: a speck, no more than a pinprick, really, on the back of her gown.

"So what? What is it?" Mr. Bigelow asked.

Dr. Fitch straightened, putting a hand to the small of his back and groaning slightly. Immediately I straightened, too, and pretended I hadn't been snooping. I smiled innocently, but I don't think my precaution was necessary. He didn't even seem to notice me.

"On her dress here. What is it?" Mr. Bigelow repeated.

"I'm not sure, but I think it's a speck of blood. And you see here?" With another groan, he bent over the body once more, and pulled back the neck of Mrs. Hartland's dress. "That speck corresponds with this tiny puncture wound here. Right here, at the base of her neck, above the left clavicle."

"Hmm."

Aha! A puncture above the left clavicle! That must mean . . . *poison!*

Hmm. I wondered what kind of poison killed people so quickly. It must have worked extremely fast, since she didn't even cry out during the séance. She only fell forward onto the table without even releasing the hands of her neighbors. It occurred to me that someone ought to ask Miss Lloyd and Mr. Carstairs if they felt a spasm in her fingers or anything like that. I hoped Mr. Bigelow would think of querying them about the possibility. Perhaps I'd just give him a hint.

"So what does that mean?" Mr. Bigelow frowned at the doctor.

"She must have been pricked with something." Dr. Fitch gently lifted Mrs. Hartland's head and gazed at her face. Her right cheek had been resting on the table, and I noticed it was turning purple. Was that a symptom of poisoning? I longed to ask, but didn't quite dare.

"I don't know if it matters. Could have been a mosquito." The doctor shrugged.

I longed to protest, but didn't want either man to kick me out of the room.

"Could be anything," Mr. Bigelow said, nodding.

The doctor sighed and reached for his black bag. "I won't be able to tell you much until I get the body to my office. I'll be able to do a more thorough examination there. Right now all I can tell you for certain is that the poor woman is deceased."

"Yeah," said Mr. Bigelow. "She sure is."

"My post-mortem examination will undoubtedly tell us more, although it's probably just a heart attack."

"But you will check into that puncture wound, won't you?" I said, unable to control myself a second longer. "She might well have been poisoned."

Both men turned to look at me, and neither one of them with

favor. I cursed my too-ready tongue even as I lifted my chin. "She was a famous woman," I declared. "She dealt in scandal and gossip. It's absolutely possible that someone wanted to stop her from revealing secrets."

Dr. Fitch and Mr. Bigelow exchanged a glance. Dr. Fitch shut his black bag with a snap. "I will perform a thorough examination, young lady. You needn't worry about my competence."

"Oh, I wasn't—"

"Yeah," said Mr. Bigelow. "If there's anything to find, Dr. Fitch will find it."

Darn it! "I wasn't questioning your competence, Dr. Fitch. Really. I only wanted to make sure that you don't overlook anything."

"I am not in the habit of overlooking things, my good woman."

Oh, boy, I guess I'd put my foot in it that time. But darn it, nobody seemed to be taking the possibility of murder seriously, and I thought it was a highly likely possibility. "I'm sure that's so," I said meekly. "I only wanted—"

"Yes, yes," said Dr. Fitch. "I understand." He stomped out of the room.

With a sigh, I gave him a couple of seconds, then left the room after him.

Mr. Bigelow followed me. He was chuckling, the rat.

I soon forgot all about the detective's inappropriate sense of humor, however. Shortly after the doctor left the house and the police had allowed the séance attendees to go, I realized I'd have to call a taxicab in order to get home since Mr. Francis Easthope, who had promised to escort me to Chloe's house, was occupied with his mother.

"Don't bother with a cab, Miss Allcutt," Mr. Bigelow said, surprising me. "I'll take you home."

A police car. With lights on the roof. "Oh, but—"

"I'll *take you home*," he repeated with such emphasis that I knew it would be useless to argue.

Thus it was that I arrived at my sister Chloe's house in a police car, driven thereto by a detective on the Los Angeles Police force, and I faced the appalling task of relating the events of my evening to Chloe and Harvey. Worse, I had to tell my mother.

At least the auto's roof lights weren't flashing and the siren wasn't blaring.

CHAPTER SEVEN

"This," declared my mother in her most austere and commanding voice, "is the limit. You are to cease disobeying your father and me at once, Mercedes Louise Allcutt. You have no business with a *job.*" She said the word *job* as if it were a crawly bug that had landed in her soup.

"I'm twenty-one years old, Mother," said I staunchly. "I love my job, and I shall keep it." At that point in time, I fear I sounded a good deal more staunch than I felt.

"You are a disobedient child," said she regally. "You are being utterly ridiculous. At your age, you need to be thinking about marrying and starting a family. You have no business pretending to be of the working classes."

"I'm not pretending to be anything," I cried, feeling beleaguered and overwhelmed. "I *am* a working woman! If that makes me one of the *working classes,* I guess I am. And I'm proud of it, too."

"You're taking a job away from someone who needs it," Mother declared. I guess she figured that if she couldn't get to me using her tried-and-true bullying tactics, she'd shame me into quitting.

Well, it wasn't working. "Mr. Templeton had been searching for weeks for a secretary before he hired me. If somebody else wanted the job, she could have had it before I even moved to California."

"Mr. Templeton." Yet another couple of words that sounded

97

dirty in her mouth. "Your precious *Mr.* Templeton is no better than a thug."

I gaped at her. "A *thug!* How do you figure that?"

She eyed me as if I'd turned into the crawly bug swimming in her soup. "You know very well what I mean, Mercedes Louise."

"No, I do not!"

"A private investigator," she said with a sniff. "What kind of occupation is that for a young man to pursue?"

"A perfectly respectable one. A useful one. A *necessary* one," I said fervently. In truth, it sounded to me as if Mother was grasping at straws, and I felt minimally more secure in my position as part of the worker proletariat. I mean, a thug? Ernie? Good heavens, what next?

"Fiddlesticks. You're being irresponsible and impulsive, and you have no business trying to persuade me that you're anything but a frivolous young woman who is behaving abominably."

"I'm sorry if you believe I'm behaving abominably, Mother, but I still see no harm in my holding a job. In fact, I believe I'm contributing more to the world by working in it than by presiding over social teas in Boston. *That* is the sort of thing *I* consider frivolous."

"Nonsense. And the people with whom you now associate are completely inappropriate."

"Inappropriate? How do you figure that?" I was both angry and curious at this point.

"Your precious employer actually carries a gun," said my mother, adding emphasis to her condemnatory statement with an eloquent shudder.

"He doesn't carry a gun all the time. Most of the time it's locked in his desk drawer."

"That doesn't make his use of a deadly weapon any more appropriate. He has a gun, and he uses it in his work." She spoke as if Ernie's owning a gun put a capper on the conversation.

I wasn't buying it. "Good heavens, Mother, Father owns a gun, if it comes to that. What's more, he and his friends go out hunting at least once a year, searching for animals they aim to kill that they don't even need for food!"

"Hunting is a sport, Mercedes Louise," said my mother coldly.

"I think hunting is disgusting," I said bravely. No matter that it was the truth and that I felt sorry for the poor deer and quail and whatever else my father and his cronies slaughtered. They had no need to slaughter anything because we had plenty of money to buy food.

"You, young woman, are being absurd. There's a vast difference between hunting for sport and carrying a gun intended to be used against human beings."

I didn't like the way she'd put that, but I went on anyhow. "Ernie needs his gun because the bad guys carry guns. Ernie has never used his gun since I've known him. That's more than you can say for the criminal element. Why, every day you read about Tommy-gun toting bootleggers shooting innocent people on the streets."

"It's the job of the police to deal with the criminal element," Mother pointed out.

"They aren't always successful." I saw no need to mention that the last three cases Ernie had worked on—all of his cases, in fact, since the Ned affair—had been spying on unfaithful spouses and attempting to gather information in divorce cases. That sort of thing sounded sordid even to me, although it was a necessary function, I guess, in some circles. Of course, the mere mention of the word *divorce* would give my mother a spasm. Divorce was unheard of in her circle. Divorced people were ostracized and—

But wait.

According to Chloe, divorce might well be the reason Mother was here right this minute, making my life miserable.

When that thought occurred to me, I blurted out, "Perhaps *you* should hire a private investigator, Mother. You could probably take Father to the cleaners if you had proof of his liaison with his secretary."

It was as if the world stopped spinning. The entire household—it only consisted of Mother, Chloe, Harvey, Buttercup (who was snuggled in my arms and giving me a necessary degree of comfort) and me—froze. A gasp went up from the human occupants of the room, and Buttercup uttered a tiny "yip," probably because I squeezed her rather tightly the next second, when I realized what I'd said. Curse my tongue!

Straight as an ancient oak, Mother sat, staring at me with eyes like frozen flames. Chloe and I had inherited our blue eyes from her, although neither Chloe nor I could make our eyes look like that. With a voice so strained it quavered slightly, Mother said, "Mercedes Louise Allcutt, I had known before I came here to visit you and your sister that you had gone wild. I never expected to discover that you had become so utterly degraded as now seems to be the case. I will thank you to keep a civil tongue in your head, young lady."

I could have said the same to her—well, except for the "young lady" part—but I'd already said entirely too much. I did not, however, lower my chin. Darn it, there was nothing wrong with my holding a job. And it certainly wasn't my fault somebody had died during the séance that night. Or that Father was having a fling with his secretary.

It was Chloe who spoke next, nearly surprising me to death. "Mother, I think you're taking this much too seriously. Mercy loves her job. Lots of women work nowadays. There's nothing wrong with it." God bless my sister as a saint.

To my absolute shock, Harvey backed her up. "We employ

many young women at the studio, Mrs. Allcutt. We couldn't run the place without them. Women have added immeasurably to the effectiveness of our workforce."

From everything I'd read, women also came cheaper than men so the studio was probably saving money, but I didn't point that out to anybody. I was too grateful to my wonderful sister and her equally wonderful husband for coming to my defense.

Eyeing the three of us with motherly scorn, Mother said, "The women in our family, Mr. Nash, do not work. They maintain their places in society by fulfilling the duties thereof."

I'd had enough. Rising, with Buttercup in my arms for the aforementioned comfort's sake, I said, "I don't care for the duties thereof, Mother. In fact, I think they're stupid. I like my job. I'm keeping it. And Ernie is a fine, upstanding man, earning his living in a profession closely allied with the one he held in the police department."

Mother's eyes went huge. "He was a *policeman?* Good God, child, how much lower can a man sink?"

Very well, so Mother was thinking of all the Irish cops in Boston—who weren't low, darn it, but you could never get Mother to admit it. It's just that back east, there's a prevailing attitude among the so-called upper crust that Irish immigrants and their offspring are somehow less proper than the rest of us. Silly prejudice if you ask me, but nobody did. Sometimes it seemed as if nobody *ever* asked my opinion about anything, but only attempted to dictate to me.

"According to you, I've already hit bottom," I said, feeling spiteful. "So you might as well write me off as a lost cause."

And with that I left the living room, climbed the stairs to my bedroom, entered it, and collapsed on my bed, hugging Buttercup the whole time. She knew I was troubled, and she kissed me to show me that she loved me. I was ever so glad I'd bought her, even though she'd cost more than I earned in a week working for Ernie.

The next day I left for my job before anybody else, except Mrs. Biddle the housekeeper and Buttercup, was out of bed. I thanked my lucky stars for it as I paid the engineer at Angel's Flight my nickel and the little railroad car made the steep descent from the heights of luxury to the middle of Los Angeles.

My chest ached, and I knew it was because the altercation with my mother had left me hurt and angry. I also knew my mother would never understand the choices I'd made for myself in life, so I might as well just forget about trying to please her. But it's difficult to write off one's mother as a lost cause, as I suggested she do with me.

I mean, we *all* want the approval of our parents, don't we? Even when we don't really approve of them.

Nuts. By the time I walked from Angel's Flight to the Figueroa Building, said good morning to Mr. Buck, and entered the lobby, I felt like crying. When I saw Lulu, who truly *was* crying, I reminded myself that I wasn't the only person in the world with problems. What's more, although I might well have family problems, at least I had money, which was more than Lulu and her brother had.

I hurried to the receptionist's desk. "Oh, Lulu, did Wilbert tell you what happened last night?"

She sniffled into her handkerchief. Lulu always wore interesting clothes. Today, she was clad in a bright pink, drop-waist dress with red flowers on it and a big red bow on the side. She nodded, and I noticed that not only had her mascara become smudged, but she hadn't repainted her fingernails. She generally spent her days filing and polishing them, but this morning she'd evidently been crying instead of fiddling with her nails.

"Oh, Mercy, Wilbert's so worried! I just know the coppers

are going to blame him for that woman's death."

Puzzled, I said, "But why would they do that? Last night they kept saying it was a heart attack."

She shook her bottle-blond head. "Oh, they'll find some way to pin it on him. They always do."

They did? I didn't understand. That being the case, I said, "I don't understand, Lulu."

She shook her head some more. "You don't know."

"Why don't you tell me, then?"

She eyed me for a second, then apparently decided I could be trusted. "Don't tell nobody, okay?"

Not only would I not tell nobody, I wouldn't tell anybody, which was more to the point. "I promise," said I, figuring I was safe in doing so, since whom would I tell?

Lowering her voice, she said in a harsh whisper, "Will has a record."

A record. I had several records myself. And a Victrola upon which to play them. Then the meaning of her words struck me. "You mean he has a *police* record?"

She nodded. "Yeah. In Oklahoma."

And neither one of the Mullins siblings had bothered to tell me. I'd placed a crook in Mr. Francis Easthope's residence, all unawares. Boy, maybe my mother was right about me. Maybe I was irresponsible and impulsive and not to be trusted on my own in the big city. How discouraging.

"Do you mean to tell me that your brother is a criminal and you didn't tell me?" I regret to say my words were shrill.

Lulu flinched. "He's not a criminal! He played a prank and got arrested. The problem is, he left the state before his trial, so he's . . . well, I guess, technically, he's a fugitive."

A fugitive from justice. Things just kept getting better. I wanted to thump Lulu and her precious brother both. "What kind of prank?"

"He and a friend knocked over an outhouse on Halloween. The bad thing is that somebody was in it at the time, and when the outhouse fell over, it landed on him and he broke his arm."

An outhouse. Good Lord. I'd heard of outhouses, but I don't believe I'd ever actually seen one. We Bostonians had indoor plumbing. "Um . . . that doesn't sound so awful to me."

"It wasn't. It was Halloween, for cripes' sake, and kids always do stuff like that on Halloween."

Kids in my life didn't, but my life and Lulu's bore scant resemblance to each other.

"But the cops locked him up overnight. Our parents had a fit. Will was only seventeen at the time, and he figured his life was over after he was arrested, and since I was living in California, he decided to run away and join me here."

"I see." I still resented the fact that neither Wilbert nor Lulu had told me about Wilbert's previous brush with the law, but I felt better about foisting him on Mr. Easthope. I mean it's not as if Wilbert Mullins had killed somebody or anything like that, and I was absolutely positive that Mr. Easthope didn't have an outhouse. "Well, I can't see that there's much chance of the Los Angeles police connecting him with a broken arm in Oklahoma, if that's any comfort. Besides, the woman at the séance probably died of a heart attack. Everybody thinks so."

Except me, who thought she'd been murdered. However, I didn't for one second think Wilbert Mullins had done it. Why should he? I'm sure he never once dreamed of such a thing. He'd seemed totally awestruck the night before. I couldn't imagine him killing Hollywood's leading gossip columnist. Such a scenario made no sense.

I patted Lulu's shoulder. "Please don't worry, Lulu. I'm sure everything will turn out all right. Wilbert seemed very happy in his job last night. It was just pure dumb luck that Mrs. Hartland died during the séance."

"Oh, Mercy," she said, worries for her brother temporarily forgotten, "is it true she was really Hedda Heartwood? And that you actually got to meet Jacqueline Lloyd?" Her smudged eyes widened, and she stared at me with hungry intensity. I reminded myself that Lulu wanted to be the next Jacqueline Lloyd herself and took pity upon her.

"Yes, indeed. Mrs. Hartland wrote her column as Hedda Heartwood. And Jacqueline Lloyd is as lovely in person as she is on the silver screen."

"Oh, my." Lulu pressed folded hands to her bosom, squashing her handkerchief and looking enraptured. "Oh, my. You're so lucky, Mercy."

Yeah, I guess I was, if you can call being at a séance where a woman died lucky. But I understood what Lulu meant. She'd give her eyeteeth to meet some of the people I've met through Chloe and Harvey.

"Well," I said upon a deep and heartfelt sigh, "I'd better get to the office. Ernie's not going to be happy about last night's affair, either."

"Thanks for helping Wilbert, Mercy," Lulu said, her rapture forgotten and her voice taking on a shaky, helpless quality. "I just hope the cops don't nab him for murder."

The elevator doors closed upon a sob from the receptionist's desk, and I sighed again as it lifted me to the third floor.

You could have knocked me over with a feather when the elevator doors opened, and there stood Ernie Templeton, fists on hips, glaring at me as if I'd murdered Hedda Heartwood myself. Startled, I jumped a little and said, "Ernie!"

"Damn it to hell and back again, Mercy Allcutt, what's this Phil tells me about a murder at that damned séance last night?"

I drew myself up stiffly, annoyed with this uncalled-for attack upon my sensibilities so early in the morning. Wasn't it enough that I had to put up with my horrid mother without having to put up with attacks from my heretofore not-too-impolite employer? Yes, it was, darn it.

"Don't you dare yell at me, Ernie Templeton," I said through clenched teeth. "And who said anything about murder?"

"Phil told me all about it, damn it."

"Stop swearing," I said crossly, swerving around Ernie and heading to the office. "And none of it was my fault." I paused and turned. "Did you say Mr. *Bigelow* is now calling Mrs. Hartland's death a homicide?"

"They think she was poisoned." Ernie stomped past me and went to the office, where he opened the door and stood scowling at me until I passed him and entered my formerly soothing place of work. Today it looked as if I was fated to find no comfort anywhere.

I must admit, however, that it was kind of nice to know my suspicions were correct and that I hadn't merely been dramatizing the events of the prior evening. Ignoring Ernie's fierce glower, I went to my desk, placed my handbag and hat in my drawer, sat in my nice rolling chair behind my desk, folded my hands and placed them on my blotter. "As I wasn't the one who poisoned her, I fail to comprehend why you're berating me, Ernest Templeton. I had absolutely nothing to do with that woman's death."

"Damn it, you're always getting mixed up in things. Why is it that whenever you show up, things happen?"

"That's not fair and you know it!" I cried, peeved and working on a glower of my own. "I've never, ever been involved in murder." Before he could contradict me, since that was something of a fib, I hurried on. "And I'd never attended a séance before last night. I'm sure no one in the entire house full of guests knew murder was contemplated before it happened. Well, except for the murderer. Anyhow, when I left Mr. Easthope's home last evening, the doctor was still calling the death a heart seizure, and so was Mr. Bigelow. What kind of poison was used?"

"Oh, no, you don't," snarled Ernie, slamming the front office door. "You're not getting involved in this."

I sighed heavily and with sarcasm. "It looks as if I'm already involved in it. Not that I want to be."

"Huh!"

"I *don't!* Darn you, Ernie Templeton, none of this is my fault!"

"She's right, Ernie," came a voice from Ernie's office. Startled, I turned and espied Mr. Phil Bigelow lounging on the doorway. "It's not technically her fault."

"Oh, good morning, Mr. Bigelow."

"Good morning, Miss Allcutt."

"My, aren't we formal today? Didn't you two share a murder just last night? What's with the 'Miss' and 'Mister' stuff?" Ernie's tone was quite nasty.

But I had just registered the latter part of Mr. Bigelow's greeting and didn't take Ernie to task. "What do you mean, it isn't *technically* my fault? *None* of last night's doings were my fault!"

Mr. Bigelow shrugged.

Ernie said, "Huh" again.

The telephone rang just then, sparing Ernie and Mr. Bigelow a tongue-lashing from me. I picked up the receiver and barked, "Mr. Templeton's office. Miss Allcutt speaking."

There was a pause on the other end of the wire. I guess the person was taken aback at my abrupt tone, and I felt at fault. Softening my voice, I asked pleasantly, "May I help you?"

That did the trick. The person who'd called began pouring out her tale of woe, and I set up an appointment for her that very day. When I asked how she'd learned of Ernie's business and she said she'd read about him in the newspaper's classified section, my mood brightened considerably. I'd been so engrossed in other matters that I hadn't even checked the *Times* to see if our ad had been printed, but this was confirmation of a most encouraging nature that it had been.

When I hung the receiver on the hook, I realized both Ernie and Mr. Bigelow still stood in my part of the office. I smiled cheerfully. "You have an appointment at ten o'clock this morning, Ernie. Miss Ethel Ginther wants you to find her missing uncle."

"Her missing uncle? How the devil did her uncle get lost?" Ernie didn't appear especially gratified to know that he had a new client. How typical of him.

"I guess he left home and never went back again. Her aunt is distraught."

"So why didn't her aunt call me?"

Irked, I snapped, "Because Miss Ginther is helping her poor aunt, who is in a total state."

"Oh, brother, this should be fun," grumbled Ernie. He and Mr. Bigelow returned to his office and closed the door behind them.

Extremely annoyed, I'd pushed myself up from my chair and intended to dash after them to get the particulars about Mrs. Hartland and why the police now believed she'd been poisoned, but the telephone rang again. Huffing, I sat once more and picked up the receiver. This time I made sure my voice was inviting when I said, "Mr. Templeton's office. Miss Allcutt speaking."

This time too, I recognized the voice on the other end of the wire. "Miss Allcutt, have you heard the news?"

It was Francis Easthope, and he sounded dreadfully shaken. My sympathy was instantly aroused. "Oh, Mr. Easthope, I just this minute heard about it. I'm so sorry."

"Oh, God." I could envision him running a hand through his splendidly groomed hair. "I need Mr. Templeton's help. Do you think he'd be willing to take the job?"

This puzzled me a trifle. I was pleased that he'd thought of Ernie in this time of crisis, but wasn't altogether sure why he'd done so. "What do you mean? Aren't the police investigating?"

"The police?" I'd never heard him sound contemptuous before. "I was there for the Taylor investigation, remember? I wouldn't trust the L.A. police department to investigate a schoolyard bully."

Oh, dear. I'd read all about the William Desmond Taylor murder and the botched job the police had made of it. In fact, I may have mentioned that it was that failure in police procedures that had led Ernie to quit the force and go into private practice. The L.A.P.D. truly did have a dismal reputation. It was a shame that good people like Mr. Bigelow had to endure being tarred with the same brush the corrupt police were.

"This awful murder is going to affect the entire picture business, and I need to know that it will be cleared up and that no taint will mar the studio."

"I understand. I'm sure Mr. Templeton will be able to help you." Knowing Ernie and his antipathy toward Mr. Easthope, I was sure of no such thing. But *I* didn't have any such prejudices, and *I* would help him if Ernie wouldn't. I had no idea how I'd do so, but I had faith in my investigative abilities.

"Are you? Then will you set up an appointment for me? I tell you, I'm nearly out of my mind, and Mother is a wreck."

"Mrs. Hartland was her good friend, wasn't she?"

"Lord, yes. They were friends from the cradle practically. Mother is inconsolable."

"I'm so sorry, Mr. Easthope. I'm sure this terrible crime will be solved soon."

"I hope so," he said, sounding as if he didn't think anything good would ever happen again in the entire future of the world.

"Can you come in at eleven this morning? Mr. Templeton

has an appointment free then." He had the whole morning free except for that one appointment at ten, but I didn't want to say so aloud.

"Thank you, Miss Allcutt. You're a godsend."

Tell that to my mother. I didn't want to say that aloud, either, so I merely closed our conversation and hung up the receiver.

And *then* I barged in on Ernie and Mr. Bigelow.

CHAPTER EIGHT

"I'll be damned if I'll work for that faggot!" I don't think Ernie had quit glaring since I'd arrived at work that morning.

"I don't know what you have against Mr. Easthope," I retorted angrily. "He's a perfectly lovely gentleman."

"He's lovely, all right," muttered Ernie, sneering.

Mr. Bigelow snickered.

I'd have stayed to argue, but I heard the outer office door open, so I whirled around and stormed out of Ernie's office. I'd have slammed the door, except that I'd been reared never to do such a thing. Sometimes I think my upbringing will oppress me forever.

My mood changed instantly when I saw Sylvia Dunstable and Mr. Carstairs in my office. "Good morning," I said, happy to see my new neighbors.

Mr. Carstairs looked as if he'd been doing some hair-mussing that morning, along with Mr. Easthope. "*Good?* It's catastrophic, if you ask me."

Oh, dear. Another distraught gentleman. "You've heard they now consider the death a homicide," I said, slumping into my chair and waving the two newcomers into the chairs facing my desk.

"Yes. Murder. And I was there with Jacqueline Lloyd." Mr. Carstairs allowed Miss Dunstable to sit before he sank into a chair.

"I keep telling Mr. Carstairs that there's nothing for him to

111

worry about," said Miss Dunstable. "After all, it's not as if *he* did anything wrong."

"I was at a *séance,* for God's sake, where a *murder* took place, for God's sake, with a *client,* for God's sake. It won't *matter* if I've done anything wrong or not. My career is ruined."

"Tut-tut." Miss Dunstable looked with disfavor upon her employer. "Haven't you ever heard that all publicity is good publicity, Mr. Carstairs?"

"Not murder," he insisted.

Miss Dunstable and I exchanged a speaking glance. Well, there were two speaking glances involved, actually, but you know what I mean. I thought she was right. I'd read about Mr. Carstairs before I'd ever met him, which meant, in my mind, that he wasn't scornful of publicity. So why should this be any different? I could imagine great opportunities for him to speak to the press about how terrified his client was, how he aimed to protect her, and all sorts of things like that. Why, the man could become something of a hero if he played his cards right.

That being the case, I added my support to that of Mr. Carstairs's secretary. "I believe Miss Dunstable is correct, Mr. Carstairs. Why don't you compose a letter to the various newspapers deploring not merely the murder—not, naturally, that there's anything *mere* about murder—but telling people how upset Miss Lloyd has been, and how you'll do everything you can to cooperate with the police, how your duty is to protect your client, how the villain must be caught and punished, how you'll do anything in your power to see that justice prevails, and things like that. You'll appear to be a logical, caring person who wants to see immorality crushed." Morality had become a big issue since the Fatty Arbuckle affair of a few years prior. Not to mention the Taylor murder and perpetual gossip about liquor and drugs—John Barrymore and Mabel Normand spring to mind—being used by people in the motion-picture industry.

Miss Dunstable practically beamed at me, so it seems I'd offered a sensible suggestion. I did admire her. She was so . . . efficient. And she looked every bit the professional secretary. That day she was clad in a sensible, lightweight gray suit with matching shoes. She was also levelheaded and didn't fall apart in a crisis as the men around us seemed to be doing.

"Miss Allcutt has a very good idea there, Mr. Carstairs. You should attack the problem, rather than allowing the problem to attack you."

Well put, I thought, although I didn't say so.

Mr. Carstairs, who had buried his head in his hands, lifted said head and peered from one of us to the other. "Do you really think so?"

"Indeed I do," said Miss Dunstable firmly.

"Yes," I said, also firmly. "Don't allow the publicity to affect you negatively. Use the newspapers for your own good and that of your client." It's a good thing my mother wasn't there to hear me say that.

Ernie's office door opened, and Mr. Bigelow took a step out, then stopped. Ernie was right behind him, and he frowned when he saw we had company.

Mr. Carstairs rose from his chair.

"Carstairs," said Ernie, not warmly.

Mr. Carstairs nodded. "Templeton."

With a sigh, Miss Dunstable stood, too. "We'd best be getting back to the office, Mr. Carstairs. I can deliver letters to the *Times* and the *Herald Examiner* this morning, and they should appear in tomorrow's editions. If I get there early enough, the evening editions might carry them."

"Right," said Mr. Carstairs.

And with a wave and a "thank you" for me, the Carstairs contingent vanished.

"What the hell was he doing here?" asked Ernie, whose mood

had not improved. He hooked a thumb at the office door.

I was spared delivering a stinging retort by the telephone, which started ringing just then. Shooting a scowl at my hateful employer, I picked up the receiver. "Mr. Templeton's office. Miss Allcutt speaking."

This time the potential client on the other end of the wire needed to hire Ernie to trace his wife's movements, since the caller suspected her of dire doings with a neighbor. I suppressed a sigh. The trouble with a private investigator's line of work is that there's so much distasteful stuff involved.

Technically, I know, murder is sordid, too. In fact, it's a heinous crime against man and God. But at least it's interesting sometimes. Mrs. Hartland's murder had definite points of interest. But trailing a straying wife only seemed repugnant to me. Nevertheless, I set up an appointment for the gentleman, Mr. Richards, to see Ernie at two o'clock that afternoon.

The telephone rang all morning. Some of the callers only wanted to ask about Ernie's fees, but some of them had what might prove to be actual cases for us. By lunchtime, the entire day was crammed with appointments and my hand was tired from writing. I still hadn't told Ernie about the advertisement I'd placed in the newspaper.

At noon his office door opened and he exited, shrugging into his coat and slapping his hat on his head. "Come on, kiddo, we're going to Chinatown for lunch."

I blinked at him. "We are?"

"Yeah. I'm sick of talking to clients and listing to the blasted telephone ring. Besides, I want you to tell me exactly what happened last night."

I sniffed even as I reached into my desk drawer to retrieve my hat and handbag. "I thought you weren't going to assist Mr. Easthope."

Francis Easthope had showed up at approximately five

minutes until eleven that morning, proving how eager he was for Ernie's help in solving Mrs. Hartland's murder. I don't know what Ernie said to him during their appointment, but poor Mr. Easthope didn't appear any too happy when he left. I'd have questioned him, but I was busy on the telephone, which truly was becoming a nuisance by that point in time. Still, my initiative proved that advertising one's services aided in attracting customers.

Ernie muttered something under his breath that I couldn't hear—I probably wasn't meant to hear it—and stood at the open office door. "Come on. We don't have all day."

As if to prove his point, the telephone rang once more.

"Leave it," he barked. "Hell, it's lunchtime. Nobody does business at lunchtime."

From what I'd gathered during dinner-table conversation at Chloe and Harvey's house, that wasn't necessarily the case, but I did understand what Ernie meant. Most businesses allowed their employees an hour for luncheon, and people expected offices to be closed during that time.

Ernie drove us to Chinatown in his old, battered Studebaker automobile, and we ate at the noodle shop where part of our last adventure had taken place. I gazed with nostalgia at the plaza as Ernie guided me lunchward. That had been an exciting time, fraught with criminals, drug-runners and even a short-lived gunfight. It had been frightening, but it was something I'd always recall with pleasure. My life had been so dull up to that point.

The noodle shop was a small place with a counter and stools. I struggled up onto mine, still lost in memories, and Ernie plunked himself down without any great effort.

"All right," he said, butting in to my nostalgic mood without apology. "Tell me what happened last night. And don't leave out anything."

So, interrupted only once when Charlie, the proprietor of the shop, took our orders for pork and noodles, I did, trying to recollect every tiny detail. When I was through speaking, our noodles had been set in front of us, and we dug in.

After taking several bites, Ernie returned to the subject of the murder. "You say Mrs. Hartland's son was supposed to be there but wasn't?"

"Yes."

"Hmm. Wonder what his story is."

"Mrs. Hartland said he was sick."

"Huh."

By George—which, by a strange coincidence, was the son's name—I hadn't considered the possibility that George Hartland might have faked his illness and done his mother in under cover of darkness as the séance progressed, probably because of some fabulous inheritance. Hedda Heartwood must have been a wealthy woman at the time of her death. Such an act would be most heartless and appalling. Imagine a child killing a parent . . .

I decided I'd best not think about children killing parents in general, but to concentrate on George Hartland's alibi for the prior evening. As I munched my pork and noodles (enlivened by a whole host of vegetables, lest you get the idea the meal wasn't healthy) I pondered what I could do to investigate this aspect of the crime.

I could call Wilbert! He'd know if anything unusual had happened outside the séance room. Perhaps. He was a new employee; it was possible he wouldn't have recognized anything out of the ordinary. But he did have access to the rest of Mr. Easthope's staff so he could ask, couldn't he?

"Well?" Ernie sounded miffed, and I realized he'd been speaking to me.

"I'm sorry, Ernie. What did you say?"

He heaved an aggrieved sigh. "For the love of God, pay attention, will you?"

"I already apologized," I snapped, miffed in my own right. After all, Ernie had been acting like a bear with a thorn in its paw all morning long. All I'd been doing was thinking.

"I said do you know for a fact that Mrs. Hartland's son was sick?"

"Of course I don't. I don't know George Hartland from Adam."

"Hmm." Ernie spooned some savory broth into his mouth.

"Anyhow, I thought you didn't want to handle Mr. Easthope's case." Poor Mr. Easthope. I felt just awful for him.

"I don't want to handle it," growled Ernie. "But I'm afraid my secretary aims to involve herself in it whether I want her to or not, so I figure I'd better know what's going on."

"Nonsense." I felt my cheeks get hot. I don't know why. After all, I should be proud of myself for my willingness to help a friend in need. But Ernie made it sound as if I were a blithering idiot for caring at all. In spite of my embarrassment, I knew myself to be in the right. I ate some more noodles.

"Phil is going to check on Hartland's whereabouts at the time of the killing, so don't you go getting involved in it."

Well, really! "Listen to me, Ernie Templeton, and listen well. You have no right to dictate my movements outside of office hours!"

He rolled his eyes, lifted his bowl, and downed the last of his broth. Before you take him to task for bad manners, this was a common practice among the residents of Chinatown and, no matter what my mother would surely say, I honor cultural traditions. In fact, when I'd finished the last of my pork and noodles, I did likewise.

When I set my bowl back on the counter, I muttered, "Well, you don't."

"I know, I know." Ernie tossed some money onto the counter and slid off his stool.

Being considerably shorter than he, I made a leap for it, landed on my feet, and followed my annoying employer to the front door of the noodle shop. Charlie called something after us. I presume it was a pleasant farewell, although he'd spoken in Cantonese, so who really knows? Not I, certainly.

Ernie held the door open for me to pass through. "But if you have a brain in your head, you'll let the police handle the matter and won't get involved. That's their job, and you don't know what you're doing."

That cut me to the quick. "Darn you, Ernie Templeton. I may not be a trained private investigator, but I'm intelligent and resourceful, and I know how to telephone people and ask questions!"

"That's exactly what I mean," growled Ernie, stomping back to Hill Street and his Studebaker. "You're liable to put yourself in danger doing stuff like that. Remember what happened last month? If you hadn't stuck your nose into the investigation, you wouldn't have got yourself in trouble."

"That's not fair! It's not my fault that Ned turned out to be crazy!"

His back was to me, but I know darned well that he rolled his eyes again. Phooey.

Ernie's appointment book was jammed for the rest of the day. He didn't seem awfully happy about it, although there was no time to ask him why. I should have thought he'd be pleased with all the new work my advertisement had generated, but all he did was scowl at me between appointments.

Finally at about ten minutes past five o'clock, after closing time, the last client left the office and I heaved a gratified sigh. Ernie might not think much of my investigative capabilities, but he couldn't fault my ingenuity in drumming up business. I had just put my hat on and slipped my handbag under my arm and was about to bid Ernie a good-night when he turned to face me—he'd just seen the client out of the office—and gave me a hideous frown.

"All right, Mercy Allcutt, what's this about an ad in the *Times*? Three people told me they heard about me through my ad in the *Times*."

I lifted my chin. "Good for you. Advertising pays."

"Maybe. What I want to know is who paid for the advertising."

Curse the man. He was still frowning. "I did. And I should think you'd be thanking me instead of frowning at me!"

He walked slowly toward my desk, looking fierce. It was an effort, but I didn't flinch. "If I ever decide to advertise my services, it will be my decision, and it will be my money that pays for it. I want that clearly understood."

"Don't be absurd."

"It's not absurd. It's the honorable way to do business. All right. How much did the ad cost?" He started fishing in his trousers pocket.

"Oh, for heaven's—"

"Damn it, how much did it cost?"

I gave up. "A dollar and a half for the week."

He slapped a dollar bill and a half-dollar onto my desk. I didn't pick up the money, but only stared at it dumbly. "Don't you ever do something like that behind my back again." And with that, he turned and exited the office before me.

Well.

I felt approximately like two cents. Perhaps less. With tears in my eyes, I scooped up the money and shoved it into my desk drawer.

Darn him, how could he make even the most helpful of

gestures seem like a wicked betrayal? I only wanted the best for his business. After all, I depended on his success for my own employment. It wasn't my fault I had money of my own, was it? What was he so angry about? I didn't understand.

Then it occurred to me that perhaps my initiative (not to mention my money) had hurt his pride. I guess I could understand that, but understanding didn't make me feel any better. In fact, I plunked myself down in my chair and hauled out my hankie to blot the tears that spilled over and ran down my face.

Curse it, why couldn't I ever do anything right? I couldn't please anyone. Not my mother, not Ernie, not anybody.

I had just settled into a state of pitiful self-contempt when a light knock came at the office door. Surprised—after all, most of the offices in the Figueroa Building were already closed—I sniffled and said, "Come in."

The door opened slowly, and Sylvia Dunstable peeked her head in. "Are you busy, Miss Allcutt?"

Was I busy? Not unless you counted feeling sorry for myself as being busy. "Not at all. Please come in, Miss Dunstable." I made a quick last swipe at my tears and hoped the ravages of self-pity weren't visible on my features.

"I just wondered if you'd seen the afternoon edition of the *Times*." She held out a newspaper. "I picked one up when I went to the newspaper's office to deliver Mr. Carstairs's letter."

"Oh, he wrote that letter?" I felt slightly better. It had been I who'd suggested he write letters to the *Times* and the *Examiner*. Perhaps I wasn't a total failure after all.

"Yes. One to the *Times* and one to the *Herald Examiner*. That was a brilliant idea of yours."

My mood lifted another tenth of an inch.

"Thank you."

"Thank *you*." She held out the paper and I took it.

The headlines slashed across my vision like a knife: HEDDA HEARTWOOD SLAIN! POLICE SUSPECT POISON!

Oh, dear. My mother was going to have fifty fits. Not only was her daughter working for a living, but she was directly involved in the largest scandal to hit the motion-picture industry since the Taylor murder.

"Good heavens," I whispered.

"Read the article," Sylvia suggested. "It gets worse."

I looked up at her, praying she hadn't really said that. "It does?"

She nodded. So I read the article and discovered she was right. There, on the front page of the *Los Angeles Times,* was my name, Mercedes Louise Allcutt, listed as an attendee at the séance during which Mrs. Hartland had been foully done to death. They'd even spelled it right. My name, I mean. Lots of times people get my last name confused with Louisa May Alcott's. Miss Alcott was supposed to be a distant relation but who really cares, besides my mother?

I wondered if I could take a room in a hotel for the night. That pleasant notion had barely skimmed my brain before I thrust it aside as cowardly and unfair to Chloe and Harvey. Not to mention Buttercup. If I didn't show up to bear the brunt of our mother's wrath, said wrath would descend upon Chloe, and she didn't deserve it. I didn't, either, but at least I wasn't pregnant.

My heart throbbing with dread, I went home.

CHAPTER NINE

The following morning when I walked to Angel's Flight, I was still smarting from last evening's crushing diatribe that had been delivered with vigor and scathing contempt by my mother. Every time I passed a newspaper stand or a kid hawking papers on the street, I cringed.

"Read all about it!" cried the urchin standing outside the Angel's Flight depot. "Hedda Heartwood murdered! Read all about it!"

Since I didn't believe I could feel any worse, I bought a newspaper and perused it after I took my seat. The article didn't add much to my knowledge of the events surrounding the crime. Hedda Heartwood was really Vivian Hartland. There were only eight people in attendance at the séance, nine if you counted Fernandez. The séance had been conducted by Angelique and Anthony d'Agostino and had been held in the home of Mr. Francis Easthope, a costumier for the Nash Studio in Los Angeles. Oh, Lord, there was Harvey's studio's name, right there in print.

Feeling as if a dart had lodged in my heart, I folded the paper on my lap, set my handbag on it, folded my hands on top of them both, and stared out the window. Three minutes later, at the bottom of Angel's Flight, I got off and walked down Broadway to the Figueroa Building, feeling perfectly awful.

My mood didn't improve when I found Lulu in tears again that morning. I wanted to turn around and run far, far away,

122

but I wasn't so poor a friend as that. Therefore, I approached the receptionist's desk in the lobby and said, "What's wrong, Lulu? Is it Wilbert?" I couldn't imagine what could have happened to Wilbert, unless the L.A.P.D. had wired Oklahoma and discovered he was wanted for tipping over an outhouse. That seemed a remote possibility to me.

She looked up. Her eyes were streaming, her mascara was smudged, and her nose was almost as red as her fingernails (which she'd managed to polish sometime in between bouts of tears, I guess). "Oh, Mercy, they questioned him *all night* at the police station!"

"Why'd they do that?" It seemed a peculiarly fatuous thing to do, since Wilbert was a brand-new employee at the Easthope establishment and didn't know anybody who'd attended the séance except me.

"I don't know," she wailed. "They're gonna pin it on him! I know they're gonna pin it on him!"

I sat in the chair in front of the receptionist's desk and patted Lulu's hand. "They won't do that, Lulu. They have no reason to. They probably only wanted to find out what Wilbert could remember of the events of that night." That made sense to me, as I intended to do the same thing.

Sniffling pathetically, Lulu's watery gaze surveyed me, for signs of sincerity I presume. "You really think so?"

"Yes, I do," I said bracingly. "In fact, I'd like to speak to Wilbert myself."

"Oh!" Lulu seemed to forget her misery. "Is Ernie investigating?"

Oh, boy, I hated to tell her that my hard-hearted employer had no intention of helping out Mr. Easthope. Ergo, I waffled. "I'm going to make a few inquiries for the firm."

"I'm so glad Ernie's going to help!" And Lulu burst into tears again.

With a sigh, I decided to take the stairs up to the third floor, figuring the exercise would do me good. By the time I reached my office I was puffing a little, but I felt virtuous, which was a definite improvement over how I had been feeling.

I entered the office cautiously, fearing that perhaps Ernie had arrived early again that day, but let out a sigh of relief when I saw no sign of him. Good. That meant I could go through my morning routine of dusting and tidying without being lectured as I did so.

As I wielded my dust cloth and tidied things that were already tidy, I mulled over what I might do to help the police catch Mrs. Hartland's killer. I definitely needed to talk to Wilbert and find out exactly what had gone on behind the scenes on the night of the murder. And if I could, I'd like to speak with Mr. George Hartland, too, and find out if he'd really been sick or had only been pretending. You never knew about people. Even if he had been faking an illness, that didn't necessarily mean he was a murderer. Maybe he just didn't like séances. Or his mother's friends. Or something.

Nuts. Investigations were so complicated.

Ernie entered the office with Phil Bigelow about a half hour after I got to work. I'd been dreading his advent since he'd been so peeved with me the day before, but both men smiled as they sailed past my desk and on into Ernie's office, so I guess I was forgiven for drumming up so much business. Men.

Mr. Bigelow didn't stay in Ernie's office for long. He lounged out of it and over to my desk maybe five minutes after the two men arrived. Ernie was right behind him. I looked up at them with trepidation. It wasn't like Mr. Bigelow to want to chat with me, since he was Ernie's friend.

"Phil has to ask you some questions, Mercy," Ernie said, clarifying matters.

"Me? You want to ask *me* questions?" I pointed at my chest.

"Yeah."

"Oh."

"For Pete's sake, Mercy, you were at the scene of the crime," Ernie explained irritably. "Of course, he wants to ask you questions. He wants to ask everybody who was there questions."

That made sense. "Oh, of course. Please, Mr. Bigelow, take a seat." I gestured at the chair beside my desk.

"Call me Phil," he said, smiling in a friendlier manner than he'd thus far exhibited since I saw him at Mr. Easthope's house.

"Thank you. Please call me Mercy." My mother would die if she knew her daughter was on a first-name acquaintanceship with a policeman.

He drew a notebook out of his coat pocket. "All right, Mercy. Ernie says you're the one who got Wilbert Mullins the job at Mr. Easthope's place. Is that correct?"

"Well . . . yes, it is. Wilbert needed a job and Mr. Easthope needed to get rid of those spiritualists who've been bleeding his mother dry. He suspected they were crooks, and I figured putting Wilbert in his home would kill two birds with one stone." Poor phrasing. "In a manner of speaking."

"Right. So this Wilbert kid was supposed to be kind of like a spy?"

I thought about that. "Kind of. I thought Wilbert Mullins and Mr. Easthope could help each other, if you see what I mean. Wilbert, as a houseboy, might unearth some of the tricks of the d'Agostinos' trade."

"d'Agostino," said Mr. Bigelow—I mean Phil. "Right."

"What do you mean by that? Isn't that their name?"

Ernie snorted. "Not by a long shot. They're really a pair of shysters by the name of Clyde and Maude O'Doyle, and they're from Saint Louis, Missouri."

"My goodness."

"And they're married."

"My *goodness!*" I don't know why I was so surprised. I guess because they looked more like brother and sister than husband and wife.

I guess Phil didn't approve of Ernie supplying me with that sort of information, because he shot Ernie a "shut-up" look. Ernie only shrugged, and I began to recall why I basically liked him. He trusted me. If he didn't trust me, he wouldn't have told me the d'Agostinos' real name and marital status, would he? No, he would not.

"But your friend Mullins isn't lily-white, either," said Phil, hurrying slightly as if he were trying to prevent Ernie from leaking any more information to me. "Turns out his mother and Mrs. Hartland grew up together. What's more, Mullins has a record."

"Not a very big one, though," I said, then wished I'd taped my mouth shut before work that morning.

Phil's eyes narrowed into little squinty slits. "And exactly what do you know about Wilbert Mullins's record?"

I sighed. "Not much. Only what Lulu told me this morning. I didn't know it before, or I would have told you. She said he knocked over an outhouse, broke somebody's arm, and left Oklahoma before his trial. I guess that makes him sort of a fugitive."

"Sort of?" Phil lifted an intimidating eyebrow.

"An outhouse?" Ernie burst into guffaws. "That makes him the outlaw of the century, Phil."

"It's not funny, Ernie. The kid's a criminal."

"A very minor one," I said, feeling sorry for Wilbert. Even his crime was silly. I mean, if you were going to be sent up the river for something, wouldn't you rather it be for—oh, I don't know—robbing a bank or something like that? How'd you like it if you had to go to court and be sentenced for tipping over an outhouse? The entire gallery would laugh, just as Ernie was doing then.

"It gives him a motive," Phil said in all seriousness.

I swallowed my burgeoning giggle. "You mean you think he might have killed Mrs. Hartland to keep her quiet about his outhouse caper?" It sounded far-fetched to me.

"People have killed for less," said Phil sententiously.

"I think you're grasping at straws," I said. "What about the O'Doyles? They seem more likely as the culprits than poor Wilbert."

"We're looking into them, don't worry. We won't leave any stones unturned."

"You won't? Then do you know whether or not George Hartland was really sick the night of the séance?"

Phil frowned at me as if he didn't appreciate my curiosity. "We're looking into it." Wooden. Very wooden.

"And what about the poison? Do you know what kind of poison killed her? It must have worked awfully fast, because I sure didn't hear anything at all. Not even a gasp or a scream or a thump when she hit the table."

"We're working on that, too. It was probably some kind of alkaloid."

"What's an alkaloid?" I asked before I could stop myself. What I should have done was keep my big mouth shut and visited the library on my luncheon break. Well, I could still do that.

"It's a poison derived from a plant," Ernie said helpfully.

"Oh. You mean like that poison that comes from apricot pits?"

"Yeah. Like that," said Phil, grunting slightly as he rose from the chair beside my desk. "Well, I can't think of anything else to ask at the moment, Mercy. If you think of anything, please give me a ring."

"I will," I promised him. "Good luck. I'm sure it wasn't Wilbert."

He said, "Hmm." Not awfully encouraging, that.

"Have fun interrogating your next witness." Ernie snickered.

"Huh," said Phil, but his face flushed slightly.

"Who's your next witness?"

"Miss Jacqueline Lloyd," Ernie said with a grin.

"Oh, are you going to her home?" I wondered where she lived, and if it was a fabulous mansion or a smaller abode, like that of Mr. Easthope.

"Naw. Phil's getting two birds with one stone this morning. Carstairs and Miss Lloyd, both, in Carstairs's office."

Oh, boy, I wish I could sit in and hear what they had to say! Since I figured it wouldn't hurt to ask, I did. "May I go with you and listen? I'll be happy to take notes for you. I'm very good at shorthand."

I was right in that it didn't hurt a bit to ask. Phil's curt refusal to allow me to accompany him, in spite of my shorthand skills, stung slightly but not too much. However, I didn't have time to fret about it, since the telephone rang. Ernie turned on his heel and headed to his office.

As Phil exited the office, I heard Ernie flap open the *Times* and clunk his shod heels on his desk.

"Mr. Templeton's office. Miss Allcutt speaking."

The rest of the morning was busy—my advertising dollar and a half at work—and I didn't have much of a chance to think about the Hartland/Heartwood murder. Ernie left for lunch a little early, claiming he was sick of the telephone bell and me "yammering" (his word) into the receiver. Therefore, I didn't feel guilty at all when, a couple of minutes before noon, I scooted down to Sylvia Dunstable's office, hoping to find out if she'd overheard any interesting tidbits when Phil interviewed Mr. Carstairs and Miss Lloyd.

You could have knocked me over with a spring zephyr when I opened the door and saw not only Sylvia Dunstable, but Jacqueline Lloyd herself, seated beside Miss Dunstable's desk. Both women turned to look at me. It appeared they'd been having a comfortable coze before I interrupted them.

You'd think that since I'd come to live with Chloe and Harvey, I'd have become accustomed to seeing actors and actresses in person, but I hadn't. Perhaps it's because the silver screen projects such large images, but I'm always taken aback when I see a screen personage in the flesh. And nervous. I'm always nervous at such times. Such is the power of the flickers.

"Oh," said I. "I'm sorry. I didn't realize you were busy."

"That's perfectly all right, Miss Allcutt," said Miss Dunstable in her pleasant, well-modulated secretarial voice. "Please come in."

Both ladies had very nice smiles. Any one of Miss Dunstable's smiles could have made its recipient feel warm and welcome, and it did the same to me. Miss Lloyd's smile could have illuminated the entire world with some light left over for Mars or Venus.

This points out a fact that I'd come to appreciate fully since I moved to Los Angeles. I've heard it said that makeup can do wonders for almost anyone, but it takes more than makeup to create a true presence on the silver screen. I first noticed this phenomenon in a small way when my uncle Threnody (it's too long to explain, so it's best not to ask about the name) purchased one of those Brownie box cameras and tormented the family with it during a Christmas get-together at my aunt Augusta's house. He took pictures of all of us, including my mother and father over my mother's strenuous protests, which points out the strength of Uncle Threnody's character.

Well, when the photographs were developed, I was most awfully disappointed by the way I looked. I'm not bad looking in person, but I decided after that unfortunate episode that I'm definitely not what they call photogenic. Chloe fared much better than I, although neither of us possessed what has become known as *star quality.*

Both Allcutt girls would have been entirely eclipsed by Miss Jacqueline Lloyd who, either in person or on film, had star quality in abundance overflowing. She was the most ethereally lovely creature I've ever beheld, on or off the screen.

It was mid-August and the temperatures in Los Angeles had hovered in the upper nineties and low hundreds for days. In deference to the weather, Miss Lloyd had dressed all in white: a perfectly splendid drop-waist white suit with a tie on the side; a pair of simple white pumps that probably cost more than the Figueroa Building; and a glorious confection of a white hat that sat atop her sleekly shining dark head. She was the loveliest thing I'd ever seen. She almost took my breath away, and I'm not easily moved by human beauty.

"Miss Allcutt," said Sylvia Dunstable, breaking into my awestricken stupor, "I believe you've met Miss Jacqueline Lloyd."

"Er," I said, coming back to my senses, "yes. We met at Mr. Easthope's house." Collecting my courage around me like a cloak, I stepped forward and held out my hand. "How do you do, Miss Lloyd? It's a pleasure to meet you again."

"Miss Allcutt," she murmured, taking my hand. "So pleased."

I sank into a chair in front of Miss Dunstable's desk. "It's been a pretty awful couple of days, hasn't it?" I asked, hoping to convey my empathy and none of my perhaps-unseemly curiosity.

Jacqueline Lloyd shuddered delicately. "It's been perfectly horrid. My nerves are shattered."

Miss Dunstable clucked her tongue in sympathy. "Mr. Carstairs has been upset too."

"I'm sure he has. It was . . . ghastly." Another delicate shudder trembled through Miss Lloyd's slender form. "To think that I was actually holding the hand of a . . . of a *dead* person." She put a white-gloved hand to her alabaster forehead. "It doesn't bear thinking of."

"I'm so sorry," said I, although I'd been there too and didn't feel particularly shuddery. On the other hand, it truly was fairly appalling to think about holding the hand of a corpse for several minutes before you realized she was dead. "Had you met Mrs. Hartland before the night of the séance?"

"Yes."

"Did you know her well?"

"No. Only slightly," said Miss Lloyd. "She was the reason Mr. Carstairs asked me to attend the wretched thing."

"Oh, really? Why is that?" I hoped she wouldn't mind my asking.

"Well, she is—that is, she was—" Another delicate shudder made the white veil on her hat tremble. "—the most important columnist in the industry. Mr. Carstairs thought it would be good publicity for me to be seen to be interested in spiritual matters, and since she was there she'd surely write about my attendance."

I considered this information for a second before blurting out, "Couldn't you just go to church or something?"

Miss Lloyd peered at me as if I'd spoken to her in one of the lesser-known Germanic dialects, if there are such things.

Sylvia Dunstable laughed softly. "Oh, my goodness, Miss All-cutt, that wouldn't do at all."

"It wouldn't?" I didn't understand.

Fortunately for me, Miss Dunstable was happy to enlighten me. "You see, it's like this: *everybody* goes to church. Only a very few of us can afford to hire spiritualists and delve into the realm of communication with the departed. To participate in a séance lifts one out of the commonplace. If you're an aspiring motion-picture star, you can't allow yourself to be lumped among the masses. You must do everything in your power to transcend the ordinary. Mr. Carstairs leaked a story to the press about Miss Lloyd seeking to communicate with her late, beloved mother."

"Ah," I said, comprehending at last. Maybe. "I think I see what you mean."

"A true star must be perceived as apart from the horde."

"Ah," I said again, in lieu of anything more cogent.

"It's the difference between . . . oh, say, Gloria Swanson or Pola Negri or Lillian Gish and a swarm of other girls who come to Los Angeles in pursuit of a career in the pictures," Miss Dunstable continued. "A thousand other girls might well be pretty, but a star has a certain exceptional excitement about her. A girl has to have it to begin with, but then it must be nurtured assiduously. Mr. Carstairs knows how to create a star, and he's leading Miss Lloyd in the right direction. She must always be seen to possess a certain quality that others lack."

"Yes. I see what you mean," I said. And I did. The quality of ambition and luminosity Miss Dunstable was describing was the difference between Jacqueline Lloyd and . . . well . . . Lulu LaBelle, although I hate to say it. Lulu was pretty and she very well might possess talent. She might even look good on the screen. But she clearly didn't have that single-minded passion to be famous that led people like Jacqueline Lloyd to do *nothing* that didn't further their careers. If she did, she wouldn't be sitting in the lobby of the Figueroa Building day after day filing her nails, but would be out pursuing stardom.

It sounded like too much work to me. I'd rather be the assistant to a private investigator and take my observations home and write books about them without always worrying over who was watching me do it. I'm not much for the limelight, I guess.

Then again, Miss Lloyd's travels on the road to fame and fortune bore some slight resemblance to my mother's societal aspirations for her daughters back home in Boston. Mother was always showing Chloe and me off at big society gatherings, hoping, I'm sure, to snabble so-called "suitable husbands" (men with money and power) for her chicks. She made us attend all the "best" parties. She was particularly pleased when she garnered an invitation to a function sponsored by Mrs. Lowell. Although the Lowells were reputed to speak only to God, Mrs. Lowell occasionally spoke to my mother, who was almost as exalted as a Lowell, at least in her own mind.

Oh, dear, I shouldn't have said that. I'm *such* an undutiful daughter.

"Um . . ." I said after a moment spent digesting the interesting differences between movie stars and the rest of us mere mortals. ". . . so you had met Mrs. Hartland before that get-together at Mr. Easthope's house?"

"Once or twice," said Miss Lloyd.

"It was very important to stay on Hedda Heartwood's good side," put in Miss Dunstable. "Mr. Carstairs has often told me that he tries always to make sure his clients are seen only under favorable conditions by her. Or he did, that is."

"Really? Why is that?"

"That woman could make a person's career," said Miss Lloyd, her voice going a bit stiffish. "She could also ruin a career. She could be vicious."

"My goodness." Perhaps that ferret-like quality I'd noticed in Mrs. Hartland's features revealed more about her character than I'd first thought. "I didn't know that."

Miss Lloyd sniffed.

Miss Dunstable said, "There are lots of pitfalls on the road to cinematic fame, Miss Allcutt."

"I guess so. Had you ever run afoul of Mrs. Hartland?" I

asked, perhaps not very diplomatically. "I mean, had she ever written anything ugly about you?"

"Certainly not," said Miss Lloyd with hauteur. "There is nothing about me that cannot stand the light of publicity."

"That's good." I felt a little ratty about having asked that question, but I really wanted to know about the business. "It must be awful to have to keep secrets."

"I wouldn't know." Miss Lloyd rose from her chair. "I really must be going," she said. "I have a perfectly hideous headache from all those questions. My nerves have been unstrung since that awful woman was murdered."

That awful woman? Hmm. I wondered what Jacqueline Lloyd knew about Mrs. Hartland that I didn't. I was on the verge of asking when she forestalled me.

"If you *must* know about Hedda Heartwood, Miss Allcutt, perhaps you should speak with Mr. Carstairs. He knows ever so much more about her than I do. I must leave now."

"Of course." Sylvia Dunstable rose to her feet, too, and skirted her desk in order to see Miss Lloyd to the door.

This points out yet another difference between people like Jacqueline Lloyd and me. Secretaries escort picture stars to doors. They let people like me find our own way.

"Well," I said to Miss Dunstable when she returned to her desk, "I truly didn't mean to interrupt you."

"Think nothing of it, please. Miss Lloyd and I were just chatting."

My goodness. To think of "just chatting" with a big name in the motion-picture business boggled my mind. Although, come to think of it, I *just chatted* with lots of people like Harvey and Mr. Easthope all the time. That wasn't the same, though. The people I knew might be of major importance in the industry, but for the most part they were behind the scenes and nobody but those who worked in the business knew who they were. The people whom everyone idolized were the stars, the actors and actresses whose faces were known worldwide.

The whole motion-picture mystique was beginning to sound silly to me, so I left Miss Dunstable's office and went to my own. There I slapped on my hat, grabbed my handbag and headed to the library.

CHAPTER TEN

I spent almost the entire hour I was allowed for lunch in the library, reading all about poisons made from plants. For instance, I learned that an alkaloid is an amine produced by a plant. That didn't mean a lot to me, but I gathered that there were a whole lot of them, and they were all toxic to a greater or lesser degree. I also learned that alkaloids tasted bitter, contained nitrogen, and occurred generally in seed plants.

After reading for nearly an hour, however, what puzzled me most about alkaloids was how someone could come by one. I mean, it's one thing if you're an explorer traveling down the Amazon River or up the Nile, but most household cupboards weren't stocked with stuff like codeine, morphine, strychnine, datura or curare. I guess some folks had supplies of codeine and morphine, but I couldn't figure out how a fatal dose of either of those substances could have been delivered by a prick to Mrs. Hartland's back. Datura and curare killed extremely fast according to the books I looked at, and many Indian tribes used arrows dipped in those two poisons. Oddly enough, when the substances were eaten, they produced no ill effects on the person doing the eating.

But where would a person living in Los Angeles, California, get his or her hands on a supply of poison-tipped arrows? I hadn't a clue, and none of the library books helped me find one.

At any rate, after almost an hour, I had a notebook full of

information about alkaloids and possessed not a single notion as to what to do with it when I left the library. I grabbed a tamale and a paper cupful of lemonade from a street vendor (in Boston, you'd probably get a Coney Island and a Nehi, but the principle's the same) and headed back to the Figueroa Building. Ernie hadn't returned from lunch yet, so I ate my own lunch at my desk and perused my notes. I didn't feel as if I'd made any appreciable progress in the solution of Mrs. Hartland's murder by the time one o'clock rolled around and the telephone started ringing again.

Since I really wanted to talk to Wilbert Mullins, during a lull in the telephone nonsense I dialed Mr. Easthope's home. Wilbert answered the phone!

"Mr. Easthope's residence," he said in a voice stiff with the importance of his job, but I recognized it anyway.

"Is this Wilbert Mullins?" I asked to be sure.

Silence greeted my question, and it occurred to me that Wilbert might be nervous about talking to people since he'd been quizzed by the police and had a record and all. Besides, it wouldn't surprise me to learn that the vultures of the press had been bothering the residents of Mr. Easthope's house all day.

"It's Mercy Allcutt, Wilbert. I don't want to bother you. I just wanted to ask a few questions."

"Oh." Wilbert's sigh of relief carried all the way from Mr. Easthope's house to my ear. "I'm glad it's you, Miss Allcutt. The police and the press have been hounding me."

"I'm sorry about that. I'm sure they're just doing their job."

"Hmm."

So much for that. "Say, Wilbert, did you see anything odd the night of the séance?"

"Odd?" He hesitated. "To tell the truth, Miss Allcutt, the whole thing was odd to me. We don't have much truck with motion-picture people and séances and such-like nonsense in

Enid, Oklahoma."

I could appreciate that. "What I mean is, did you see anyone hanging around the house who didn't seem to belong to the household or be one of the guests or anything?" That was a stupid question—after all, everyone there would have been new to Wilbert—and I was about to withdraw it when Wilbert surprised me.

"Well, there was this guy."

I perked up instantly. "What guy?"

"I'm not sure. Updegraff—he's the cook's husband—went outside for a smoke and saw this guy smoking and slouching. That's what Updegraff said. Slouching—in the shrubbery. He— Updegraff—asked the guy what he was doing there, and he— the guy—said he was supposed to be at the séance, but didn't feel well. I thought that was kind of funny."

I did, too, and my mind instantly fixed upon George Hartland. Had he been at Mr. Easthope's house all along? Could it be George Hartland who'd perpetrated the dastardly deed? "Did Mr. Updegraff ask the . . . the guy for his name?"

"Yeah. I think he was a George something or other."

Aha! I knew it! "Thank you very much, Wilbert. This information is most helpful."

Very well, so now I knew that George Hartland hadn't been ill at his home that night. He'd been at Mr. Easthope's house. Furthermore, he hadn't come inside, but had skulked in the shrubbery. Fishy. Very fishy. I knew I ought to tell Phil Bigelow immediately, but I wanted to talk to Mr. George Hartland first. Phil would be upset with me if he ever found out, but that was just too bad. Let him do his own detective work.

During the very first case on which I'd worked—good heavens, had it been only a month ago?—I'd had good luck with the telephone book. Hoping luck would again prove to be my friend, I reached for said book and thumbed through it until

I got to the H section.

Drat. No listing for George Hartland. What did that mean?

He lived with his mother! That's probably what it meant. With thundering heart, I peered at the pages again, and *voila!* There she was, bold as brass: Vivian Hartland. I guess since she used another name for her column, she didn't worry about getting too many idle telephone calls.

With trembling fingers, I lifted the receiver from the hook and dialed the number listed in the phone book. Some male person on the other end picked up his own receiver on my third ring. My heart soared into my throat.

"This is the Hartland residence," said the voice. I thought it sounded rather tired and wan, but perhaps I was projecting.

"May I please speak to Mr. George Hartland? This is Miss Mercedes Allcutt calling." My tone was very formal and unemotional, although my insides were leaping about like ballet dancers, and my nerves were jumping like several children on pogo sticks.

Silence greeted my polite inquiry. My insides jangled louder, and my heart started to sink.

And then, to my utter relief, the voice on the other end of the wire spoke again. "Miss Allcutt? Are you the Miss Allcutt who was at Mr. Easthope's house the evening of my mother's death?"

Hallelujah!

"The very one," I assured him. "Is this Mr. George Hartland?"

"Yes."

"I just wanted to convey my heartfelt sympathy, Mr. Hartland. I'd only met your mother earlier that evening, but her death was an awful shock. I'm sure it's even more horrid for you."

"Thank you, Miss Allcutt."

He sounded as if he was on the verge of tears, and I didn't

want him to be. I mean to say, if he was the killer, he should be happy, not crying, curse it. On the other hand, he lived in Los Angeles, and his mother had made a fortune (I presume she had, anyhow) from the motion-picture business, albeit in an ancillary profession. Perhaps George Hartland was a good actor after having been exposed to acting all these years. Or perhaps he'd done her in because he didn't like her and only afterward realized that he'd killed the goose that laid the golden egg.

That last scenario sounded pretty far-fetched, so I settled on the actor possibility as the more probable.

Before I could analyze things further, Mr. Hartland spoke again. "I'm very glad you called, Miss Allcutt. You were among the last people to see my mother alive. You were one of the people who were with her when she died, and I wish you could tell me what happened."

Hmm. Such an ingenuous question from a probable murderer. Then again, perhaps he wanted to ascertain exactly what people had seen in order to find out if anyone saw *him* on the fateful night.

"Well . . ." I said, starting off slowly and not quite knowing how much to tell him. Then I realized that I didn't know a single thing about what had happened other than what I'd seen, so it wouldn't hurt to tell him everything I did know. "I'm afraid I must tell you that I didn't see much. I don't suppose any of us did, because the room was pitch black. All the lights were out, you see, and the medium was . . . um . . . in a trance." I decided that mentioning my personal skepticism to Mr. Hartland would serve no useful purpose. Better to stick strictly to the facts— which were that I hadn't seen a solitary thing.

"You didn't hear anything?"

"I'm sorry, but no, I didn't."

"And you didn't see anything?"

"No. It was dark."

"You didn't hear any doors opening or anything like that?"

Interesting question. I wracked my brain, but it was empty. Well, you know what I mean. "No. I'm sorry."

A sigh whiffled across the phone lines to my ear. "I figured as much."

All right. His questions had been answered. It was time for some questions of my own before he decided to hang up his receiver. "But I understand that you were supposed to be there, Mr. Hartland."

"Yes," he said. "And now I'm terribly sorry I couldn't make it."

"You couldn't make it?"

"I had a terrible cold in my chest."

"Really?" I kept my tone of voice as sweet as I could. "I understand from the houseboy that you were seen by another employee at the house that night."

Silence again. I hoped he wouldn't hang up on me.

"That fellow Updegraff, I expect," he said at last, contempt in his voice.

"Well, yes, Mr. Updegraff did say he saw you in the shrubbery."

"Hmph. I wasn't 'in the shrubbery,' for heaven's sake. I had thought to go to the séance in spite of my illness in order to make my mother happy, but I felt too awful, so after lingering outside for a while to assess my ability to participate, I went home before knocking on the door."

"Ah," I said. "I see." What I didn't say was what I was thinking: *a likely story.* "Um . . . are you feeling better now?"

"Feeling better? Of course, I'm not feeling better! My mother was murdered!"

Touchy, touchy. "Yes. I'm so sorry, Mr. Hartland. It was a perfectly dreadful thing to have happened."

"Dreadful, indeed."

"Um . . . do you think it's wise to be smoking when you have a lung ailment?"

"Beg pardon?"

"Well, Mr. Updegraff told the houseboy, who told me, that you were smoking in the shrubbery. I should think that would have aggravated the cold in your chest."

A second or two of silence ensued. "I . . ." More silence. Then he blurted out, "Listen, Miss Allcutt, this is nobody's business, and certainly not yours, but I'll tell you anyway. I didn't attend that ridiculous séance because I saw that ass Carstairs going up to the door. I'd just arrived, and I decided I wasn't going to go anywhere Carstairs went."

Odd. "You don't like Mr. Carstairs?"

"He's a damned shark!" A pause. A sigh. "Sorry, Miss Allcutt, I didn't mean to swear. But the man is after me, and I didn't want to be in the same house as he. I didn't trust him not to make a scene."

"Why ever not? He's after you? What do you mean? Is Mr. Carstairs some kind of criminal?"

"No, no, no. But he thinks I am."

Perhaps this telephone call hadn't been such a good idea after all. It only seemed to be confusing me more than I was already. "I . . . um . . . don't understand."

"I owe the man money, if you *have* to know. I'd hired him for some legal work a while back, and I haven't yet come up with the funds to pay him back. And I didn't want him dunning me at a party, for God's sake!"

"Ah. I see. Well, I guess I can understand that."

"The cops won't understand. You can bet on that."

Oh, I was sure they would.

At last Mr. Hartland said, "Well, I really need to go, Miss Allcutt. There are so many preparations to be made."

"Yes, I'm sure there are. Please accept my most sincere

condolences, Mr. Hartland. I didn't know your mother well, but she seemed a lovely woman." Oh, very well, so she'd seemed kind of sharp and foxy. That doesn't mean she wasn't nice, too, does it?

"Thank you. And thank you for your call." It sounded to me as if he only tacked on the latter because he believed he should be polite.

With a sigh, I hung up the receiver. Then I picked it up again and dialed the number for the Los Angeles Police Department and asked to speak to Detective Bigelow. When I was told that Detective Bigelow wasn't in and was asked if I'd like to speak to another detective, I hesitated for only a heartbeat before I politely declined the switchboard operator's offer. Best not to entrust my intelligence to another detective since, according to Ernie, everyone in the L.A.P.D. except Phil Bigelow was a crook. I wasn't sure I believed that blanket condemnation of an entire city department, but I doubted that keeping my intelligence to myself for an hour or so would matter much.

It turned out not to matter at all, since Phil Bigelow strolled into the office with Ernie Templeton approximately five minutes after my conversation with George Hartland ended. They went directly to Ernie's office and I followed them. I was pretty excited for about the first minute and a half of my revelations, and I hadn't even arrived at the telephone call yet.

Ernie interrupted first. "You did *what?* Why the devil would you spend any time at all in the library looking up alkaloid poisons, much less the entire hour?"

I frowned at him, annoyed by so trivial a question. "Well, you're going to have to know what kind of poison did her in, aren't you?"

"Not I," said Ernie, the fiend. "That's Phil's job. It's assuredly not yours."

"Well, I'm interested!"

143

"Mercy, the police are on the job, believe me. And the pathologist will probably be able to tell us what kind of poison killed the woman pretty soon."

I felt like an idiot, and I didn't like the feeling one tiny bit. "It doesn't hurt to do independent research," I said stolidly, lifting my chin.

"It might hurt *you,* damn it," said Ernie, determined to be annoying. "Butt out, Mercy. This is a job for the police."

Glaring, wishing I could throw my secretarial notebook at his head, I said, "According to you, there's only one honest policeman on the entire force, and that's Mr. Bigelow here." I didn't mean to whack Phil on the shoulder when I made that broad gesture with my hand. And I'm sure I didn't hurt him, since I do believe I connected with a shoulder pad, but the incident was embarrassing nonetheless. I said stiffly, "I beg your pardon."

"Think nothing of it." Phil was trying not to laugh, blast him.

"He is the only honest cop on the force, but that doesn't mean the others can't do their jobs if there's no bribery involved."

"Hey," said Phil in mock outrage.

Ernie shrugged. "It's the truth. But I do trust the force to work on this one. There's no incentive for them not to. Who cares enough about Hedda Heartwood's murder to pay anybody to cover it up?"

"How can you say that?" I demanded, stung. "According to everyone I've talked to, she was the gossip center of the Hollywood universe."

"Yeah, but unless they break into her house and steal her notes, nobody's going to know what she knew."

That hadn't occurred to me, but it sounded like a plausible thing for a murdering gossipee to do. "Do you think they might?"

"Naw. The cops have the place under surveillance and Phil's

in charge. He's got men he trusts, more or less, not to accept bribes."

I turned to Phil. "So you really do trust them?"

Laughing, Ernie said, "He ought to. Easthope paid them a bundle to investigate the case and find the murderer."

I think I gasped. "That's awful, Ernie Templeton." My own personal outrage was genuine and was clear to hear in my voice. "The police department has to be bribed to do its job?"

Ernie only nodded.

"Well, then, if you truly believe law enforcement in Los Angeles is so very corrupt, I will *not* butt out of the case." Boy, I'm glad my mother didn't hear me say that. "I will persist in attempting to bring the villain to justice."

"Really, Mercy, it's probably best if you don't meddle—um, I mean, it's probably best if you don't get involved in this. We're talking murder here, you know." I got the feeling Phil was attempting diplomacy, but his words fell far short of his goal.

"I am *not* meddling, Detective Bigelow. I am attempting to assist your precious police department in solving a crime. I should think you'd appreciate my involvement. Aren't the newspapers always writing about the public being apathetic to the growing crime situation? Well, I'm not apathetic! And I don't have to be bribed, either!"

Ernie leaned back in his chair, rolled his eyes, and muttered, "Christ."

"And *you*," I said, pointing at him, thereby breaking another cardinal rule of my childhood, "can just stay out of it!"

The front legs of Ernie's chair hit the floor with a thump, and he leaned forward on his elbows. "You're my secretary. I'll be damned if I'll sit back and let you get yourself into trouble again."

"What do you mean, *again?*" cried I, even more outraged. "I

145

caught your blasted murderer for you last month, if you'll recollect."

"How could I forget," muttered Ernie. "You damned near scared me to death."

"You damned near got *yourself* done to death," added Phil.

"Oh, bother the both of you!" I started to storm out of Ernie's office, but then I remembered the conversation I'd had with George Hartland. Pausing at the door to the outer office, I pondered whether or not to reveal my information. I didn't want to. Not to those two beastly men.

However, my job was to serve the public . . . Well, technically, my job was secretary to a private investigator, but I *wanted* to serve the public, so I swallowed my pride and turned to face my tormentors once more. I thought rapidly as I struggled to decide on the best way to reveal my news. If Phil already knew all about it, I'd be embarrassed. If he didn't, I'd feel great triumph. Determining to frame my intelligence carefully, my jaw was stiff when I said, "Did you know that Mrs. Hartland's son was at Mr. Easthope's residence on the night of the murder?"

The starts of surprise from Ernie and Phil gratified something deep within me. Petty, I know.

Phil said, "Huh?"

Ernie said, "What the hell?" Then he frowned at me. He would. "How the devil do you know that?"

By that time my chin was so high, it almost pointed at the ceiling. Lowering it only enough to make my words understood, I explained. "I know that because I spoke to Wilbert Mullins. He told me that Mr. Hartland was discovered by Mr. Updegraff in the shrubbery, smoking a cigarette."

"By God," muttered Phil.

Ernie only sputtered.

I forged onward. "So, upon that intelligence, I took the initiative and placed a telephone call to Mr. Hartland's residence, which is really his mother's home. There, I am pleased to report, I spoke to the man himself. And before you interrupt me—" I spoke more loudly, because I could tell that Ernie was set to spring—"let me tell you that Mr. Hartland told me himself that he was *not* ill the night of the séance."

"*Damn* it, Mercy!" cried Ernie, furious.

I paid him no mind. "He saw Mr. Carstairs entering Mr. Easthope's house and detoured to the garden, where he smoked a cigarette and pondered. It turns out that he owes Mr. Carstairs money from when Mr. Carstairs represented him in a legal matter. He was afraid Mr. Carstairs would bring the matter up during the party." I felt like adding a *so there* to my narrative, but I restrained myself.

Both men stared at me for several seconds. It felt like several hours to me, but I wouldn't let on. Finally, Phil murmured, "Well, I'll be . . . um . . . That's very interesting, Mercy. Thank you." Phil has the instincts of a gentleman, even though he persists in keeping low company.

I turned toward said low company to find him still in a state of incoherent fury. Deciding it would behoove me to remove myself from Ernie's office before he recovered enough to holler, I did so, closing the door smartly behind me.

The ringing of the telephone saved me from contemplating my moment of triumph, which was probably a good thing since I might have become smug, and the truth was that I really hadn't helped the investigation along a whole lot.

Or perhaps I had. The more I looked at what I now knew, the more George Hartland surged to the forefront of possible suspects.

On the other hand, what did I *really* know? Only what George Hartland had told me. I had no confirmation from anyone else that his story was true. Bother.

However, confirmation or denial was as near as two offices

away, and I decided I'd jolly well go seek out a definitive answer to my question regarding George Hartland. When there was a lull in the telephone's ringing, I tapped softly at Ernie's office door. Phil was still in there. God alone knew what they were talking about. According to accepted reasoning men don't gossip, but according to my own personal observations they were worse than women when it came to slinging mud, only men didn't call it *gossip*. But we needn't get into that right now. Suffice it to say that I tapped softly on Ernie's door.

"Yeah?" came his inelegant response to my knock.

I peeked in. "I need to go down the hall for a moment, Ernie. I'll be right back."

"Okay."

He naturally assumed I was going to visit the powder room, and I figured what he didn't know wouldn't hurt me; therefore, I didn't clarify my purpose in leaving my desk. I did, however, hurry down the hall.

Miss Dunstable looked up as I entered her office, and smiled her pleasant, professional smile. "How do you do, Miss Allcutt?"

"I'm fine, thanks. I actually came here to ask a question, if I may. Um . . . is Mr. Carstairs available?"

"I'm not—"

She didn't get to finish her sentence, because Mr. Carstairs himself appeared in his office doorway. "Did I hear my name taken in vain?" His smile seemed slightly predatory to me, but perhaps I was allowing my reading of detective fiction to color my opinion.

"Good afternoon, Mr. Carstairs," I said brightly. "I was hoping you could answer a question for me."

"Fire away," said he.

"Is it true that Mr. George Hartland owes you money?" As soon as the question left my lips, I felt my face flame. What kind of question was that to ask of a gentleman? My mother would be horrified. In truth, *I* was faintly horrified.

So was Mr. Carstairs, whose smile vanished instantly.

I hastened on, stumbling as I went. "You see, the police believed Mr. Hartland was ill the night of the séance during which his mother died, but according to Mr. Hartland himself, he saw you enter the house and didn't want to go in after you because he owes you money. I . . . I know it sounds awful, but I'm checking on his alibi. I mean his lack of alibi. I mean . . ." Good heavens, what a pickle I'd managed to talk myself in to.

"Ah," said Mr. Carstairs, his frown easing, which made me feel better. "I see." After a pause of several seconds, he added, "Yes. He told you the truth. He does owe me money, and he doesn't seem inclined to pay. Services rendered, you understand."

I really wanted to know what sorts of legal services Mr. Carstairs had rendered to Mr. Hartland, but I didn't feel right in asking. I think there are laws of confidentiality or something like that, and it was more than likely that Mr. Carstairs wouldn't take kindly to more probing. I'd already asked enough awkward questions for one day.

"I see. Thank you very much."

I'd probably have made a fool of myself by thanking him several more times, but the office door opened, and Ernie Templeton walked in, looking rather like I'd expect an angry bear to look if somebody snatched his blueberry bush from his paw. I jumped an inch or two.

"So there you are," Ernie said, glowering at me and ignoring the room's other two occupants. "I thought you'd left the office for something important."

"I did!" I cried indignantly.

"Well, I'd say your job is more important, Miss Allcutt. And the telephone's ringing off the hook so you'd better get back to it."

My face felt as if it would burst into flame, and my temper soared into the stratosphere, but I didn't make a scene in front of strangers—well, relative strangers. Instead, I said primly, "I was just finishing my business here, Mr. Templeton, and I shall return to the office at once."

"Good thing," growled my infuriating employer. And he gave Mr. Carstairs an unpleasant sneer, bobbed his head at Miss Dunstable, and stood at the door, waiting for me.

Longing to kick him in the shins as I passed, I suppressed my desire and returned to the office.

There wasn't much of the workday left after that, thank goodness, since I didn't stop steaming until I'd ridden up Angel's Flight and walked the two blocks to Chloe's house. The thought that soon I would see my darling Buttercup cheered me until the realization that I'd also see my not-so-darling mother spoiled it for me. Nevertheless, I was more cheerful than not when I opened the door to Chloe's house and was greeted by my adorable poodle, who leaped into my arms and wiggled all over. There's nothing quite like the love of a dog to elate one's sagging spirits.

My sense of well-being lasted until I looked up, Buttercup in my arms, discovered Mother standing in Chloe's beautiful tiled hallway, and heard her say, "Mr. Easthope telephoned, Mercedes Louise. There will be another séance at his house tomorrow evening, and I shall attend it with you."

CHAPTER ELEVEN

Not only did my mother declare her intention of attending the next séance with me, but she positively *grilled* me on the Hartland case. I couldn't understand her enthusiasm for something that, as far as I knew, she considered a profession crafted in hell and that only yesterday she'd been dead-set against.

"But . . . I thought you didn't approve of my job, Mother," I said, still reeling from shock and forgetting for the moment that it was unwise to feed my mother weapons with which to smack me.

She surprised me. "I do not at all approve of your decision to remain in the employ of a person so far beneath you socially, Mercedes. However, if you are determined to hold on to this so-called *job* of yours, I believe it is my duty to assure your safety."

My *mother* aimed to ensure my *safety?*

"Um . . . by attending the séance at Mr. Easthope's home?"

"Certainly. You shouldn't be running around the countryside without proper supervision."

"Proper supervision?" I repeated faintly.

"Yes."

It was only then that I noticed a suspicious gleam in Mother's generally steely eyes. I peered more closely until she frowned at me and accused me of staring. I guess I was, too, but darned if it didn't look as if my mother—*my mother*—was interested in the case!

To test out my theory, I asked tentatively, "Um . . . do you have any theories about who might have killed Mrs. Hartland, Mother?" Then I braced myself.

"How can I possibly have any *theories,* as you call them, until I have acquainted myself with the venue in which the deed took place and the inhabitants of the place?"

"Um . . . I guess you can't."

From anyone else in the world, the sound she next made would have been a snort. From my mother . . . well, I guess it was still a snort. "The situation needs merely to be studied," she said with dignity. "I'm sure that, as a disinterested party, I can shed some light on the case."

"But aren't the police disinterested? I mean, they weren't involved in the séance or anything."

She made that noise again. "The police are individuals of limited abilities, Mercedes, or they would be doing something else with their lives. This situation needs to be studied by someone with intelligence and standards."

"Oh. And you don't believe the Los Angeles Police Department has standards?"

"Not proper ones." Her tone of voice left no room for argument.

Oh, boy. Just what I wanted. My mother. At Mr. Easthope's house. During a séance. Well, I supposed it was always possible that the murderer, if there was one and he or she was present at this next séance, might mistake my mother for his or her next victim.

How remarkably mean of me. I beg your pardon.

At any rate, the conversation appeared to be over. Meekly, I carried Buttercup into the living room where Chloe sat, looking as if she'd just as soon be somewhere else. I felt exactly the same way, although it was really our mother we both wished elsewhere. Casting a quick peek over my shoulder to determine

Mother's whereabouts, I whispered, "What's going on?"

Chloe looked up at me and shrugged her shoulders as if she didn't understand this sudden enthusiasm our mutual mother was taking in my work, either. Then she whispered, too. "She's been going on about the case all day long, Mercy. She's read all the newspaper articles about it. She even made poor Mrs. Biddle buy a copy of the *Examiner* at the market this morning. I think she's actually interested."

"Good Lord." Buttercup and I sank onto the sofa next to Chloe, and Chloe and I exchanged puzzled glances. "Do you suppose she's turning human?" I gave Buttercup a hug to let her know I didn't consider being human any more or less good than being a poodle.

Chloe thought about it for a second, then shrugged again. "Too soon to tell. It's difficult to imagine something like that happening, though, isn't it?"

"Boy, ain't *that* the truth?" Quickly I scanned the room, hoping Mother hadn't heard my misuse of the English language. Fortunately, she wasn't there yet. Before I could say anything else that might get me in trouble, I hustled Buttercup, my handbag, and myself up to my room, where I changed into a nice evening frock for dinner. My mother might not like me much, but she couldn't fault my wardrobe.

All through dinner and afterward, Mother declaimed on the impending events at Mr. Easthope's house. By the time I escaped to my bedroom, not only had she dictated my costume for the following evening, her costume for the following evening, and what I should and should not say during the get-together, but she'd even picked out what she wanted me to wear to work the next day.

I sat on my bed, hugging Buttercup and silently cursing my father for this whole mess.

★ ★ ★ ★ ★

There was an uncomfortable consequence of placing an advertisement in the *Los Angeles Times* aside from Ernie's anger. I didn't fully realize it at first, because I was already uncomfortable thanks to my mother. She'd selected a woolen suit of dark brown tweed, infinitely more suitable to a Boston winter than a Los Angeles summer, but I was feeling so intimidated by the time morning rolled around that I didn't have the gumption to select a more suitable costume.

By the time I got to the office I was very nearly wilted, and I did something I'd never done before. I removed the jacket to my suit and draped it neatly over the back of my chair. Fortunately, I'd had sense enough to select a short-sleeved, sheer white shirtwaist to wear with the costume, so that helped revive me a bit. About nine o'clock, I decided I'd run out and purchase one of those little rotating fans from the local Kress Drug Store during my lunch hour. I also swore I wouldn't allow my mother to interfere in my choice of clothing again.

But the uncomfortable consequence to which I referred before was that we were now so busy at Ernest Templeton, P.I.'s office that Ernie was hardly ever there. I missed him. Even when he was grouchy, which he'd been a lot lately.

I didn't see him at all that morning for the first hour or so. Then, along about nine-thirty, the outer office door opened, and I looked up expectantly. I was disappointed when James Quincy Carstairs, Esquire, popped in. I greeted him warmly nevertheless.

"Good morning, Mr. Carstairs."

"How do you do, Miss Allcutt?" He came over to my desk and hesitated a second before I gestured that he should take one of the chairs there.

"I'm fine, thank you." I smiled reassuringly, noting that he seemed to need encouragement. I'd never seen him less than entirely at ease before.

He sat, slumping slightly. "I'm not sure I'm fine," said he, sounding worried. "Miss Jacqueline Lloyd just telephoned to tell me that there's going to be another séance tonight, and that she wants me to accompany her again." He didn't seem one bit pleased by anything he'd said.

Since I had problems of my own, I only said, "Yes. I'll be there, too."

At this intelligence he perked up a little bit. "Oh, I'm pleased to hear it." His perkiness faded almost immediately. "However, I still don't like it."

"Oh? Why is that?"

He shook his head. "It just seems . . . I don't know. Unwise, perhaps. Certainly it's disrespectful of Miss Hedda Heartwood." He looked at me almost beseechingly. "For heaven's sake, she was murdered during a séance there only a few days ago. It seems to me that Easthope is not merely pressing his luck by holding another one so soon, but is . . . oh, I don't know. Guilty of bad taste, I guess."

Especially since the spiritualists in question had been shown to be not quite what they'd portrayed themselves as being. I wondered if Mr. Carstairs knew that.

I didn't have to ask him.

"Even those spiritualists are phony, for the love of God," he went on. "I understand their name is really O'Doyle."

"Yes, I heard that, too."

"Miss Lloyd claims they only changed their name because d'Agostino sounded better than O'Doyle, but I have my doubts. I don't really buy into this spiritualism craze." He'd been glaring at his beautifully manicured hands, which rested lightly in his lap, but he looked up after he delivered that last line. "I don't mean to disparage any of your personal beliefs, of course, Miss Allcutt."

I shook my head. "They aren't mine, believe me. I don't buy it, either. I was only there to begin with because Mr. Easthope was attempting to talk some sense into his mother, who is enthralled with the d'Agostinos. O'Doyles. Whoever they are. Neither my presence nor the exposure of their fake name seems to have worked."

"Do you know why there's going to be another séance, by the way?"

I did, actually, but I wasn't sure I wanted to spread the news. There seemed to be no reason not to, but still I said, "Haven't a clue."

Mr. Carstairs sighed soulfully.

I went on, "But I'm sure Mr. Easthope would never be guilty of doing anything in bad taste. There's got to be a good reason he agreed to hold this séance tonight. I know Mr. Easthope quite well, and I can assure you he'd never do anything like this unless it was necessary."

"You really think so?"

"I'm sure of it."

He didn't appear to be convinced and opened his mouth to speak again, perhaps to voice his doubt, but our conversation was interrupted abruptly when Ernie shoved open the outer office door, took a step inside, saw Mr. Carstairs, stopped where he stood, and glowered at the both of us. "Don't you have an office of your own, Carstairs?"

With another sigh, Mr. Carstairs rose from his chair. "Indeed I do, and I'm headed there now." And with that, and with a polite nod for me, he departed.

I frowned at Ernie. "There's no need to be rude, Ernest Templeton. The man was only chatting."

"Why the hell is he chatting with *you?*"

"He's concerned about another séance that's being held tonight at Mr. Easthope's house. Miss Lloyd wants him to attend it with her. I'll be there, too."

Without removing his hat, Ernie plunked himself down beside my desk. "Another séance? At that faggot Easthope's place? And you're *going* to it? Are you nuts?"

Through clenched teeth, I said, "Yes, yes, yes, and no. And don't you dare call Francis Easthope names!"

"He's a faggot whether you like it or not, and you're a damned fool to go to another séance at his house. Don't you understand that a *murder* took place there, for God's sake?"

"Of course I understand that. And I don't know what you're so worried about. I'm sure nothing else will happen. And anyhow, the murder wasn't Mr. Easthope's fault." Drawing upon intelligence gleaned from my mother the night before and that I hadn't divulged to Mr. Carstairs, I said, "It's his mother. She's hoping anther séance will draw forth the name of Mrs. Hartland's murderer from the Other Side. Whatever that is," I added a trifle snidely.

"Oh, brother. Does she know her precious spiritualists are phonies?"

I sighed heavily. "Yes, she knows they changed their name. But she thinks they only did it because d'Agostino sounds better for a pair of spiritualists than O'Doyle. They claim d'Agostino is a family name on their mother's side, although how that can be, I have no idea, since they're married and not brother and sister." I frowned. "Maybe it's her mother's name or something. It's vaguely possible that d'Agostino is her maiden name, I suppose."

Ernie's head tilted slightly and he gave me another one of his "oh, brother" expressions.

I reacted negatively. "The whole thing is nothing to do with me! I only told Mr. Easthope I'd help him debunk the d'Agostinos. O'Doyles. Whoever they are. I told him I'd help him, and I don't break my word."

"Listen, kiddo, if his mother isn't convinced yet that those two are fakers, no amount of hanging around the house on your part will convince her."

"I suppose it won't, but I owe it to Mr. Easthope to try."

"You're stupid."

That *really* burned me up. "I am not! It's not as if Mr. East-hope is secretly housing a vile murderer who aims to kill off everybody who attends séances there one by one! What would be the point of killing off the clientele?"

Standing as precipitately as he'd sat and whipping off his hat, Ernie strode to his office. "You never know. I still say you're an idiot to go."

"If you had condescended to help the man, I wouldn't have to!" I flung at his back.

"Nuts."

"Anyhow, this time his mother might listen, because *my* mother insists upon attending the stupid thing with me."

Ernie, his hand on his doorknob, turned and stared at me for a second or two, then vanished into his office.

The door slammed behind him. I think I heard him laughing, the rat.

The rest of my workday was every bit as awful as the beginning had been. In fact, if you can believe it, it got worse.

At approximately nine forty-five, Miss Ethel Ginther, the lady whose uncle had disappeared and who'd called Ernie's office when she saw my ad in the *Times,* presented herself in the outer office. We'd met before and I have to admit that, while I was delighted she'd seen my newspaper ad and decided to hire Ernie to find her missing uncle, I wasn't terribly impressed with Miss Ginther herself, who tended to flutter.

She was fluttering like a hummingbird when she entered the outer office. I sighed, although I doubt that she noticed. She didn't notice anything that wasn't directly connected to herself, as nearly as I can possibly understand a woman like that.

"Oh, Miss Allcutt, I simply *must* see Mr. Templeton!" It wasn't merely she who fluttered, but her clothing did, too. That day, she'd clad herself in a morning dress of pink taffeta (did I mention that the woman was in her forties and was relatively sallow? Well, she was, and pink was *not* an appropriate choice for her), covered with a darker pink cape-like thing that flipped and flapped around her so violently that I had to rescue the inkpot on my desk from flying off onto the carpet. Fortunately, being a neat person by nature, not to mention having very little work to do, I'd already made sure the inkpot was securely capped.

In spite of her irritating mannerisms I smiled at Miss Ginther, whom I considered a success of sorts. "I don't recall your calling to make an appointment, Miss Ginther."

"No, no, no, I didn't. I didn't because there was no time, you see, and I just truly need—*desperately* need—to see Mr. Templeton. It's vitally important. *Vitally* important. It's about my uncle."

See what I mean? Even her words fluttered around in the air like confetti. Or grapeshot, perhaps.

Still smiling, I gestured at a chair in front of my desk. "Please have a seat, Miss Ginther. I'll see if Mr. Templeton is available to see you."

I knew darned well Ernie was available, since he'd been turning down work right and left lately, claiming there was only one of him and he couldn't possibly take on all the jobs my ad had generated. When I'd pointed out that he had a capable assistant in the person of my very own self who could certainly conduct interviews and minor investigations, he'd only sneered, snapped open his *Times* and said, "I don't think so."

Annoying man. That morning I confounded him by not giving him a chance to think of an excuse to ignore Miss Ginther.

I rapped smartly on his door, stepped into his office, and said, "Miss Ginther is here to see you, Mr. Templeton." Then, almost before he could lower his feet from his desk to the floor, I swung his door wide and smiled at our visitor.

"Come right in, Miss Ginther."

Ernie was still glowering and folding up his newspaper when the woman, with much waving of hands and flapping of capes and juggling of handbags and other accessories, tripped into the office with a trilled, "Oh, Mr. Templeton!" I shut the door and smiled to myself. Petty, I know, but satisfying.

Miss Ginther was still babbling at Ernie, I suppose, when, at ten-fifteen, Lulu LaBelle burst, sobbing, into my office. Startled, I took one look at her, jumped to my feet, and hurried to her side. "Lulu! Whatever is the matter?" Gently, I guided her to the chair beside my desk. "Do you need a glass of water?"

"They arrested Wilbert!" she wailed, sounding to my untrained ears as a banshee on an Irish moor might sound.

Her news shocked me so much that I didn't even quail at the intensity of its delivery. "Th-they arrested him?" I forgot all about the water I'd offered and sank numbly into my desk chair.

She nodded. "They arrested him! Oh, Mercy, he's going to hang for a murder he didn't commit! I just know it! They're railroading him!"

It wasn't the time to point out that California used the electric chair to execute murderers. This was bad news. It was bad all around, actually, since I was almost, if not entirely, positive that Wilbert Mullins had nothing to do with Mrs. Hartland's demise.

"But why?" I asked, feeling out of my depth. "Why did they arrest him?"

"They learned that Mrs. Hartland used to live near us in Enid, and the coppers think that Wilbert killed her to keep her from spilling the beans about his record!"

Mind you, Lulu wasn't quite that coherent in her exposition, but that's what she meant. I stared at her. "His record of turning over an *outhouse?*" I don't know about you, but it seemed to me that Wilbert's so-called "record" was so minor as to make his committing murder to prevent its becoming known akin to somebody shooting an elephant because he didn't like peanuts. "That doesn't make sense."

"You tell them that," Lulu wailed. "They did it!"

"Good heavens."

Lulu had a good cry in my office chair, then pulled herself together enough to go back to her job in the lobby. My head was spinning when Phil waltzed in about the time Ernie finally got rid of Miss Ginther. I was grateful for that since it saved me from receiving a lecture from Ernie about allowing crazed clients into his office when he didn't want to be disturbed.

Anyhow, just in case Ernie planned to scold me in Phil's presence, I turned my own queries upon Phil before he had a chance. "Why in the name of heaven did the police arrest Wilbert Mullins?" My voice was a trifle louder than propriety called for.

Phil and Ernie both eyed me with something that looked rather like trepidation. Did they think I was going to have hysterics? Idiots, both of them.

"Um . . . because they think he did it," said Phil.

I squinted at him. "I notice you say *they* think he did it. Does this mean that you don't?"

"Haven't made up my mind yet," said Phil, looking less nervous and more policeman-like. "We have to sift through all the evidence."

"What about Mr. Hartland?" I demanded. "He lied about not being there, and he had a lot to gain from his mother's demise."

"We know that. We're looking into all aspects of the case and all possible suspects."

"Then why did you arrest Wilbert?"

"He was considered a flight risk."

"A *flight* risk?" I stared at the man, incredulous.

"He fled from Oklahoma to avoid a lesser charge than murder."

I didn't really have an answer to that one, so I merely said, "Hmph," and pointedly turned away from Phil to busy myself with some paperwork. At least when an unwelcome client came to call, I got to document his or her appointment in the appropriate file, which would take a minute or two. I trusted the men would vanish before I ran out of work again.

They did. Phil and Ernie retired into Ernie's office and closed the door. I breathed a sigh of frustration. Wilbert Mullins? He didn't kill Mrs. Hartland. It was insane to think he did.

I had to admit, if only to myself, that given his past reluctance to deal with the police in his home state, he might actually *be* a flight risk. It was difficult to believe that Wilbert Mullins was much of a danger to society, however. Especially here in Los Angeles, where outhouses were a rarity in this modern day and age.

And *then,* right as I prepared to lock up the office and head to the Kress drugstore for a fountain luncheon, who should appear in the office but a gentleman I'd never seen before. He looked quite angry, too.

Glad I hadn't moved from behind my desk since I felt safer with a broad expanse of wood between angry clients and me, I smiled my efficient secretary's smile and said, "Good morning. May I help you?"

"I need Templeton," said the man, whom I'd guess was in his late fifties or early sixties. He was quite distinguished looking, with thick salt-and-pepper hair, a well-made suit of summer seersucker, an ebony walking stick with an ivory handle and a fine derby hat.

So many people did seem to need Mr. Templeton that day. However, I'd never met this particular one before and didn't think he should be able to barge into the office and consult with Ernie without my intervention. "I will be happy to make an appointment for you," I said, fibbing only a little. At least this particular person looked as if he were well off and could afford Ernie's services.

"Damn the appointment." That shocked me. We didn't even *know* each other, and he was swearing at me. "I need to see him *now.*" He glanced at Ernie's closed door. "Is that his office?"

"Yes, but . . ."

He didn't wait for me to finish, but marched over to Ernie's office, lifted his walking stick and thumped on the door.

"Now wait a minute here!" I cried, leaping up and racing to my employer's office in an attempt to fend off this offensive, if well-groomed, individual.

Ernie hollered, "Yeah?" He would.

Before the interloper could shove the door open and barge right on in, I, in a deft move of which I'm proud to this day, maneuvered myself in front of him, put on my haughtiest Boston persona, and said, "Stop that this instant!"

Believe it or not, the man stepped back a pace.

Without giving him time to recover his wits, I went on, borrowing heavily from my mother for the performance. "How dare you? You sit yourself right down there and behave properly. First of all, give me your name." With erect posture and forbidding (I hope) features, I stared him in the eye and began moving inexorably forward. He had no choice but to back up. Well, technically, I guess he had a choice. He could have thrust me aside and continued his assault on Ernie's office door, but I suspect he'd been reared with manners as had I, so he didn't.

Behind us, the office door opened and Ernie said, "What's up?"

Curse him. That gave the intruder just the chance he needed. Without heeding my command to sit and stay (a command Buttercup learned in our first week together, proving yet again that poodles are better than people), he darted around me and came face to face with Ernie. The only good thing about that maneuver was that Ernie was a good deal taller than he, and the newcomer didn't appear quite so imposing by comparison.

"Are you Templeton?" Imperious.

Ernie said, "Yeah." Insouciant.

I rolled my eyes.

It didn't matter. The man said, "I'm Conrad Blythe, and I'm here to tell you to stop dogging my footsteps."

Conrad Blythe. Who in the world was Conrad Blythe?

From the grin that spread over Ernie's face, I presumed he knew. "Well, well, well. Come right on in, Mr. Blythe. We have a lot to talk about." And he let the man into his private office, winked at me, and closed the door in my face.

Well!

Only after luncheon did I learn that Mr. Conrad Blythe was Miss Ginther's missing uncle and that he was missing because he wanted to be. He hadn't wandered off and become lost or been kidnapped or Shanghaied or murdered or anything of that nature. He'd simply had enough of Miss Ginther's aunt, who, if she was anything like her niece, must have been difficult to live with, and set up housekeeping elsewhere. He'd evidently been sending money for the support of his wife, but he didn't want to live with her any longer, and he didn't want to reveal his present address because he didn't want her bothering him. I hate to admit it, but I understood his dilemma. In fact, I'd probably have done the same thing if I'd been saddled with Miss Ginther and her aunt.

So much for Miss Ginther's missing uncle. Still, it was a case, and it had generated income for the firm. And I was responsible for it. So there.

But the events of the morning, while upsetting, paled when compared to those of the afternoon. Not only was Ernie inundated with unwanted clients, all of whom demanded updates on their open cases ("Thanks to that damned ad you placed"), but right before I was about to put on my hat, grab my handbag, lock up the office and head to Angel's Flight, Miss Sylvia Dunstable opened the office door. She didn't come in. She only stood there holding onto the jamb, swaying slightly, pale and trembling and looking tragic.

I gaped at her and hurried around my desk, fearful lest she faint right there in the doorway. "Whatever is the matter, Miss Dunstable? You look as if you've seen a ghost!" I took her hand and led her to one of the chairs in front of my desk. I liked Miss Dunstable and wouldn't have minded if she'd sat in the chair beside the desk, but she looked too shaken to make it that far.

"It's . . . it's . . ." She gulped and sat with a thump.

Good heavens. I'd never seen the unflappable Miss Dunstable in this state. I hadn't known she was capable of such an exhibition of naked emotion in public—or in the office. I guess we weren't really public.

Ernie, who generally departed for home before five o'clock rolled around, but who had been much busier than usual lately thanks to me, opened his office door. "What's going on? Is anything the matter?"

I glanced up at him. "It's Miss Dunstable. I don't know what's wrong, but she's terribly upset."

Miss Dunstable looked from Ernie to me, and I was horrified to see tears pooling in her eyes. I chafed one of her hands with one of mine and fumbled to find a hankie in my handbag with the other. "Oh, Miss Dunstable, please tell me what's the matter! What is it? I've never seen anyone looking so upset!"

Pulling her hand away from mine, she took the handkerchief I offered her and wiped her eyes. Then she swallowed twice, cleared her throat and said, "Rudolph Valentino is dead."

CHAPTER TWELVE

The news spread like wildfire. Lulu, already upset by her brother's arrest, was inconsolable. I know, because I tried to console her before I left the building. My efforts went for naught and, with a deep and heartfelt sigh, I left the Figueroa Building carrying my suit jacket. Not even for my mother would I wear heavy tweed in hundred-degree heat.

Even as I walked to Angel's Flight, I saw people sobbing in clusters on street corners or gathered around newsstands reading the headlines, numb or in tears. Red cars rolled by filled with shocked and weeping people. The newsboy on the corner couldn't even give voice to his "Extra!" for the lump in his throat. I myself was reeling from the news. Not physically, of course, but emotionally.

I wasn't as in love with Rudolf Valentino as many of the other girls I knew, but I have to admit to a secret "pash," as Lulu calls it, for the fellow. I think it was his burning eyes that drew one to him. Or perhaps it had been the vehicles in which he'd starred. I know one isn't supposed to talk about such things, but I doubt there's a young woman alive who doesn't occasionally dream of being swept off her feet by an intriguing fellow from the mysterious East. That's as opposed to my own personal East, which was Boston and about as mysterious as a stalk of celery.

Valentino had been a very young man, too. Well, to me he'd seemed a little old, but I was only twenty-one. Ernie told me that thirty-two, Mr. Valentino's age, was young. Ernie was about twenty-eight or twenty-nine, I imagine, although he hadn't told me so.

When I opened the door to Chloe's house, feeling sad and thinking about my own mortality for perhaps the very first time, I was glad to discover the horrible news hadn't affected Buttercup's mood. She raced to greet me, wagging her whole body as always. I picked her up, even more thankful than usual for her comforting presence in my life.

The living room contained Chloe, who was pale and looking ill; Francis Easthope, who was patting her shoulder and saying soothing things; and my mother, who sat as still, upright and poised as a marble statue, with a critical expression on her face. No surprise there.

Clutching Buttercup to my bosom, I said softly, "You heard the news?"

Chloe nodded. "It's . . . ghastly."

Mr. Easthope straightened and looked as if he was going to do the polite thing and come to greet me. I shook my head and he understood. In her condition, Chloe needed his attention more than I did.

"Good afternoon, Mr. Easthope. It was so kind of you to come over."

"I 'phoned him," said Chloe in a weak voice. "It was just . . . so shocking."

"It certainly was." I plopped onto the sofa with Buttercup still cradled in my arms, and put my handbag on the side table. My hat soon joined it.

My mother looked at this activity with patent disapproval. She believed in constant vigilance in the tidiness department, and according to her rules one should never use interim measures to achieve it. If I were obeying the dictates of my upbringing, I would have gone upstairs, put my hat and handbag in my room, and only then joined the family. And I'd never have bought Buttercup, who would probably be relegated to the backyard for all eternity. Nonsensical rules, if you ask me. Chloe needed my support.

"May I get you anything, Chloe?" I wondered if she needed Buttercup, but didn't dare ask in front of my mother. Mother didn't approve of people requiring solace in times of trouble, either. She believed one's strength of character was supposed to carry one through life. And that, if you ask me, would be a very lonely existence.

Hmm. Perhaps my father'd had a point when he'd left the woman.

"Maybe . . . maybe a glass of water." She glanced at me, and I could see she'd been trying with all her strength not to cry in front of our mother. I wished my mother in Hades at that moment. Or at least Boston.

"Sure. I'll be right back." Carefully setting Buttercup down on the floor (Mother would have had seven fits if I'd set her on the sofa), I went to the kitchen, my faithful pup following. "Oh, Buttercup, whatever are we going to do? Mother can't possibly mean to stay here. *Can* she?"

Buttercup, bless her heart, gave me a significant whine to indicate that she understood my distress even if she couldn't respond in English.

When I took Chloe her water, I decided to work the conversation around to the business aspects of Mr. Valentino's death. I couldn't think of anything less conducive to melancholy than business, unless one's own were failing or something like that. "What is this going to mean for Harvey's studio?"

After nearly draining the glass, Chloe set it carefully on a doily, thereby forestalling a lecture from our mother. "I don't know. Valentino isn't one of Harvey's stars, but it's still such a terrible blow to the industry. And all of his fans. Oh, it doesn't bear thinking of."

So much for business. I sighed. "No, it doesn't. Do you know what's going to happen now?"

She shook her head. "Harvey telephoned. He said he thinks they'll send his body back to Los Angeles by train for burial."

"Hmm. I suppose the newspapers will give a schedule. I expect there will be people lining the railroad tracks." I vaguely recalled when Theodore Roosevelt's body was transported for burial. The newspapers had run photographs of people flocking along the tracks, hats over their hearts, heads bowed in respect. They were quite touching pictures of a nation in mourning.

As if she couldn't contain her contempt a second longer, Mother spoke. "I think it's a disgrace that people should give a motion-picture actor such adulation. Lining the tracks. Disgusting."

We all looked at her, but none of us said a word.

Fortunately, we heard Harvey's machine make its way down the drive at that point and Chloe perked up considerably. Defying Mother, she rushed straight into Harvey's arms when he appeared in the archway between the hall and the living room. He greeted her warmly and with the affection that was the hallmark of their union.

Needless to say, our mother looked upon this tender reunion with asperity. The old cow. If she'd shown more overt affection for our father, perhaps he wouldn't have sought it elsewhere.

But I don't suppose that was fair. Even though our mother was far from a cuddly person, there was no possible excuse for flouting one's marriage vows. I know people have been doing it since the beginning of time, but that didn't make it right.

Oh, nuts. It was all too deep for me.

Dinner that night was probably quite tasty, but the mood was somber. I wasn't sorry when the meal was over and I could retire to my room and prepare for the ordeal to come.

It was a definite ordeal, too. Mr. Easthope himself drove Mother and me to his house after dinner. The staff, already upset by Wilbert's arrest, was in shock over Rudolph Valentino's demise. The little housemaid, who had been teaching Wilbert the tricks of the serving trade, had swollen, red-rimmed eyes and looked as if she'd been crying since she'd heard the news. Updegraff, who was acting as a butler since Rupert had been arrested and couldn't perform his duties as houseboy, and whose demeanor was always grave, that evening looked as if he were attending a funeral rather than a séance.

When Mr. Easthope escorted us into the living room, I was a little surprised to see a youngish man seated beside Mrs. Easthope. He appeared strained, but she looked positively haggard. Mr. Easthope, suavity itself, guided my mother over to his mother and the fellow.

"Miss Allcutt, you already know my mother."

"Yes. How do you do, Mrs. Easthope?" I held out my hand politely.

She took my hand but only shook her head, as if speaking was too much of a chore for her to contemplate, much less attempt.

"And this, Mrs. Allcutt and Miss Allcutt, is George Hartland, the late Mrs. Hartland's son."

"Oh!" Good gracious, this was wonderful. I could investigate a suspect at close range. I didn't reveal my joy. "Good evening, Mr. Hartland. I'm so terribly sorry about your mother."

George Hartland had stood upon our entry into the room. "I'm as well as I can be, Miss Allcutt. Thank you," he said, casting a nervous glance at the door to the living room, searching, I presume, for Mr. Carstairs. I also presume he didn't dare *not* attend this particular séance, no matter to whom he owed money, since it had been set up specifically to unveil the identity of his mother's murderer.

"Mother, please allow me to introduce you to Miss Allcutt's mother, Mrs. Allcutt."

Mrs. Easthope held out a limp hand once more, and this time she managed to speak. "So pleased to meet you." She didn't yet know my mother or I'm sure her pleasure would have dimmed considerably. She turned to me and gave me a wan smile. "I'm so glad you could attend this evening, my dear. It's always a good idea to have continuity, in spite of the dreadful news the day has brought."

Whatever that meant. I smiled and said, "It's very good to see you again, Mrs. Easthope, although I'm still very sorry about the reason for this séance." I shook her hand again, and warmly, deciding my mother, while insensitive, was basically correct in that a motion-picture actor, no matter how handsome and appealing, really shouldn't have such an impact on the citizens of the great United States of America. It seemed frivolous somehow that the world should be cast into a gloom over Valentino's untimely passing.

Of course it's always a tragedy when a young man or woman dies, but . . . oh, bother. You know what I mean.

Mr. Carstairs and Miss Lloyd showed up at the same time the d'Agostinos did, and I do believe I saw a look of relief wash over Mr. Hartland's face when the meeting was almost immediately called to order. So to speak. In actual fact, Mr. d'Agostino murmured something to Fernandez, who vanished like a spirit himself. Then we were all herded to the dining room (this time Updegraff did the honors, since Wilbert was languishing in the pokey) and we took our places around the table. That night I sat next to my mother and had to hold her hand. Mr. Carstairs was on my other side. Across from us were Jacqueline Lloyd, Mr. Hartland, and Mrs. Easthope. Mr. Easthope sat next to Miss d'Agostino, who sat at one end of the table. Mr. d'Agostino was at the other.

The same folderol ensued. You know: dimmed lights, courtesy Fernandez; admonitions from Mr. d'Agostino to be silent; a good deal of writhing and moaning on Miss d'Agostino's part; and then her classic slump. The deepness and resonant quality of her so-called "trance" voice still impressed me.

What impressed me even more was when, about ten minutes into Ms. d'Agostino's trance, as her control was holding a breathy conversation with the late Mrs. Hartland, Mr. Hartland suddenly leaped to his feet, screeched, *"No!"* and collapsed to the floor.

Fernandez must have been standing right smack at the light switch because the lights went on instantly. Sure enough, there was a hole in the seating arrangement across from me where George Hartland had been sitting. I muttered, "Oh, no, not again," which I guess was callous. But honestly, how much of this sort of thing is a person supposed to take?

I anticipated what happened next. Jacqueline Lloyd, who had been holding Mr. Hartland's hand, glanced at her own empty hand, then at Mr. Hartland's body on the floor, rose to her feet, cast a hysterical glance around the table, shrieked like yet another banshee on yet another Irish moor, and flopped to the floor like a beached flounder.

"For heaven's sake," my mother muttered. For once, I didn't blame her for her sour tone of voice.

I heaved a large sigh as Mr. Easthope raced around to the other side of the table, hesitated in the face of two fallen bodies, and decided to eschew gentlemanliness for the nonce as he knelt beside Mr. Hartland. Knowing he needed my support, if only because I was a commonsensical person, I rose and hurried to assist him.

My mother barked, "Mercedes Louise!"

I ignored her.

"Thank God you're here, Miss Allcutt," he whispered. "I can't believe this has happened again."

I knelt beside him. "Do you know what exactly *did* happen?"

"No."

Since Mr. Easthope appeared to be on shaky emotional ground, I pressed two fingers to the side of Mr. Hartland's neck. Surprised and gratified, I said, "He's got a pulse!"

"Thank God," came Mr. Easthope's heartfelt response.

"Updegraff," I called, remaining beside Mr. Hartland. "Will you please call a doctor and the police?"

"Yes, ma'am," said Updegraff, and he left in more of a rush than I'd heretofore believed him capable of.

Because we'd determined that George Hartland lived, even if we didn't know for how long or what had happened to him, Mr. Easthope turned his attention to Jacqueline Lloyd. Luckily, Miss Lloyd already had a couple of champions at hand in the persons of Mr. Carstairs, who was on his knees beside her, chafing her hands and looking otherwise helpless; and Mr. d'Agostino, who's expression was more pinched and angry than fearful or worried. I wondered if that meant anything.

Mr. Easthope took charge, bless him. "Let us get her to a sofa, fellows. I believe she only fainted."

"I think you're right." I could hear the relief in Mr. Carstairs's voice.

"I'm sure that's it," agreed Mr. d'Agostino. "I expect Mr. Hartland only fainted too." He sounded grumpy. I guess he didn't appreciate people dropping like flies during his séances. I doubt that he cared much about the individuals involved, but I'm sure he didn't want to garner a reputation as a medium who killed off his clients, even by accident.

Speaking of mediums (or should that be media? Well, who cares?) I glanced over to see what the other half of the team was doing. Miss d'Agostino sat, looking almost as statue-like as my mother, and with an expression almost as grim as Mother's on her face. Mother's gaze was fixed firmly upon her errant daughter, naturally.

If the two spiritualists *were* behind these occurrences, they gave no indication of it. If I read the expressions on their faces right, they were more peeved than pleased by this latest interruption of their mystical twaddle. Then again, what did I know?

I was still on my knees, wishing I knew more about first aid and medical techniques so that I might be of more assistance to Mr. Hartland, when I heard my mother's voice. Unfortunately, it was closer than it would have been if she still sat at the table. I sent up a silent prayer for strength and patience.

"Mercedes Louise Allcutt, get up from the floor this instant and telephone for a taxicab. We must get out of here before the police arrive."

I squinted up at her, astounded by her order. "We can't do that, Mother. No one can leave the scene before the police get here."

Her bosom swelled and her chin would have lifted if she weren't still glaring down upon me. "And why not?" she demanded. "I am *not* accustomed to these sorts of goings on."

"Neither am I," I said, feeling not the least bit obedient at the moment. "And you're the one who wanted to come here tonight."

"How *dare* you speak to your mother like that?"

"Oh, go sit down, Mother. We can't do anything until the police get here."

To my utter amazement, not to mention my eternal gratitude, she did, giving me only one last irate huff before doing so.

That gave me time to think, and I instantly thought of the back of Mr. Hartland's neck. Well, I don't mean that exactly, but I recollected the little pinprick on the back of Mrs. Hartland's neck, so I looked for one on her son.

I didn't find one, which might well account for the fact that Mr. Hartland, while unconscious, yet breathed. Hmm. I didn't know what the lack of a pinprick signified, if anything. Maybe he *did* just faint.

Or . . . merciful heavens, what if George Hartland had staged this scene simply for the purpose of diverting attention from himself as the killer of his mother? If everyone believed an attempt had been made on his life, they'd be less likely to think of him as a murderer.

Except that I just had. And I'm sure the police would think about the matter in that light, too.

So what did this mean? Was George Hartland another innocent victim of a crazed fiend who haunted séances—so to speak? Or was he a cold-blooded murderer who was only acting the part of a victim?

Bother. I had no earthly idea.

"Can't you stay out of trouble for a single damned day?"

Ernie. He'd just opened the outer office door and didn't even bother to remove his hat or shut the door before bellowing his question at me. I'd arrived at work a little earlier than usual in order to escape Chloe's house before my mother could renew her inquisition and vilify me some more for being undutiful and rude and a disgrace to the family.

She and I hadn't left Mr. Easthope's house until well after midnight and she'd rebuked me all the way home, into the house, and even up the stairs. She covered every single aspect of what she considered my sinfulness until I honestly believe she was on the verge of accusing me of Rudolph Valentino's unfortunate passing. I finally escaped to my room and shut the door in her face but it was a truly miserable evening and night, and it took me a long time to get to sleep, even with the faithful and fluffy Buttercup to give me succor and companionship.

The police—in the person of Phil Bigelow, who wasn't happy to see me, and a couple of uniformed officers—had arrived about twenty minutes after they'd been called. The doctor was already there and had called an ambulance to transport Mr. Hartland to the hospital on Hill and College. Mr. Carstairs said he was going to take Miss Lloyd there, too, since she was so shaken up, and the doctor said he believed that was a good idea. Nobody, to my knowledge, had figured out what happened to Mr. Hartland by the time Mother and I finally got to go home.

Then on my way to work I saw black bunting everywhere, in honor of Rudolph Valentino's decease, I presumed. The two women who rode Angel's Flight with me that morning looked as if they'd been crying all night long, and the entire city of Los Angeles seemed to have been cast into a state of terminal gloom.

Therefore, I was already feeling abused, mistreated and unhappy, not to mention exhausted, and I didn't appreciate Ernie's attack on me first thing in the morning. I reacted negatively.

"Curse you, Ernie Templeton, don't you dare swear at me! And it's not my fault George Hartland collapsed last night *or* that Jacqueline Lloyd fainted! She seems to faint all the time, for heaven's sake!" That wasn't really fair, but I wasn't feeling fair and didn't give a fig.

"I swear to God, Mercy Allcutt, you've got to stay out of this sort of thing! Don't you understand that it might be *you* next time?"

"What do you mean, it might be me? And what do you mean *next* time?" I regret to say my voice was quite loud. But so was Ernie's and, darn it, if I couldn't yell at my mother—and I couldn't. It was all I could do to stand up to her at all—I'd jolly well yell at him. "No one in the entire world has any reason *whatsoever* to kill me!"

177

"How the hell do you know that?"

The blasted man loomed over my desk with a hand on each of the chairs I'd set there for clients. I was standing, too, but he was much taller than I and I felt intimidated.

Before I could tell him how I knew that, he continued his rant. "If you keep sticking your nose into dangerous business, somebody might just take it in mind to get rid of you, damn it! You don't have a single, solitary notion of what to do to stay out of trouble! I swear to God, you drive me *crazy!*"

"Well, you drive me crazy, too, curse it! How *dare* you yell at me?"

"I'm not yelling, damn it!" he bellowed.

The outer office door, which Ernie had left standing open, opened a little wider and Phil Bigelow appeared. "Jeez, you guys, I could hear you on the elevator."

I knew my face was blazing with fury. Now it blazed with embarrassment, too. I turned on Phil in reaction. "Then *you* tell Ernie nothing that happened last night was my fault! He's blaming *me!*"

"I'm not blaming you!" Ernie roared. "I'm telling you to stay the hell out of police business!"

"I'm not *in* police business!" I roared back heatedly. "I was only helping a friend! You wouldn't know about that sort of thing, I suppose!"

Phil held up both of his hands. "Hey, kids, calm down. Let's all just relax for a minute here."

Ernie snatched his hat from his head and slapped the back of a chair with it. I winced. It was a hard blow. "She drives me nuts," he said more softly.

"He drives *me* nuts," I said, also softly. I'd opened my drawer in order to stow my hat and handbag, and now I slammed it shut. I don't believe I'd ever done such a thing before in my whole life. Ernest Templeton, P.I., was the most aggravating man I'd ever known. And I'm including my idiot, awful brother in the bunch, too. My brother was only a snob and a bore. Ernie truly rattled my cage.

Phil placed a hand on Ernie's shoulder. "Let's you and me go into your office, Ern. It'll give you a chance to cool down."

And how was *I* supposed to cool down? I guess *I* was on my own. Nobody cared about *secretaries*, did they? Of course not. They yelled at them and then left and went off to chat with their friends, leaving *secretaries* to their own devices.

Well, that was fine with me. I had a device of my own. Picking myself up out of my chair, I fairly flounced to the office door and stamped down two offices to that of John Quincy Carstairs, Esquire. There I opened the door and stood on the threshold, probably looking a good deal as Miss Dunstable had when she'd conveyed the news of Rudolph Valentino's death to me the day before.

She looked up, registered my presence, and stood. "Oh, Miss Allcutt, I heard! How perfectly ghastly for you!"

And bless the woman, she came to me with her hands outstretched. I crumbled like stale bread as she led me to the chair beside her desk.

After sniffling and blowing my nose, I apologized. "I'm sorry. It's just all so upsetting," I said, trying to explain my breakdown, which was truly out of character for the usually stoic me.

"Nonsense. You suffered a great shock," Miss Dunstable said bracingly. "I understand Miss Lloyd actually fainted."

I sniffled again, not entirely because of my tears. "Yes, well, she faints at everything, I guess. She fainted before, too."

"The artistic temperament," Miss Dunstable murmured. I could tell she didn't want to dwell on Miss Lloyd's shortcomings.

I didn't either. In fact I was a little ashamed of myself for that one fairly mild barb. Ernie Templeton had clearly been a worse influence on me than I'd heretofore guessed. That being the case, I said, in an effort to change the subject, "If you want to know what I think, it's that Mr. Hartland staged his collapse last night in order to draw attention away from himself as his mother's murderer."

Miss Dunstable's mouth dropped open, and I realized I'd just accused a man of murder out loud. Good Lord, if my mother could see me now, she'd disown me entirely.

Hmm . . .

But I didn't have a chance to ponder that pleasant possibility because Miss Dunstable said rather breathlessly, "My goodness, I wonder if you're right."

"I don't know," I admitted. "It only just occurred to me. I shouldn't have said anything. After all, the poor man might well have been only upset by his mother's death and reacted to something innocent—if you can call a séance innocent—a little dramatically."

"I just don't know," said Miss Dunstable. "It's all so puzzling."

"It is that," I agreed, and then I sighed. "Well, I suppose I ought to get back to work. If today is anything like the last several days, the phone will be ringing off the hook."

"You're busy then?" queried Miss Dunstable, sounding faintly surprised.

Her tone irked me. "Oh, yes, we have a very busy office," I assured her, fibbing only a little bit. Since my ad came out in the *Times,* we actually had been busier than before. I didn't like having to admit that so far the ad hadn't yielded a whole lot of billable work, but it had at least generated interest. Interest is the first step toward getting more work, isn't it? I wasn't sure, but it made sense to me, so I didn't feel guilty.

As I walked down the hallway to Ernie's office, I decided that I liked Sylvia Dunstable ever so well. She was not merely a competent secretary and one to be emulated, but she was a real comfort to a person in a time of need. Kind of like Buttercup, only without the fur.

And, boy, did I need comfort a few minutes later when I walked into Ernie's office to find Ernie and Phil standing there, staring at my empty desk. I stopped in the doorway and surveyed the men unhappily. If I'd only come back a minute or so earlier, they probably wouldn't have noticed I was missing. Oh, well.

Brazening it out, I smiled and lifted my chin. "Gentlemen. May I help you with anything?"

They turned and stared at me. Flustered, I brushed past them and went behind my desk, wishing one of them would say something. Whatever was wrong? Ernie couldn't be angry because I'd left the office for a minute or two, could he?

As I usually do when anxious, I began to talk. "You know, gentlemen, I've been thinking about last night's dramatic events, and it occurred to me that perhaps Mr. Hartland staged the whole thing so as to divert suspicion from himself. If we thought someone was trying to kill him after killing his mother, no one would look at him closely as the murderer of Mrs. Hartland, would they?"

Ernie and Phil exchanged a glance I couldn't read, but which made me nervous. "Well?" said I, sharply. "It's possible, isn't it?"

Frowning down at me—I'd taken a seat in my chair and folded my hands on my desk—Ernie said, "Yeah, it might have been possible. But Hartland's dead. Somebody smothered him with a pillow in the hospital during the night."

As I gawped at my employer, my brain spun, repeating the same refrain several times: *So much for that fine theory, Mercedes Louise Allcutt. Come up with another one, why don't you?*

CHAPTER THIRTEEN

"He's d-dead?" I glanced from Ernie to Phil and back again, my mind in a whirl.

"He's dead."

"But . . . but . . . how? Was it from natural causes? Oh, wait, you said he was smothered, didn't you?" And then an idea struck me. Before I could mull it over, I blurted it out. "Well, then, the killer must be Miss Lloyd! Have you checked into her background? Perhaps she has a long history of assault." With pillows? I shook my head hard. "Perhaps there's insanity in the family or—"

"She was drugged and unconscious all night long," said Phil, bursting my balloon before it had even begun to float.

Gathering my scattered resources, I demanded, "And how, exactly, do you know that?"

"Because our guys were there first thing this morning and questioned the staff at the hospital. The nurses on duty during the night—when they weren't crying on each other's shoulders over Rudolph Valentino—said they gave Miss Lloyd a hypo along about midnight last night, and she's still out cold."

"Well, when was Mr. Hartland smothered? Perhaps she did it at eleven."

"He was still alive at a quarter past twelve."

"How do you know that?"

"One of the nurses gave him a pill to help him sleep at twelve-fifteen. The time is right there on his chart."

"Hmm. I don't suppose it was the pill that did it." I only suggested it because I couldn't think of anything else to say.

"It wasn't the pill. It was a pillow."

"I suppose you can tell the difference between when someone dies of a drug overdose and when one is smothered with a pillow?" Hope still faintly glowed in me, although it was fading fast.

"Yes." There wasn't a shred of uncertainty in his voice.

"Oh." Blast it, that blew *that* theory sky high. Then I thought of something that boosted my morale considerably. "But at least you can't blame Mr. Hartland's murder on Wilbert Mullins, can you?"

Phil and Ernie glanced at each other, and my triumph soared. I recognized those expressions. They were expressions indicating that, no matter how much they hated to admit it, they had to agree with me.

"*Can* you," I persisted.

"No," Phil admitted.

"So are you going to release him? I'm sure Mr. Easthope would be happy to have him back as houseboy." That was a barefaced lie. I didn't have a single, solitary clue what Mr. Easthope's views on rehiring Rupert Mullins might be.

"No, we aren't going to release him yet."

"But why not?" I was building up to outrage, but hadn't quite made it there yet.

"We can't release him until after we find out who killed Hartland."

"Which Hartland?"

Phil heaved an aggrieved sigh I consider totally unjustified. "Both of them."

"But *why?* It's obvious that Wilbert didn't have anything thing to do with Mr. Hartland's death. It is logical, therefore, to conclude he didn't kill his mother, but that one other person killed the both of them. I should think you'd be looking at the same perpetrator for both crimes."

"Yeah, well, have you ever heard of accomplices?" This question was delivered by a sneering Ernie.

"Probably only one accomplice," amended Phil. Just in case I missed Ernie's sneer, he gave me one of his own.

Accomplices?

Ernie and Phil exchanged an expressive look.

Accomplices? Hmm. I hadn't actually thought about possible accomplices, unless Ernie and Phil were talking about—

One accomplice?

I gaped at the two men standing before my desk and my jaw dropped open and stayed that way for several seconds as the implications of what they'd said flipped over and over in my mind. When I shut my mouth, my teeth clacked so loudly, I'm sure Ernie and Phil heard them. I'd finally made it to outrage. Perhaps even beyond it.

Livid, I stood, flattened my palms on my desk and demanded, "*An accomplice?* Are you two going to stand there and tell me that you think for one minute *I* helped *murder* a man? Of all the contemptible, revolting, inconceivable—"

As I sputtered, hardly believing what I'd heard, Ernie looked at me, puzzled.

So did Phil.

Then Ernie's expression of puzzlement changed to one of exasperation. "For Christ's sake, Mercy, we're not talking about you!"

My mouth clacked shut again. My rage was so all-consuming that it took me a couple of seconds to settle down a trifle. Then I said, "Oh." Then I swallowed more bile and tried to control my heartbeat using a method Mr. Easthope had explained to me once. He claimed the relaxation technique was practiced by Buddhist monks somewhere in the East. Wherever those monks were from, they were considerably east of Boston I guess, because the technique didn't work on me for several tense moments.

When I thought I could speak without shrieking, I asked, feigning Oriental calm, "Then whom do you suspect of being Mr. Mullins's accomplice?"

"She's been working downstairs in the lobby for a couple of years now, for Pete's sake," said Ernie in patent disgust. "I can't believe you thought we were talking about you."

"You mean *Lulu?*" I cried, any semblance of calm, eastern or otherwise, evaporating in yet another flash of ire. "Don't be ridiculous! Lulu would no more murder a man than *I* would!"

Another meaningful glance passed between the two men, creating in me an urge to batter them both with a blunt instrument. The only instrument to hand was the telephone, so I didn't. Besides, I'm not violent by nature. Instead, I said, "That's the most asinine thing I've ever heard."

"Yeah?" Phil appeared peeved, and for the first time since I'd met him, he reminded me of a policeman. "Well, I've seen lots of stuff more asinine than that, believe me."

"I sincerely doubt that. Have you spoken with Lulu?"

"Not yet."

"Phil's on his way downstairs to question her now," Ernie said.

"Suspecting Lulu of murder is utter nonsense. What about those two wretched spiritualists? What about the O'Doyles? Have you questioned them? They've already proved themselves to be liars and crooks. To me, they're much more likely to be the perpetrators than poor Lulu or her brother." I thought of something else. "Or Fernandez! That man gives me the willies, and he's already an accomplice of the O'Doyles! He's in their employ, for heaven's sake! I wouldn't put it past him to kill someone if *Angelique,* or whatever her real name is, asked him to."

I thought it was a brilliant point, but Ernie only rolled his eyes. "The police are questioning everybody, Mercy, including the O'Doyles and Fernandez. They aren't only concentrating on Lulu LaBelle."

I sniffed. "It's a good thing." Although I was still seething, there didn't seem to be an appropriate target to impale with my pointed remarks, so I asked something about which I was curious. "Why'd he faint, anyway?"

Phil answered me. "He said he thought he felt someone stick him with something."

"Stick him with something? Stick him with what?"

Phil only shrugged, and I guess that was my answer. Some answer.

Ernie and Phil toddled off to Ernie's office to commiserate and, probably, discuss how irrational women were, always flying off the handle and so forth. It wasn't fair. Women were certainly no more irrational than men, and men caused all the trouble in the world they were so proud of being in charge of. Besides, Phil was supposed to be going downstairs to question Lulu, not gossiping with Ernie. Stupid men.

After sitting at my desk and fuming for a few seconds, I was interrupted by the telephone ringing, and I had to answer it. "Mr. Templeton's office. Miss Allcutt speaking."

A soft voice, one that sounded as if it might be slinky if it weren't clogged with tears, answered my greeting. "Oh, is this the private investigator's office?"

Who'd she think she was calling, a dentist? Rather than take my wrath out on a possible client, I said sweetly, "Yes it is. Mr. Ernest Templeton, discreet private investigations."

"Oh, I read his ad in the *Times.*"

My ad, thought I. And if she read the ad, why'd she think

this was a dentist's office? Still sweet, I said, "May I help you?"

"Oh, I hope so!"

I rolled my eyes. Clearly, this woman thought she had problems, but I didn't feel like mollycoddling anybody, and especially not someone who sounded as if she might be young and lovely and, perhaps, vamp-like when she wasn't crying. I'd had my fill of vamps during my first case with Ernie. "Would you like to set up an appointment to see Mr. Templeton?"

"Oh, I don't know."

I wasn't Houdini. I couldn't get her out of a scrape telepathically. In fact, I don't think even Houdini could do that. Possessing myself in patience with some difficulty, I said, still sweet, darn it, "If you have a problem with which you believe a private investigator might be able to help, Mr. Templeton is the man for you. He's tops in the business." I didn't know that, of course, since I didn't know any other private investigators, but at least I trusted Ernie. When he wasn't being a pill to me.

"Oh, do you really think so?"

If she said "Oh," in that breathy voice one more time . . . I gave myself a hard mental slap. "Yes, indeed. Mr. Templeton is the best."

"Oh."

I gritted my teeth.

"Well, then . . ."

I ground said teeth together.

"Oh, I don't know."

I finally lost my patience. "If you have a problem, I will be happy to make an appointment for you to see Mr. Templeton. This morning. If you're close by the office, you can come in at nine-thirty." It was then eight-thirty. I couldn't imagine that even a vamp would need more than an hour to prepare herself to see a P.I. "If you're not sure, perhaps you should telephone later, when you *are* sure."

Evidently, my snappish tone of voice startled her, because silence prevailed on the other end of the wire. It lasted so long, I was about to hang up the receiver, feeling guilty but justified, when the breathy voice came again.

"Oh, yes. Please. Nine-thirty will be fine."

I think she probably heard me exhale, but I couldn't help myself. Regaining my composure along with my faintly tainted sweetness, I said, "Very well. What is your name, please?"

"Persephone Chalmers."

Persephone Chalmers? Good grief. "Excellent, Miss Chal—"

"Missus. Missus Chalmers."

Who'd'a thunk it? "Very well, Mrs. Chalmers. We'll see you at nine-thirty. You have our address from the advertisement, correct?"

"Oh, yes. Yes, I do."

"Fine, then. We'll see you at nine-thirty." Because I really didn't want to make her life worse than it evidently already was, I added, "Please try not to worry. Mr. Templeton will be happy to help you." Especially if she was young and pretty and had money and what everyone was calling SA, an acronym for sex appeal, at which descriptive phrase my stuffy Boston soul cringed even though I didn't want it to.

Because I was still irked with both Ernie and Phil—Lulu La-Belle as an accomplice, indeed—and because I'd been told that Phil was on his way down to interview Lulu, which was his job, blast it, and which he wasn't doing as he sat and blabbed with Ernie, I decided to interrupt the two irritating men. Therefore, I strode to Ernie's door, gave a quick rap, and without waiting for Ernie's usual, "Yeah?" I marched right on in.

". . . blue pictures. I'm not sure about that, though. My men are checking into it."

"Lucky then." Ernie's chuckle was cut short by the door opening.

Phil sat up with a start. He'd been leaning on his elbows over Ernie's desk, and it looked as if the two men had been whispering. Just like a couple of silly schoolgirls. Schoolboys, I mean.

Ernie's head snapped up. He'd been leaning over his desk, too. Men. "Yeah?" he said to me, clearly irked by my intrusion.

"A young woman named *Missus* Persephone Chalmers has an appointment to see you at nine-thirty, Ernie." Even her name made me want to gag.

Ernie lifted an eyebrow. "Persephone?" He grinned at Phil. "There's a name suitable for blue movies if you ask me."

Phil grinned back.

I didn't have any idea what the beastly men were talking about.

"Okay, kiddo," said Ernie, dismissing me with a wave.

Furious, I stamped back to my desk, although, since I'm a good secretary no matter what the provocation, I did close the door behind me. And without slamming it, too.

As I waited for Mrs. Persephone Chalmers (and shouldn't she be using her husband's first name? Mrs. Adonis Chalmers, or whatever?) to show herself in the office, I strained all my powers trying to figure out what "blue pictures" and "blue movies" were and if they might possibly pertain to the Heartwood/Hartland murders or if the two men had gone on to other topics altogether. I had planned to ask Phil when he finally went downstairs to do his policemanly duty, but what with one thing and another, primarily the telephone's constant interruptions, I was unable to do so. On my own I had come to no definite conclusion about them when, at precisely nine-thirty, the outer office door opened and a young woman floated in as if borne on a cloud.

I had just replaced the telephone receiver in the cradle, and I looked up. My heart sank. "Mrs. Persephone Chalmers?" I said.

It had to be she, and, if anything, she was worse than a vamp.

Clad head to toe in cream-colored fabric from her veiled hat to her lovely linen summer suit to her silk stockings to her dyed-to-match pumps, she radiated both money and distress. One or the other of those commodities and Ernie, who was a sucker for distressed females and who had no aversion to money, was sunk. When both were added to the face discernible through the veil, which was young and lovely and fragile and frightened, not to mention blond-haired, and Ernie had no chance at all of remaining unmoved. I sensed it in my bones, which felt particularly cold as I watched Mrs. Chalmers waft to a chair before my desk.

"Oh," she whispered. "Yes. I am Mrs. Chalmers." She hovered near the chair, as if afraid to touch it or sit in it.

With a sigh, I rose from my desk feeling entirely too sturdy, brunette and self-sufficient, and wishing it were otherwise. Oh, well . . .

I tapped lightly at Ernie's door.

"Yeah?"

I heaved another sigh as I opened the door a crack.

"Mrs. Persephone Chalmers is here to see you, Mr. Templeton."

"Ah. Right. Send her in."

So I drew his door wider, smiled at Mrs. Chalmers even though it was a struggle to do so, and said, "Please come this way, Mrs. Chalmers."

"Oh," she said. It was more of a whisper, actually. "Thank you." And she drifted across the floor and into Ernie's office, leaving an only-faintly-discernible trace of a captivating fragrance in her wake. I didn't slam the door that time, either.

As Ernie spoke with Mrs. Chalmers, I made appointments for a woman who wanted Ernie to spy on her husband, a husband who wanted Ernie to spy on his wife, and an insurance firm that wanted Ernie to determine if a man really had been badly injured in a mishap at the Broadway Department Store or if he was merely faking. Evidently, he'd tripped getting out of an elevator on the third floor, and he claimed the elevator operator hadn't leveled the elevator cage properly. The insurance company clearly believed the man was lying. Personally, I didn't care, although I thought he should have been more careful.

I felt particularly grumpy during that period and I knew why. I didn't want my boss, Mr. Ernest Templeton, to succumb to any more beautiful clients, darn it. Last month's flirtation with a black-clad siren who was being blackmailed had been bad enough. This month's cream-clad seraph with her air of delicate innocence seemed to me to be even more dangerous.

Not, naturally, that I cared on a personal level. I was only concerned about Ernie's welfare and the state of the business.

Oh, whom am I trying to kid?

But I don't want to think about that now.

I didn't want to think about it then, either, and the task was made easier for me when Lulu burst into the office while Ernie was sequestered with the lovely Mrs. Chalmers.

"Oh, Mercy!" cried she, her face awash with tears.

"Oh, Lulu!" I cried in return, and I rushed out from behind my desk to embrace the poor thing.

"They think *I* did it!"

"I'm sure they don't, really," I said, sure of no such thing. I was beginning to think Phil was, if not as corrupt, then at least as stupid as his fellow cohorts in the police department. Not a single thinking human being could believe that Lulu LaBelle *or* her brother could kill the two Heartwoods. Hartlands. Whoever they were.

Guiding Lulu to the chair beside my desk, I sat her down, then reached into my desk drawer (not the one I kept my handbag and hat in, but the other one, which was deeper) and withdrew a water glass. "Stay right there, Lulu. I'll get you a drink of water."

"Th-thank you, Mercy."

I dashed down the hallway to the ladies' powder room and filled the glass. By the time I got back to the office, Lulu had stopped sobbing hysterically and was mopping her cheeks with an already-soggy handkerchief. She took the water with a shaking hand. "Thank you." She sipped the water between hiccups.

"Lulu," I said gently. "Try not to worry too much about this. I'm on the job, and I *know* neither you nor Rupert could commit cold-blooded murder."

I expected her to thank me again. Instead, she lifted her head abruptly—she'd had it bowed as she wiped tears and mascara from her cheeks—and said, *"You?"*

She sounded incredulous and I resented her tone, but she was already upset so I didn't take her to task for it. "I." Since she still gaped, I said tartly, "I'm the only one who's tried to help you and Rupert so far, am I not?"

Lulu bit her lower lip for a second, then nodded.

"I'm the one who got him the job with Mr. Easthope, am I not?"

Her head sagged again. "But that's when all the trouble started!" she wailed pitifully.

Shocked by the note of accusation in Lulu's voice, I did a little sagging of my own. "But . . . I was trying to *help* you. I didn't know some fiend was going to murder Mrs. Heartwood. Hartland. Whatever her name was."

Lulu put her hand on mine and appeared chastened. "I know it, Mercy. I'm sorry. I'm just so upset."

Hmm. "Of course." I still felt as if she'd slapped me.

Ernie's door opened at that point, however, and I didn't have time to brood. Lulu jumped up from the chair, muttered, "I'd better get downstairs," and raced from the office, leaving Ernie, Mrs. Chalmers and me all to gape after her. I guess Lulu didn't want to be seen with her makeup smeared. And she hadn't even taken a good gander at Mrs. Chalmers first, either. I hate to admit it, but Mrs. Chalmers in all her cream-colored loveliness made me want to hide somewhere, too.

However, I am an Allcutt, and we Allcutts are made of stern stuff, whether we want to be or not, so I turned and smiled at the duo exiting Ernie's office.

Ernie hooked a thumb at the door. "What's the matter with her?"

I wanted to shriek at him that having been falsely accused of a vicious crime was the matter with her, but since Mrs. Chalmers was present I didn't. "She's upset."

"I guess."

And that was it for me as far as Ernie's attention went. As if he were guiding a fragile spun-glass angel, he walked Mrs. Chalmers to the door. Chalmers herself didn't bother to say good-bye to me—or even say, "Oh," once more. She just gazed up at Ernie through that stupid veil with wide blue eyes and smiled tremulously. I wanted to heave a brick at her.

Ernie was straightening his tie when he turned from the door after her exit. He had a sappy grin on his face, making me want to heave a brick at *him*.

"What's her problem?" My voice sounded faintly caustic.

"Jewel theft," said Ernie. And he swaggered to his office and shut the door.

Curse all men.

CHAPTER FOURTEEN

Buttercup had been banished to Chloe and Harvey's beautifully landscaped backyard—Mother, who didn't like dogs in the first place, detested it when they begged at the table, not that Buttercup ever did anything so unrefined—and we were all sitting around the dinner table wondering what to talk about. Since Mother's advent into our lives, the general flow of cheerful, inconsequential dinner-table chatter had dried up completely.

I already felt fairly glum. Valentino's death had cast a pall of melancholy over the entire nation, it would seem. Ernie Templeton, my boss, whom I . . . respected, had evidently fallen under the spell of another *femme fatale*. Lulu LaBelle and her brother Rupert Mullins had been falsely accused of murder. As for me, I didn't have a solitary idea in my muddled brain what to do about any of those things. This was particularly true since my prime suspect, George Hartland, and my second-prime suspect, Jacqueline Lloyd, were out of the murder stakes.

"Mercedes Louise Allcutt, stop toying with your food."

I dropped my spoon, startled by Mother's booming accusation. As I hadn't been toying with my food, I dared to frown at her. "I wasn't toying with my food, Mother. I was trying to fish out a cucumber bit." Mrs. Biddle had served us a cold soup called *gazpacho*, which she claimed was a Spanish concoction, for dinner. It was quite tasty and refreshing on such a hot August evening.

"Nonsense," said Mother, completely uncowed by my defiance. "*Fishing* out cucumber bits is toying with your food, and it is impolite."

I heaved a sigh as big as I was, and internally acknowledged defeat. Nobody, and especially nobody as inconsequential as a daughter, would ever get my mother to admit to being wrong about anything at all, ever. Therefore, I gave up the fight and turned to Chloe and Harvey, determined to clear up at least one puzzle.

"What's a blue picture?" I asked in all innocence.

Chloe gasped. "I beg your pardon?" She stared at me, plainly horrified.

Harvey apparently swallowed the wrong way, because he started to cough and Chloe had to slap him on the back. Mother, naturally, glowered at all of us.

Realizing I'd said something wrong, although I didn't know what—well, I guess I knew what, but I sure didn't know why—I stammered, "I-I mean . . . um . . ."

Quickly, in an attempt to rescue the moment and me both, Chloe said, "We'll talk about it later, all right?"

"Certainly," said I, relieved. "That's fine."

"And why would you talk about it later, young woman?" Mother scowled at me as she asked the question. Of course. I, being the least obedient of her children, *always* got the brunt of her wrath. "If you have introduced another topic unfit for dinner-table conversation, Mercedes Louise Allcutt, you should be ashamed of yourself. Your father and I didn't rear you to be such a hoyden."

Oh, brother. "I just asked a question, Mother," I said in my own defense, knowing it was useless. "I didn't mean to bring up an unfit topic."

"I'm beginning to think you're a lost cause, young woman."

"Fiddlesticks," I said, losing what was left of my ragged temper. "At least I didn't leave my husband!"

Mother's hard, marble-blue eyes widened amid a duet of gasps from Harvey and Chloe.

Uh-oh. I'd really done it this time. I saw Mother's jaw bunch as she clenched her teeth and knew I was in for it. Why hadn't I just kept my fat mouth shut?

Thank the good Lord, a knock came at the front door just then, and Mrs. Biddle, muttering under her breath—she didn't care to have her dinner-serving duties interrupted—hurried to answer it. I silently blessed whoever was at the front door for saving me, at least temporarily, from my mother's wrath.

After sending me a last fulminating glance—evidently she was going to save the worst of her fury for later, probably to deliver in private—Mother said, "You need to hire another servant, Clovilla. Your poor housekeeper is being run off her feet." She sniffed regally.

"Good idea, Mother," said Chloe in a bright voice. "What do you think, Harvey?"

Harvey also attempted lightness of demeanor. "I think that's a brilliant suggestion, Mrs. Allcutt. Perhaps you can call the agency tomorrow, Chloe, dear."

"Of course, darling."

Now I knew that Harvey and Chloe were very fond of each other. In fact, Chloe had told me more than once that Harvey was the man of her dreams. But I'd never heard them utter such banal endearments before. Their relationship generally tended to express itself with teasing amusement. Mother brings out the worst in all of us.

And then Francis Easthope staggered into the dining room and we all lost our train of thought. Even Mother did, I think.

"Francis!" Chloe cried, leaping from her seat and rushing to him.

"Francis, what in the world is the matter?" asked Harvey, also rising and going to him.

"Mr. Easthope!" I rose, too, and did likewise.

With the exception of Mother, who clusters for no one, we all clustered around Mr. Easthope, who looked less than perfectly put together for the first time since I'd met him.

"I'm terribly sorry to barge in on you like this," he said in a shaky voice. "But the police are at my house, executing a search warrant. They're going through *everything*. I think they believe *I* killed the Hartland woman and her son!"

"Oh, they couldn't!" Chloe.

"But that's ridiculous!" Harvey.

"No, they don't." Me.

They all looked at me, and I elaborated.

"They've already got Rupert Mullins locked up, and they interviewed his sister Lulu today at the Figueroa Building. I imagine they're only going through your home because Rupert works there. Worked there." Oh, Lord, what a dreadful mess!

"Do you really think so?"

Mr. Easthope seemed faintly relieved, which I think was awfully generous of him. After all, it had been I who'd introduced the accused murderer to his household. Not that Rupert had killed the woman or that it was my fault she'd been murdered in the first place, but . . . Oh, never mind.

"I'm sure of it." I was fairly sure of it, anyhow.

Wiping his brow, Mr. Easthope whispered, "I do so hope you're right, Miss Allcutt. Thank God Mother is out of the house tonight."

Even as I wished I could say the same thing of my own mother, she cleared her throat meaningfully and we all jumped a little bit.

Mr. Easthope started guiltily. "I'm so sorry, Chloe and Harvey. I shouldn't have come and interrupted your evening meal."

"Don't be ridiculous, dear boy," said Harvey stoutly. He was such a good fellow. "In fact, pull up a chair, and I'll have Mrs.

Biddle set another place."

"Oh, no, I shouldn't."

"Don't be silly, Francis," said Chloe. She took his arm. "You need to be with friends at a time like this."

I agreed wholeheartedly. So did I need to be with friends. However, recalling Mother's comment on the state of Chloe and Harvey's service staff, I whispered, "I'll go fetch another place setting. No sense in aggravating—" I jerked my head toward the table.

Chloe pressed my arm. "Thanks, Mercy." She rolled her eyes ceilingward. "How long is this going to go on?"

It was a cry for help, but I didn't have an answer for her. I gave her arm a little squeeze before I took off for the kitchen. "Not much longer, I hope."

We all hoped so. But we didn't dare hope too hard.

Fortunately for me, Mr. Easthope's arrival thwarted Mother from scolding me about all her grievances against me. Thank the good Lord, conversation turned to neutral topics. Naturally, Rudolph Valentino's death and the elaborate arrangements being made for his funeral shared top billing, along with how sad Theda Bara and the rest of Valentino's former lovers were sure to be. Not that we used the word "lover" in Mother's presence.

After dinner, it was Francis Easthope who finally satisfied my curiosity about blue pictures. He seemed a trifle embarrassed when I asked him the question. Since he was the third person I'd asked who'd appeared embarrassed by the subject, I'd already begun formulating my own theory.

"Blue movies?" He reached up and fiddled with his collar as if he suddenly found it too tight—which it probably was, since the weather that night must have been eighty degrees. Chloe and Harvey had big fans running, but we were all still quite warm.

"Let me guess," I told him dryly. "They're improper sorts of pictures, right?"

He nodded. "Most improper."

"With naked ladies?"

You don't often see grown men blushing—at least I don't—but Mr. Francis Easthope blushed then. I shot a quick glance Motherward, but she was frowning at somebody else for a change, so I figured it was safe to continue our conversation. She'd kill me if she knew I'd made a man blush.

"Er . . . yes. And, sometimes, gentlemen."

Naked ladies *and* naked gentlemen? Good heavens. Not, I suppose, that one could properly call them ladies and gentlemen if they allowed themselves to be photographed without their clothes on. "My word," I said, at a loss to come up with anything more cogent to say.

"Yes," said Mr. Easthope. His color had begun to fade, thank the good Lord. If Mother saw that I'd made a man blush, I'd never hear the end of it. Not that it would matter much, I guess, since I already had so many sins against me, according to Mother, that I'd never hear the end of them anyway.

"Hmm." I'd begun to think about this blue-picture thing. Ernie would probably say something sarcastic about how dangerous it was for me to think at all, but he'd have been wrong. "Is it common for young actresses coming to Los Angeles to end up in such pictures?" I asked Mr. Easthope, praying he wouldn't blush again.

He didn't, bless his heart. "Well, I don't know if one could call it *common,* but I do know that some young women have been led astray by the unscrupulous producers of illicit pictures who promise them stardom and then lead them into posing for scurrilous stills and even more scurrilous moving pictures."

"Hmm." I thought harder. "I suppose that if someone were to start making a name for herself in legitimate pictures and it was discovered that she'd acted in blue movies, such a thing would be bad for her career, wouldn't it?"

"Disastrous. As good as a death knell. You remember what happened to Fatty Arbuckle, and he was acquitted of any wrongdoing. The mere fact that a woman died in his hotel room and he'd participated in a wild party was enough to ruin his career."

"Yes. I do remember." Who didn't?

But how, I asked myself, could Jacqueline Lloyd have smothered George Hartland if, as the nurses swore, she was out cold all night long? Clearly, since she was the one sitting next to Vivian Hartland the night of the first séance, she could have poisoned her with whatever alkaloid poison she favored. But how could she have smothered her son? Hmm . . .

An accomplice.

Phil and Ernie had said something about an accomplice. But who could be Jacqueline Lloyd's accomplice? Mr. Carstairs? Unlikely, I should think. He was a successful Hollywood attorney. Why would he want to get mixed up in murder?

Well, for that matter, why would *anyone* want to get mixed up in murder?

I suppose it was vaguely possible that Mr. Carstairs had assisted Miss Lloyd because he didn't want her career ruined. That same reasoning might apply to any one of a number of other people who depended on Miss Lloyd as a source of income. Perhaps I should ask Harvey about who else might be harmed if Miss Lloyd's career took a nosedive.

Or perhaps an enraged fan of Jacqueline Lloyd had done in the Hartlands for some reason as yet unknown to anyone. To keep Miss Lloyd from meeting eligible men? To ruin her career so that another star could take her place in the Hollywood firmament?

Oh, bother. I wasn't coming to any conclusions, but I was definitely confusing myself.

"Mercedes Louise Allcutt, have you heard a single word I've spoken to you?"

I think I broke the record for the sitting high jump when Mother's voice finally penetrated my musings. Slamming a hand over my heart, I stammered, "I-I beg your pardon?"

Mother gave me one of her patented, daughter-killing scowls. "I asked if the police have discovered who killed that poor, misguided woman. Pay attention, Mercedes."

"Yes, Mother. I mean no, Mother. I mean the police aren't sure yet who killed Mrs. Hartland. And now somebody's murdered her son. George Hartland was smothered with a pillow last night in his hospital bed."

A general gasp arose, and yet once more I wished I'd kept my mouth shut. However, Mother surprised me. Although she still scowled, she had a certain gleam in her eyes that I'd only seen there once before, on the night she'd told me about the second séance.

Was it possible that my mother—*my mother*—was becoming interested in crime? Unlikely.

"I must say that since you've moved west, you've managed to become embroiled in some excessively unsavory events, Mercedes Louise."

Fudge. However, I said meekly, "Yes, Mother."

"I have to admit that the events do possess a modicum of intrigue to the casual observer, however."

Chloe and I exchanged a quick, shocked glance. "Um . . . yes, I guess they do." Maybe my earlier thought wasn't so unlikely after all.

"I suspect those nonsensical people who call themselves *spiritualists* of having perpetrated the evil deeds. They're clearly individuals of no moral worth or they wouldn't be trying to bilk people of their money in the first place."

"The police are looking very hard at the d'Agostinos.

O'Doyles, I mean." I determined that it would be better for me not to propound the notion that killing the clientele would be bad for the spiritualists' business. Mother didn't take kindly to having her opinions doubted.

"O'Doyle?" Chloe asked, a note of incredulity in her voice. "Did you say their name is really *O'Doyle?*" She burst into tinkling laughter, and it occurred to me that it was the first time in a couple of days I'd heard anyone laugh. National and local events seemed to have stripped people of their senses of humor.

"You mean d'Agostino is an . . . whatever do they call it? An . . . alibi?"

"I think you mean an alias, Mother."

She sniffed. "I suppose you *would* know that, wouldn't you?"

"Yes, indeedy."

And *then* it occurred to me that there were a whole bunch of people included in this investigation who were going by names other than their own. I wondered if Jacqueline Lloyd was Jacqueline Lloyd's real name. I knew for a fact, since I lived with a man involved in the flickers, that often both men and women will select names other than those given to them at birth as screen names. I hardly blamed some of them, especially if their last name was Mullins, as poor Lulu's was. Not that there's anything wrong with the name Mullins, but you must admit it would look queer on a marquee.

Good heavens, what if Jacqueline Lloyd had been born a Mullins? In Enid, Oklahoma? Or an O'Doyle in St. Louis, Missouri? Or even a Hartland? If she were Vivian Hartland's daughter, for instance, would she be in line for a big inheritance? That would account for her having bumped off George as well as Mrs. Hartland, wouldn't it?

Whom could I ask about this interesting new possibility? Mr. Carstairs would probably know, but since Miss Lloyd was his client her real name might be considered privileged information. I wouldn't want for him to break any laws or anything. More to the point, I'd feel really stupid if I asked him and he gave me a long lecture on attorney–client confidentiality rules.

Sylvia Dunstable. I could ask her. Mind you, she was an excellent private secretary and she might believe herself to be bound by the same rules of confidentiality her employer had to obey, but at least I wouldn't feel like an idiot asking her.

My mother, who had no access to my secret thoughts and wouldn't care anyway, said, "I do believe the police are being deplorably dilatory in the case. It's clear to me that the medium and her brother are responsible for the evil doings."

"Do you really think so?" Mr. Easthope posed his question politely.

"Who else would possibly do such a thing?" Mother demanded.

Silly me, I forgot my earlier resolution and stuck my oar in. "I should think they'd want to keep their customers alive and well. It doesn't do to kill off your clients if you want to earn a living, does it?"

"Really, Mercedes Louise! You have learned to speak very crudely since you left Boston. Your grandmother must be spinning in her grave."

I shut my eyes for a second and offered a quick prayer for patience. Mother was right, however. If Grandmother Powell, Mother's mother, had heard me say that my ear would be smarting for days from the wallop she'd have delivered. I was glad I wasn't sitting next to Mother, since she'd been known to deliver the same punishment when annoyed beyond enduring. I fear I'd been annoying my mother a whole lot since she'd arrived at Chloe and Harvey's front door.

That being the case and because it was always possible, if not probable, that if I irked her enough she'd go back home, I said, "Well, both of my grandmothers are buried in Boston, so I don't suppose they heard me. Besides, they're dead."

Chloe pressed a hand over her mouth, either in horror or to smother a laugh. I couldn't be sure. Francis Easthope cleared his throat. Harvey didn't even try to hide his grin.

Mother said, "Well, really!"

Buttercup and I retired shortly after that. I couldn't bear listening to any more of my faults being revealed to the assembled company. And it had been *she* who, all my life, had told us never to air our dirty linen in public.

I'd have called her a hypocrite to her face, but I feared for my life.

CHAPTER FIFTEEN

The report of George Hartland's death was headline news the following morning. It might have been headline news in the prior day's afternoon editions, too, but I hadn't checked.

All the newspapers played up the irony of George's murder following so closely upon the heels of his mother's. As I rode down Angel's Flight, I read what I considered a rather wild theory propounded in the *Examiner*. According to the reporter, Vivian Hartland in her guise as Hedda Heartwood had dug up so much dirt on so many people that somebody had killed her to keep her from spilling the beans. Which wasn't the wild part. The wild part was that, according to the reporter, Hedda Heartwood had exacted payment from certain parties in order to keep her quiet.

Hedda Heartwood a *blackmailer?* Nonsense! Anyhow, what did George have to do with any such fell scheme?

The train came to a halt and I refolded my paper, smiled at the engineer and walked the few short blocks to the Figueroa Building. Every time I approached my place of work these days, I smiled, and not merely because my job meant escape from my mother. The building looked *so* much spiffier now than it had when Ernie first hired me.

I braced myself before entering the lobby, but I needn't have. Although she didn't look any too chipper, at least Lulu wasn't crying this morning. Nevertheless, I approached her in a gingerly manner. "Good morning, Lulu. I hope you're feeling better today."

She left off filing her fingernails and glanced up at me. Her face bore such an expression of tragedy, I wondered if she was practicing for the silver screen or if she really felt that despondent about being suspected of murder along with her brother, the hapless Rupert. I guess I couldn't fault her if the latter was the case. Or the former, either, for that matter.

"I feel awful," she said gloomily.

Lulu generally wore very interesting costumes to work. That day she looked positively drab in a gray, drop-waisted dress with no adornment whatsoever. Even her bottle-blond hair seemed dull. What's more, her fingernails, generally painted with blood-red enamel, today were bare of polish. She couldn't have looked more funereal if she'd tried.

My heart tugged for her. Patting her hand, I said, "Try not to worry too much, Lulu. I have another theory that I intend to check out this morning. I'm sure we'll have the real culprit soon."

She gazed up at me, and I think she'd have appeared surprised if she'd had the energy. "You? You have another theory? What about Ernie and that copper friend of his? Are they both just going to let Rupert and me hang?"

Although I resented her evident lack of faith in my investigative talents, I didn't take her to task. She already felt puny enough. "I'm sure Ernie and Phil are working hard on your behalf, Lulu."

She said, "Huh," which was pretty much how I felt.

After sighing deeply and patting her hand once more, I headed for the staircase. I tried to walk the three flights of stairs to Ernie's office at least three or four times a week in order to get exercise, which I understand is good for one's circulation.

When I unlocked the office door, I got a shock when I realized Ernie had been to the office and left again already. On the usual morning, I got to work a half-hour before he did. Not today. He'd even left a note on my desk:

Mercy,
   Gone to meet with Mrs. Chalmers about her stolen jewelry.
Don't know when I'll be back. Stay out of trouble.
                                                    E. T.

Stay out of trouble, indeed. Scowling, I crumpled the note and threw it at the wastebasket. It bounced off the rim, and I had to scoop it up and throw it out more carefully. I'll just bet he *was* meeting with Mrs. Chalmers, although I had my doubts about the stolen-jewelry scenario. Although I didn't want to think that Ernie Templeton, my employer, would do anything so wicked as have an illicit liaison with a married woman, I wasn't altogether certain. He was a man, after all, and Chloe had told me shocking tales of how little some men value the sacred bonds of matrimony. Look at our father, for heaven's sake.

Bother. As I stuffed my hat and handbag into the desk drawer, I felt quite morose and crabby.

For the first time since it had begun doing so, I didn't appreciate the telephone ringing its stupid head off that day. I needed time to think, and it's difficult for one to think when the 'phone is constantly jangling in one's ear.

In between calls, I did manage to get a little thinking done. Ernie and Phil had been discussing blue movies. Who, besides Jacqueline Lloyd, who had an alibi, might be involved in blue movies?

Darned near anyone in Los Angeles, I concluded dismally. I mean a body didn't have to be a movie star or a famous director or anything like that to break the law in other fields. What commandment of the motion-picture industry declared lawbreakers needed to be in the legitimate motion picture business in order to create illegitimate motion pictures? None that I knew of, although I wasn't up-to-date on the laws in California. Or anywhere else.

But were blue movies illegal? Darned if I knew. Perhaps they were merely not respectable. I suppose that would be enough to ruin a career or two if the facts ever leaked out. Fiddlesticks.

During a lull in the morning's 'phone duties, I dashed down the hallway to Sylvia Dunstable's office. She was on the telephone when I entered the room, so I took a seat in front of her desk and waited patiently. She smiled and gave me a finger wave, and I was privy to her side of a rather boring conversation.

"Yes, Mr. Goldfish. I'll be sure to tell him."

Whoever Mr. Goldfish was, he babbled something on the other end of the wire.

"Yes, Mr. Goldfish. I'm sure that's true."

More babbling on the other end of the wire.

"I'll be sure to tell him, Mr. Goldfish, and he'll be out to your studio this afternoon at three."

A little more babbling, then Miss Dunstable offered Mr. Goldfish a polite good-bye. To my surprise she gave a comical little roll of her eyes as she hung the receiver on the candlestick.

"A bothersome client?" I asked.

"You have no idea." She didn't continue on that vein, so I never did get to know who Mr. Goldfish was or what Mr. Carstairs aimed to be at his studio for. "May I help you with something, Miss Allcutt?"

Now that I was here, I discovered myself embarrassed to continue. Nevertheless, for the sake of Lulu and Rupert Mullins, I felt obliged to do so. "Um . . . do you know anything about blue movies, Miss Dunstable?"

Her eyes opened so wide, my embarrassment deepened to chagrin. "Blue movies?" she said in something of a squeak. "Why on earth do you want to know about blue movies?"

"Oh, dear. I'm sorry. I know that sounded stupid. But I interrupted Ernie and his policeman friend, Detective Bigelow, yesterday, and they were talking about blue movies. Since they'd been cloistered together about the Hartland case, I thought the reference might have some significance to the case."

"I can't imagine why." Miss Dunstable's tone had turned rather chilly.

"Well, but . . ." I hesitated, mainly because my upbringing was getting in my way. Again. But, really, in Boston, one never asked people about other people whom they suspect of acting in blue movies, for heaven's sake. I told myself to snap out of it. "But if Miss Lloyd used to act in blue movies and Hedda Hartwood found out about it, do you think she might have killed Mrs. Hartwood to keep her from spilling the beans?"

"Good heavens, Miss Allcutt! Miss Lloyd has done no such thing!"

I felt really stupid. "Oh. Are you sure?"

"Absolutely."

I sighed heavily. "Then there's probably no significance to the reference to blue movies, but the police insist upon believing that Rupert Mullins killed Mrs. Hartland and that an accomplice of his must have killed Mr. Hartland, and I was hoping to find another culprit."

Softening, Miss Dunstable folded her hands and laid them on her desk. "Well . . . I know you're a friend of Miss LaBelle—"

"Sort of," I said, interrupting. Then I was ashamed of myself. I *was* Lulu's friend, darn it, no matter what my mother might think of her. "I mean, yes, I am. And I'm sure neither she nor Rupert Mullins had anything to do with the Hartlands' murders. Why would they want to kill them?"

"I'm sure I have no idea," responded Miss Dunstable. "But you must know that murders are committed for the silliest of reasons. Sometimes for no reason at all. Motive is about the last thing the police look for in your average, everyday murder."

I felt my eyes widen. This was new stuff to me. "They *don't?* My word! Why not?"

A little sigh preceded Miss Dunstable's next words. "Because most murders are committed in fits of passion, when a person isn't thinking clearly. When one is carried away with emotion, one doesn't necessarily react sensibly to a situation."

"Ah," said I. "You may be right."

"Oh, I'm right," she averred positively. "Believe me. I've been Mr. Carstairs's secretary for some time now, even before his clientele became more . . . um . . . respectable, I guess is a good word, than it used to be. He used to have to defend perfectly detestable people, most of whom didn't have a motive for living from day to day, much less for doing an evil deed or committing a violent crime."

"Hmm." I sat there in silence for another minute or two, and Miss Dunstable continued to gaze at me through her terribly professional-looking spectacles. I don't know what she was doing besides that, but I was thinking furiously. "I suppose you mean . . . people of a . . ." Lord, this was tricky. "Um . . . people of a . . . well, a lower social order who go out drinking and doing other unfortunate things and who get into fights and such." I'd read about such happenings in Boston. I was sure Los Angeles was no different.

"Not just people from the lower social orders," she said stoutly. "You'd be surprised."

"Ah." I thought some more. "But don't you think that these Hartland murders have an air of . . . well . . . premeditation about them? That would signify a motive, wouldn't it? I mean, if we could figure out what that motive might be?"

Miss Dunstable heaved a sigh. "I'm certainly no expert on crime, Miss Allcutt. Perhaps you ought to ask your policeman friend."

And a whole lot of good *that* would do, I thought bitterly. Phil and Ernie had their sights set on Rupert and Lulu, and no amount of talking on my part would sway them, the pigheaded so-and-sos. Nevertheless, Miss Dunstable didn't need to learn of Ernie's intransigence from me. Let her keep thinking he was a levelheaded private investigator—if she did. From everything I'd gathered thus far in my month-long career as a private investigator's assistant, P.I.s weren't held in high regard in much of what passes for society in Los Angeles.

I heaved a sigh of my own. "Yes, of course. I'll do that."

Her telephone rang then, startling the both of us, and I decided to go back to my own job. I was far from satisfied, however, and feeling very much alone in my quest for the truth. While I'm sure that Sylvia Dunstable was absolutely correct about your run-of-the-mill murder, if there is such a thing, I was also sure these particular murders had a motive, and probably a juicy one. It wasn't as if someone had killed Mrs. Hartland and her son in a drunken rage or anything like that. Both of their murders had been carefully planned—premeditated, if you will—and executed. And what an appropriate word *that* was.

Which got my thoughts spinning in another direction entirely. Gangsters in New York City and Chicago were always murdering each other in what the newspapers called "execution-style slayings." What if Mrs. Hartland or her son had run afoul of some gangsters? It had probably been her son, actually, since Mrs. Hartland had a successful career as a gossip columnist. I didn't know a lot about George Hartland, but I did know that he owed money to Mr. Carstairs and was worried about the unpaid debt. Perhaps he was a hardened gambler. Or a drug addict! Now there was an interesting prospect. Perhaps the leader of the drug gang had decided to kill Mrs. Hartland as a warning to George.

Mind you, I wouldn't consider being poisoned during a séance particularly execution-style, but I knew about as much about gangsters as I did about blue movies.

Which made my mind spin back in its original direction. I was getting downright dizzy. If gangsters were responsible for the murders, where did the blue movies fit in? Or did they fit in at all? Not that gangsters couldn't make smutty movies *and* peddle alcohol and drugs. In fact, perhaps they did both all the time. If you're dealing in one type of crime, I suppose it would be a small step to get into another one. Maybe.

Blast. I was getting nowhere fast, and the knowledge left me feeling helpless. I didn't like the feeling one little bit. I opened the door to the office—the 'phone was ringing—and decided crime-solving wasn't my forte.

"Mr. Templeton's office. Miss Allcutt speaking."

"Oh."

Mrs. Persephone Chalmers. Joy and rapture unbounded.

"Yes, Mrs. Chalmers?" My tone was polite, even if I wanted to shriek at her to loosen her talons and free my boss from her clutches.

"Oh."

My teeth were going to be ground down to a mere nub by the time Ernie finished Mrs. Chalmers' case.

"How did you know it was I?"

Because you're the only person I know who begins her every utterance with that darned breathy "Oh." Naturally, I didn't say that. "I recognized your voice."

"Oh."

Eye-roll time.

"Oh. You're very clever, Miss Allcutt. Mr. Templeton told me so."

He did, did he? That actually made me feel a teensy bit better. "How kind of him. May I help you?" I wanted to get the stupid woman off the wire so I could think some more, even though thinking didn't seem to be getting me anywhere.

"Oh. Mr. Templeton and I met this morning. I wondered if he was back in his office yet. If he is, I should like to speak with him."

"I'm sorry. He hasn't returned to the office."

Ernie turned me into a liar at that very moment when he opened the office door and strode inside. He was smirking, the rat, and gave me a cat-in-the-cream-pot grin. I didn't react, although it was an effort.

"Mrs. Chalmers," I said, instead of throwing my notebook at Ernie. "He just this second arrived. Will you hold the wire for a moment?"

"Oh, yes, thank you."

I covered the receiver with my hand and hissed at Ernie. "Mrs. Chalmers wishes to speak with you."

The wretched man had the audacity to wink at me before he went into his office and picked up his receiver. I squelched an unseemly desire to eavesdrop on their conversation and went back to thinking about Rupert and Lulu and the two Hartlands. I *knew* Rupert hadn't committed the second murder, and in my heart I knew he hadn't committed the first one. Also, Lulu was the very last person on earth whom I would suspect of being anyone's accomplice to a violent act. Not only that, but I didn't think she was strong enough to smother a full-grown man with a hospital pillow if he were to struggle against it, and what able-bodied human being wouldn't struggle against being smothered? No one whom I could think of.

Hmm. I suppose Lulu could have donned a nurse's uniform and given the man a hypo injection before smothering him. Oh, but wait. Hadn't Ernie or Phil said that he'd already have been given a hypo by a real nurse? I do believe they had. Or maybe it had merely been a pill. Sill and all, a pill might do the trick. In that case, Lulu could have crept into his room wearing her nurse's uniform and smothered him as he lay in his bed, helpless.

I felt my brows furrow and stopped frowning. My mother always said that a lady never wrinkled her brows. Not that what a lady might do with her brows had ever stopped Mother from frowning, especially at me. However, my notion about Lulu in a costume made me think that there were others in the world who probably had better access to nurses' outfits than Lulu LaBelle. And who better than someone working in the motion-picture business?

No one. That's who. And that pointed straight to Jacqueline Lloyd.

And she, according to expert testimony—I mean Phil Bigelow—had been out cold all night long. So if it was she who'd perpetrated the first evil deed, she must have had an accomplice to perpetrate the second one. Who that accomplice was remained unknown at this point.

Bother.

Before I could scream in frustration, Ernie exited his office and slapped his hat on his head. "Have to go out for a while, kiddo. Hold down the fort."

"Do you have an appointment with someone?" I asked. It might not have been any of my business, but I thought a confidential secretary should have access to her employer's schedule. Besides, I didn't want him consorting with the ethereal Mrs. Chalmers any more than necessary.

"Got to meet somebody downtown."

I thought we were already downtown. "Very well. Do you know when you will return?"

"My, my, aren't we formal today?"

I frowned at him in spite of the possibility of a wrinkled forehead. "Darn it, Ernie, I'm your secretary, and I make your appointments. I need to know when you'll be in the office and when you won't be in the office."

He chuckled. He would. "Calm down, kiddo. I was only teasing you. I'll be back by one-thirty, I should think."

I sniffed. "Thank you *ever* so much."

And he left me to my fuddled thoughts. I knew he was going to see that wretched Persephone Chalmers person. I *knew* it.

Just before noon, I made another trip down the hall, craving information that I wasn't sure anybody would—or even could—give me.

Miss Dunstable looked up from her typewriter, which got a lot more work than mine did, and smiled a welcome. She was such a nice person, and so professional she made me feel inferior by comparison. I trusted myself, however, and knew that I would eventually develop that same degree of secretarial confidence if I kept working at it.

"Good morning again, Miss Allcutt."

"Miss Dunstable, I hate to keep bothering you, but—"

"Nonsense," she said, removing her fingers from the keys. She had been typing *very* fast, and I decided to practice more. While I didn't have a whole lot of work to practice on, I could bring some of my old typewriting books to work and do the exercises. "I'm about to go to lunch, and I only wanted to finish that last page."

I guess she'd done so, because she took it out of the typewriter and laid it face down on her desk. Client confidentiality at work, by gum.

"In fact," she said, "I've been pondering what you said earlier in the day, and I think you might be on to something important."

"You do?" I'm sure my wide-open eyes and similarly gaping mouth conveyed my shock. Sylvia Dunstable, bless her professional secretarial heart, was the first person so far in my entire life who had taken any of my suggestions seriously. Which just goes to show. I'd known from the moment I first set eyes on her that she was a person of discernment and intellect.

"Yes. About Miss Lloyd. I might be able to give you some information." She glanced over her shoulder and lowered her voice. "But we can't talk here."

I looked around, too, although I don't know why. "Of course not."

She donned a bright smile. "Say, have you had lunch yet? Maybe we can catch a bite and discuss this matter."

"Oh, I'd love to," I said, thinking that having luncheon with a fellow secretary was a wonderful idea. Who knew? This might be the beginning of a long friendship. Chloe was always going out to lunch with her women friends. Thus far during my sojourn in Los Angeles, I hadn't met too many women since most of Ernie's female clients hadn't struck me as potential candidates, and most of Chloe and Harvey's dinner guests have been married couples or single men. But Sylvia Dunstable . . . well, she was what I aspired to be. "Just let me run down the hall and get my hat and handbag."

"I'll lock up here and join you," she said.

I tripped merrily down to Ernie's office, happy not merely to be taken seriously for once, but also to be dining out with a real potential friend.

We took the elevator to the lobby and both smiled at Lulu when we passed her desk. She still looked glum, so I stopped for a second. "Try not to worry too much, Lulu. We're working very hard to find the culprit."

Looking up at me with hopeless blue eyes, she asked, "Who's we?"

A trifle disconcerted, I said, "Why, Ernie and me, of course."

She nodded and said "Thanks," but I don't think she meant it.

I sighed deeply and Miss Dunstable and I left the building.

"We can take my car," said she. "It's right down the block a bit."

I'd thought we were going to walk to Chinatown or eat in one of the little drugstores or sandwich shops on Figueroa, but I was certainly not averse to traveling farther afield. "Sounds good to me."

"I know a perfectly darling little place off of Sunset. Have you ever eaten Mexican food before?"

Thinking of a trip Ernie and I had taken to Pasadena the previous month, I said confidently, "Yes, and I loved it."

"Good. Then you'll really like the place I have in mind." She stopped beside a nice-looking Ford Model T. "Here's my car. Hop in."

"Thanks."

Sylvia started the engine and pulled out onto Figueroa Street, where the lunchtime traffic was starting to thicken.

I was most impressed with her driving ability. I had seldom driven an automobile, since I'd grown up with chauffeurs and Chloe always drove when we went shopping or anything. I knew that you had to put your foot on the clutch and move the shift lever, and that there was a gear called neutral, in which you should never leave your car since it might roll away from you. And I think there's a reverse gear if you want to back up, but so far nobody I've ridden with has ever had to back up. Chloe had given me a couple of lessons in her Roadster, but I had no confidence that I'd ever be able to drive in traffic.

Therefore, I watched Sylvia Dunstable with interest. "How long have you been driving?"

"Oh, years and years." She downshifted without a single grind of a gear.

"My sister has begun teaching me to drive."

"Mmm."

Since she was watching the other cars on the road and didn't seem interested in my driving ambitions, I decided to start a conversation about the case. "I've thought a good deal about the murders, and I've come to the conclusion that they were both premeditated. Therefore, I think that in this case motive might be a factor." I hoped she wouldn't disparage my conclusion, given her greater experience in the murder line.

To my gratification, Sylvia nodded vigorously. "Yes, I think you're right. After you left my office this morning, I thought some more about the matter and came to the same conclusion."

That made me feel good, because it meant I didn't have to try to convince her that these murders weren't spur-of-the-moment violent acts. "Do you suppose there's any possibility—I know this will sound silly—but . . . well, it occurred to me that perhaps Mrs. Hartland, who made her living from gossip, might have unearthed some truly scandalous stuff about Jacqueline Lloyd." I hastened to add, "Not that I have anything against Miss Lloyd, you understand, but she seemed the most likely candidate. I mean, her career is only just starting, and it could be cut short if any kind of scandal hit the light of day. Plus, she was there both times. That is to say she was there for the first séance when Mrs. Hartland was killed and at the second one, when Mr. Hartland collapsed."

"Hmm."

"I overheard Ernie—Mr. Templeton, I mean—and Mr. Bigelow talking about blue movies, and the only person I could think of who might be hurt if the public learned about her involvement in such things was Jacqueline Lloyd."

"I see," said Sylvia Dunstable. "You may be right."

"Of course, since she couldn't possibly have committed Mr. Hartland's murder, she'd need an accomplice."

"Ah. Yes."

"Then it occurred to me that Mrs. Hartland might possibly—I know this sounds silly, too—have been blackmailing

Miss Lloyd."

I waited for Miss Dunstable to laugh, but she didn't. Rather, she turned left onto a little street a few miles away from the Figueroa Building that looked to me as if not many people traversed it on a regular basis. It was kind of twisty and led up a hill. "I don't think that sounds silly at all," she said. "It actually sounds quite plausible."

Shocked and grateful, I exclaimed, "You really think so?" Wouldn't Ernie be dumbfounded when I unearthed the truth before he did! The notion made my heart sing, which I suppose wasn't kind of it. But, darn it, I was tired of him always disparaging my efforts at detection.

"Oh, my, yes. In fact, I've thought about nothing else since you visited me earlier in the day."

Better and better. "*I* think Mrs. Hartland found out about Miss Lloyd acting in those blue movies Mr. Templeton and Mr. Bigelow were talking about, and that she was blackmailing her." I waited a second for a reaction. When one didn't come, I said less confidently, "What do you think?"

"I think you've hit the nail square on the head."

"And then, when Mrs. Hartland died, George Hartland went through her papers, discovered Miss Lloyd's dark secret, and took over the blackmail scheme from his late mother."

"That seems supremely logical to me."

My heart glowed. When I glanced at the scenery, I noticed that we were kind of up in the hills and that there wasn't much of anything around us but sagebrush and straggly trees. I'd never been in this part of Los Angeles before. Yet it was very close to the office. We hadn't traveled far at all. It seemed an unlikely place for a restaurant. "Say, where is this place we're going?"

"Not much farther. It's a darling place. You'll love it. And the scenery is wonderful. You can see almost all of Los Angeles from the top of the hill."

"My goodness." I looked around eagerly, hoping to catch a glimpse of something that struck me as restaurant-like. I had no luck, because there was nothing around but . . . well, nothing. Not only that, but the twisty road had become extremely narrow, with a scrubby slope heading upward on my side and a sheer drop-off on Miss Dunstable's side. What an odd place for a restaurant to be.

But that didn't much matter, and since Miss Dunstable seemed to be an expert driver and unconcerned about the steep decline on her side, I resumed the conversation. "Anyway, if my theory is correct about Miss Lloyd, as I said before, she must have had an accomplice who killed Mr. Hartland, because the nurses said she was under sedation and sound asleep all night."

"Absolutely."

"The only problem is that I can't figure out who her accomplice might be," I admitted.

The car slowed to a crawl. "You can't?"

There was a smile in Miss Dunstable's voice that I couldn't account for. I'd been gazing out the car's window at the sagebrush and Spanish broom—that stuff smells positively heavenly in the early summer, by the way, but now the plants were brown and shriveled and heavy with dried-up seed pods—so I turned to glance at her.

And there, staring me in the face, was a revolver, held by none other than Miss Sylvia Dunstable!

CHAPTER SIXTEEN

Astonished, I said, "What . . . ?"

"I'm really sorry you started snooping, Miss Allcutt, because so far you seem to be the only one with a brain who has been."

"What?" I said again, sounding, I'm sure, as stupid as I felt.

"And I regret having to do what I have to do, because I honestly like you."

"But . . ." Not a bit better. In my defense, however, Sylvia Dunstable *was* pointing a gun at me. I believe I can be forgiven if my brain was swirling and I couldn't think clearly.

The car stopped on the twisty dirt path halfway up the hill. Unfortunately, once Sylvia pulled the emergency brake lever she was able to hold the gun steady and it was still pointed at my face. "But I honestly don't have any choice. Don't you see? You ought to have taken Mr. Templeton's advice and stayed out of it."

"But why are you doing this? Why are you pointing a gun at me?" I cried, finally able to form coherent, if unhelpful, sentences.

"I have to do this because you've come too close to the truth."

"What truth? I don't understand."

She sighed with what seemed like genuine regret, although my facility for judgment wasn't at its best at that moment. "Jacqueline Lloyd and I are sisters, Miss Allcutt."

"*Sisters!*"

"Yes, indeedy. We came here from Tennessee about five years ago."

"T-Tennessee? You did?"

"Oh, my, yes. We had to, you see, because life had become intolerable for us at home." She sneered and repeated the word *home* as if it tasted bad.

My mouth had been hanging open pretty much ever since the word *sisters* had escaped it. I shut with a clack. "I'm . . . you did? It was?"

"It was, and we did."

"Oh. Um . . . you went through quite a bit in Tennessee, you say?" As you can probably tell, my thinking processes hadn't fully regained their full strength and vigor.

"Quite a bit?" Her laugh was positively ugly. I hadn't believed a noise so sardonic could issue from her ever-so-professional-and-proper lips. "It was hell, pure and simple. Our parents were dead, and our uncle, who was supposed to take care of us and protect us . . . well, let's just say he didn't, and that he wasn't the only man around who had noticed my sister's beauty."

Although I wasn't sure since my own background was so pristine, I got the impression that Miss Dunstable referred to something sordid and unnatural, and I felt sorry for her. Until my eyes lit on that blasted gun once more. However, in the interest of self-preservation, I said, "I'm sorry you had such a difficult time."

Again the bitter laugh. "You have absolutely no idea, Miss Allcutt. You've clearly been protected from the wicked, wicked world." The sneer looked as ugly as the laughter sounded. "Suffice it to say that we came west to Los Angeles, thinking that Jacqueline might be able to break into the pictures. And she did, eventually. Jacqueline—she's the elder of the two of us—had to work at all sorts of strange jobs to put food on the table before she hit the big time. It wasn't her fault that she had to do some things we aren't proud of. She was forced to work very, very hard. She was only sixteen years old, for heaven's sake."

"Sixteen?" If what I was inferring was correct, I was horrified.

"Sixteen. I was fourteen. Jacqueline worked like a slave to put me through secretarial school. I won't sully your pure little ears telling you what she had to do to keep us in food and clothing."

"How . . . how awful."

She laughed another unpleasant laugh. "You have no idea. You," she repeated scornfully, "know nothing about how to survive in this world, do you?"

"Um . . . I . . . um, don't guess I do." It was a miserable confession, but it was also the truth.

"Anyhow, eventually Jacqueline got a break. I was already Mr. Carstairs's secretary by that time—and what a miserable creature *he* is, by the way, always groping and grasping and pretending to be a gentleman."

I gulped but didn't speak. It would appear, however, that Ernie had been correct about Mr. Carstairs.

"After those first few blue pictures, Jacqueline acted as an extra in a couple of cowboy pictures. Then Mr. Goldfish saw her and cast her in *Whispering Oaks*."

"Oh, I saw that, and she was wonderful. In fact, the entire picture was wonderful. My sister and I went to see it, and—" I stopped babbling.

"Everybody saw it. Including Hedda Heartwood." She gave me another sour look. "You don't know anything about blackmailers, either, I suppose. In fact, you don't know a single thing about how the real world works do you, Miss High and Mighty Boston Allcutt?"

That hurt. "But I'm trying!" I cried. "I truly am trying to

learn how the rest of the world lives. I want to fit in. Truly, I do!"

"I suppose you are." She heaved a big sigh. "And you're really quite nice. In fact, in spite of yourself, I actually like you."

"Th-thank you. I like . . . liked you, too."

She heaved another huge sigh. "But I'm sorry, Miss Allcutt. You won't be able to work at learning about life any longer."

"Um . . . I don't think I understand." What with that gun pointing at me and all, I thought I comprehended her meaning quite well, but I was hoping to be surprised.

"I'm afraid I'm going to have to kill you."

No surprise there. My heart, which had been hovering around my knees, sank to the earth beneath the automobile. "You don't really need to do that, you know."

"Oh, yes I do."

"But why? I'm not going to say anything to anybody. Honest! I never would have come up with the sister motif. Truly, I wouldn't."

"Don't be ridiculous. You'll have to tell somebody, because you're too much of a Goody Two-Shoes not to."

"Oh, no I'm not," I assured her. "This will be a lesson in survival for me. A salutary lesson, in fact. I won't breathe a word to anyone. It will be our secret." Even I could tell I was lying. Talk about innocence of the world! I was disgusted with myself. Darn it, I was fighting for my life here, and I couldn't even tell a decent fib!

Her smile this time was actually rather kind. "You're a lousy liar, Miss Allcutt."

I already knew that.

"The thing that amuses me is that you can't seem to help yourself. You're an honestly good person."

Feeling defensive as well as scared to death, I asked tartly, "What's wrong with that?"

"Not a thing, my dear. You should consider yourself lucky have achieved your present age with your goodness intact. N all of us have been so fortunate."

"Lots of people from unfortunate circumstances don't l other people," I muttered.

"Not all that many."

"I don't believe that for a minute. Why only last month— sensed Miss Dunstable's lack of interest in my detectival care so I ceased talking about it.

Choosing another tactic, which would probably prove unproductive as the last one, I said, "Well, if you're going to me in anyway, won't you please tell me why you killed the Ha lands? I gather that Mrs. Hartland was blackmailing your siste

"She was, indeed, the miserable cow."

"Ah." I still couldn't quite grasp that the two women, M Lloyd and Miss Dunstable, were siblings. "But why did j have to *kill* her? Didn't Miss Lloyd make enough money to well, to pay her off?"

"Don't be such a baby. There's no paying off blackmail Miss Allcutt. If you give in to them, they'll bleed you forevei

"Oh." I guess that made sense. If a person viewed anot person as a source of income, I don't suppose a one-time p ment would dissuade him or her from tapping that source ag if money got tight. "But why did you have to kill her son?"

"You hit the nail on the head earlier today. He decidec carry on the family business," she said dryly. "He suspected queline had killed his mother. Then he went through her pap and discovered the reason. I'm sure Jacqueline wasn't the one, either. Really, Miss Allcutt, Jacqueline and I did the w of motion pictures a favor."

"Were you the one who killed Mr. Hartland? I mean, your sister truly knocked out at the hospital?" My voice small, and I asked out of faint hope. If she wasn't alrea

225

seasoned murderer, perhaps she'd balk at killing me.

No such luck. "Of course I did. I donned a white outfit and pretended to be a nurse." She uttered a short laugh. "I guess acting runs in the family. He was out as cold as Jacqueline was, so I just used a pillow to smother him. The fool."

Feeling hopeless but curious, I asked, "And Miss Lloyd killed his mother."

"Precisely."

"There was a prick on her back. Was that where the poison was administered?"

"Heavens no! That was a red herring." She squinted at me doubtfully. "Do you know what a red herring is?"

"Yes. I read detective fiction." I'd wanted to *write* detective fiction, but it didn't look as if my wants would be met. And I was only twenty-one, for heaven's sake!

Another sardonic bark of laughter met this statement. "Oh, my, Miss Allcutt, you don't know how lucky you are, to have to learn about these things through works of fiction."

"I don't feel very lucky at the moment."

She sobered. "No, I'm sure you don't."

"What poison did you use?"

"Datura."

"I read about that at the library. How'd you get it? I mean, you can't just walk into a pharmacy and ask for datura, can you?"

"Goodness, no. Jacqueline had to snitch a couple of darts from Amory Jordan's collection of artifacts."

I'm pretty sure I gasped. Amory Jordan was one of the biggest names in the picture business, being a producer and director of all sorts of movies. He was also a well-known world traveler who was always going on African safaris and trips down the Amazon and things like that. I'd read about him in the newspapers even before I moved to Los Angeles.

"I think he got the darts in some God-awful South American country when he went on an Amazon trip." She snorted. "Some people have more money than sense. Why in the name of everything holy somebody would want to visit a tropical hell like that is beyond me."

I could have enlightened her, being of an adventurous nature myself, but I sensed she didn't really care. "How did she get the poison from the dart?"

Miss Dunstable gave a careless shrug. "Soaked it."

"So where was the point of entry of the poison if it wasn't that prick on the back of her neck?"

She smiled. "Why, on her wrist, just under her bracelet. Jacqueline had to hold the old witch's hand, if you'll recall. All it took was a little prick, and *voila!* No more Hedda Heartwood. She pricked that place on her back to throw the coppers off the scent."

"How did she do that when she was holding her hand?"

"Jacqueline is extremely nimble-fingered, Miss Allcutt." Again the sneer.

I decided not to ask when and where Miss Lloyd had practiced her finger agility. "Then she poked Mrs. Hartland's neck when she pretended to faint?"

"Exactly."

"I think she succeeded in throwing the police off the track," I said, sounding as defeated as I felt.

"I think she did, too."

"Was it she who caused Mr. Hartland to faint?"

"Yes. Again proving her dexterity. Gave him a whiff of chloroform." Miss Dunstable looked bemused for a second. "I'm surprised no one else smelled it."

"So am I." Blast it, if I'd sat next to him, I'll bet I'd have smelled it before it dissipated. But Jacqueline Lloyd wasn't about to give herself away, and poor Mrs. Easthope had probably been too rattled to notice anything out of the ordinary.

Miss Dunstable heaved yet another sigh. I sensed she really didn't much want to kill me but knew where her duty lay. I understood all about doing things out of a sense of duty, oddly enough, but it didn't make me feel any better. "But it's time we got this over with. I only have an hour for lunch."

"You're going to murder me and then go back to work as if nothing happened?" My mind boggled. It had been misbehaving for some time.

She didn't react to the word *murder,* which I'd used on purpose in order to jar her. "Why, yes. As I said, I'm every bit as good an actress as Jacqueline is. She was the prettier of the two of us, though, so we decided she should be the one to go into the pictures, and I'd be the one to snag a job in a Hollywood attorney's office."

"Ah." Their foresight and planning might have garnered my admiration if it weren't for the murder thing.

"Therefore, as much as I don't really want to kill you, I have to, you see. It's a pity, but there you go."

There I went, indeed. Nuts. I eyed her gun. "Are you sure you know how to use that?"

She laughed again. I didn't like her laugh at all. And to think I used to admire her so. "Miss Allcutt, my sister and I learned to shoot before we could read. We had to in order to put food on the table. We had a *very* hard life in Tennessee."

Good Lord. And I'd never held a gun in my entire life. It wasn't the first time I'd considered the disparity between people like me, who were born into wealth, and everybody else. If I got out of this one alive, I'd definitely increase my donations to various good causes.

She'd put the car in neutral, pulled the emergency brake handle—it pulled up from the floor—and held the gun steady when she opened the driver's-side door. Keeping an eagle eye on me as she exited the automobile, she said, "Get out of the car now, Miss Allcutt. We need to finish this up so I can get back to work."

Finish this up? *Damn* the woman!

The fact that I'd actually thought a real, honest-to-goodness swear word shocked me. That was a good thing, because my befuddlement about my situation suddenly vanished in a puff of ire and pure rage took its place. I decided it didn't matter if she had a gun and I didn't. She was going to have to *work* to kill *me,* curse her black heart.

Slowly I opened the car door. All things considered, it looked to me as if I might actually have a chance if I were daring, something I hadn't had much experience being thus far in my life. Still, if I could only . . .

"Oh!" I cried, stumbling on the running board and catching myself on the car's seat.

"Stop that!" bellowed Miss Dunstable. "Get up this instant!"

"I think I sprained my ankle," I lied in a shaky voice. The shakiness was unfeigned, believe me.

"Get up and I'll put you out of your misery." To spur me on my way, I presume, she fired a shot that would have killed me had I still been standing.

"Don't do that! I'm getting up. It hurts, is all."

"Hurry up. I don't have any more time to waste on you."

From my crouched position, I could tell that Miss Dunstable was expecting to see me rise up from the passenger side of the machine. She wasn't looking below the window. Therefore, as quickly as I'd ever moved in my life, I darted across the seat, released the emergency brake and leaped back out of the car. Well, it was more of a scuttle than a leap, but you know what I mean.

"What are you *doing?*" Shrieked Sylvia Dunstable, again pulling that wretched trigger and frightening me out of my skin.

229

Alice Duncan

I didn't answer. Rather, I pushed that stupid Model-T Ford as hard as I could from my very precarious crouched position, using the frame of the driver's side door and the running board, as well as all the strength in my body.

Darned if it didn't work! The car started sliding slowly downhill.

"Wait! *Wait!* What are you doing?"

By that time I'd flattened myself on the ground, figuring that with the car in the way and moving she'd have a harder time fixing an aim on my body. With my heart in my throat, I could only see Miss Dunstable's feet as she danced on the edge of the embankment trying to avoid being struck by her car. I think she attempted to get into the automobile so she could put it into gear and pull out the emergency brake, because I saw the door open but then, with a terrible crunching sound, the car's tires slipped over the ledge and slid right downhill, taking Miss Dunstable with it, carried along by the open door. I heard her screech in astonishment, and then I heard one last explosion as she pulled the trigger a final time. I don't know where that shot went, but it was nowhere near me, thank God.

I didn't stick around to see what had happened to Miss Dunstable or if her Model T had stopped somewhere on the down side of the hill. Rather, to the crashings and scrapings of metal against loose rock as the car slid and skidded, I picked myself up from my dusty refuge and ran like a madwoman down the hill toward Figueroa where I hoped like anything some kindhearted pedestrian or driver would rescue me.

To my horror, I hadn't run past the first bend in that cursed twisty road before I saw another automobile winding its way up the hill. Instantly my thoughts fastened upon Jacqueline Lloyd, and I turned and tried to scrabble my way up the side of the hill away from the drop-off. I wasn't making much headway since the earth was dry and crumbly, and every time I grabbed on to a bush to pull myself up, it dislodged and we both tumbled backward. Nevertheless, those wretched murdering people were going to have to labor valiantly if they intended to kill me. I wasn't about to give up until I was dead, blast it. And if Jacqueline Lloyd dared to grab one of my feet to keep me from climbing, I'd—

"*Damn it to hell and back again, Mercy Allcutt, come down from there!*"

Stunned, I slid backward down the slope, landing on my bottom in the rocky dirt road. It hurt.

"Ernie?"

He reached down and grabbed my arm. "Are you all right?"

"I-I think so. But, Ernie, it's Miss—"

"Dunstable. I know. Dammit, how did you end up here? We were following you all the way from Chinatown. Didn't you suspect anything, dammit?"

I tried to brush myself off, but Ernie still held one of my arms. Anyhow, the task was impossible. It looked as if I'd managed to accumulate a whole acre or more of Southern California dirt during my various adventures.

"Don't swear at me." My voice was small, though. I'd started having a reaction to everything and there was a lump in my throat. "I thought you were going to meet—" I decided I'd better not finish that sentence.

"Better not stand there jawing, Ernie. We've got to pick up the other sister."

Phil Bigelow. I'd no sooner registered his presence than I found myself lifted into Ernie's arms. There was nothing romantic about the gesture, believe me. He handled me as if I were a sack of potatoes, dumped me in the back seat of Phil's police vehicle, and leaped into the front next to Phil. I hadn't even stopped bouncing when Phil gunned the engine and the heavy car plowed ahead up the hill.

231

"Where's Dunstable?" Ernie growled.

He was being so mean, I didn't want to tell him. But I, like Sylvia Dunstable, knew where my duty lay. Besides, the horrible woman had tried to killed me. "I left her up the road a bit." I'd scold Ernie after Miss Dunstable had been picked up and jailed. If her Model T hadn't squashed her. I shuddered at that thought.

I needn't have worried. We had no sooner rounded the bend in that stupid narrow road than we saw Miss Dunstable, looking a good deal less professional than usual, scrambling up to the road. Her spectacles were askew, she was bleeding from several cuts and scratches, and it looked to me as if she'd torn her stockings in her tumble downhill. What had been a perfectly lovely gray business suit was a dirty mess, and one of her sensible shoes was missing. If I didn't know better, I'd have felt sorry for her.

"What the hell happened here?" growled Ernie.

Without waiting for an answer, he jumped out of the car and raced toward Miss Dunstable. Phil did likewise. What's more, he drew his police weapon and yelled at the top of his lungs, "Stop in the name of the law, or I'll shoot!"

I hadn't known policemen actually said things like that.

We ended up with Phil driving back to the Los Angeles Police Station with me squished between him and Ernie in the front seat and Sylvia Dunstable, handcuffed and looking very upset, in the back seat. The only thing she said the whole way back was, "What about my machine?"

Phil merely grunted. I presume that meant he didn't give a rap about her car.

It was only when I saw Jacqueline Lloyd stripped of her makeup did it register with me that she and Sylvia Dunstable, without her spectacles, looked somewhat alike. Some kind of detective *I* was.

CHAPTER SEVENTEEN

I knew I'd be in for it when I returned to Chloe's that day no matter what I did, as my clothing was wrecked, my fingernails showed definite evidence of having tried to climb a mountain, and there was dirt caked all over various parts of me. With Mother there, it wasn't possible to sneak in and wash up before facing the family. I wish I had an apartment of my own to run away and hide in.

But I didn't.

Therefore, since I knew I was going to be late getting home and I didn't want to worry anyone, I telephoned Chloe from the police station to explain what had happened. Chloe gasped a couple of times, but she didn't scold me.

"Are you sure you're all right?" was all she said.

She sounded so concerned, I almost cried. You could bet any amount of money you wanted to, if you did such things, that our mother wasn't going to be sweet like that.

"I'm fine," I said upon a deep and heartfelt sigh. "A little dirty, is all." That wasn't quite true, since I had numerous cuts and scrapes here and there, but none of them were serious.

"Well, take care of yourself, and I'll try to keep Mother calm."

"Thank you." This time we both sighed. "Do your best, anyhow," I said, feeling hopeless and almost hating our father for putting us through this ordeal with Mother.

After my telephone call the interrogation process (Ernie said it was only questioning, but I know what it felt like to me) took hours and hours.

"If you'd bothered to tell me what you were working on and what you'd discovered at the case, this wouldn't have happened," I told Ernie at one point.

After rolling his eyes, Ernie said, "Dammit, Mercy, you're not a copper *or* a trained investigator. You're a secretary, and you have no business questioning people involved in the case, much less haring off to have lunch with the suspects."

"I didn't suspect her," I said in my own defense. "Did *you* know she was Miss Lloyd's sister?"

"Not then. But you should have wondered why she was being so chummy with you that she offered to drive you to hell and gone to eat lunch."

"That's unfair, Ernie Templeton! If *you* didn't suspect her, how was *I* supposed to suspect her?"

"Suspicion has nothing to do with it!"

"You're being completely irrational. I thought Sylvia Dunstable and I were friends. It's perfectly natural to take a meal with a friend!"

"Children, children," said Phil before either of us could say anything else.

I glared at Ernie, who glared back at me. He was being *so* unfair.

After clearing his throat, Phil hurried to speak as if he was afraid to leave any spaces of silence that Ernie or I might choose to fill with accusations. I kept glaring. So did Ernie.

Phil said, "We picked Miss Lloyd up for questioning, because it seemed to us that she was the only person who could possibly have killed Mrs. Hartland the way she was killed."

"That makes sense to me. And do you know what she used? It was—"

"*Mercy!*" That was Ernie, and he stomped my words flat. "Let Phil explain, why don't you?"

I glared some more, but recognized the validity of his comment, blast it.

Phil went on. "After we picked her up and questioned her extensively, Miss Lloyd told us that she and Miss Dunstable are sisters. We wore her down, you see," Phil said placatingly. I guess he was afraid Ernie and I might have a knock-down, drag-out fight right there in the police station. "She told us about the datura."

"Did she tell you how she got it?"

"She said he soaked some poisoned arrow tips she'd taken from some director's house."

"Amory Jordan's," I said, glad to tell him something he didn't already know.

"Oh, was it Jordan?"

"Yes, according to Miss Dunstable."

Phil wrote it down.

"Okay. She told us about the datura and how she'd pricked Mrs. Hartland under her bracelet with a needle dipped in the stuff, and how she'd made another pinprick in the back of her neck. I guess the coroner didn't find the prick under her bracelet, or he thought it had been made by the clasp or something."

"And just exactly when did you first suspect Miss Lloyd?" I asked, feeling cranky as all get out.

"When we checked out her past and discovered she'd acted in blue picture." I'm pretty sure Phil colored a little bit when he said the bit about the blue movies.

"And yet nobody bothered to tell me," I grumbled.

"Why should anybody tell you?" demanded Ernie. "You're a damned secretary! You're not supposed to be investigating anything at all, much less murder!"

"I wouldn't have had to investigate anything if you'd helped Mr. Easthope when he asked you to! Or if you'd bothered to tell me what was going on!" I retorted hotly. "All I knew was that Rupert Mullins was no murderer, but he was being held in jail for committing murder anyway, and then you started suspecting *Lulu*, of all people!"

"Nuts," bellowed Ernie. "You just can't keep out of the damned way, can you?"

"Hey," said Phil. "Let's all calm down, all right?"

Ernie huffed. So did I.

Phil continued, "When we got to the Figueroa Building to bring Miss Lloyd in—"

"Why did you go to the Figueroa Building?" I asked. "Why didn't you pick her up at her house?"

Ernie snarled something incoherent, but Phil only sighed and explained. "We called her home, and her maid told us she'd gone to the Figueroa Building to consult with her attorney."

"I see," I said formally. "Thank you."

"Anyhow, when we got there, Miss LaBelle told us the two of you had gone out to lunch."

"And if Lulu hadn't told us what kind of car Dunstable drove, you'd probably be a dead duck right now," Ernie growled.

"I would not be a dead duck, Ernest Templeton! I saved myself from being shot by being quick and resourceful, curse you! *You* sure as anything didn't rescue me! I was already rescued!" I was so angry that if it hadn't been for my early childhood training, I'd probably have bopped Ernie with the candlestick telephone sitting on Phil's desk.

"You call that rescuing yourself? You were scrambling up a damned hill when I found you, remember!"

"That's only because I thought you were Miss Lloyd and Miss Dunstable's accomplices! If you hadn't taken up the whole blasted roadway, I'd have run down to Figueroa and hailed somebody!"

"You'd have hailed *somebody*? Is that your idea of rescuing yourself?"

"Ernest Templeton, you're the most obnoxious, pigheaded—"

"Cut it out, both of you."

Phil sounded more than a trifle tense, so I glowered at him next. Darn it, none of this was my fault, and I considered that I'd behaved downright heroically in thinking of that stupid brake lever in that stupid machine. Would it *kill* Ernest Templeton, P.I., to acknowledge that I'd done something worthwhile? Blast the man.

"How did you know where Miss Dunstable took me?"

"We had a hell of a time tracing that one stupid car in all the traffic. You were almost out of sight by the time we got to the Figueroa Building. Then we almost lost it three or four times. We had to backtrack a couple of times, but a guy selling tamales on a street corner finally told us he'd seen a car of that description going up the hill."

"Oh."

"We found you in time, and that's the important part," Phil added in a softer tone.

"I was already safe," I muttered, wanting *someone* to recognize my pluck.

"Yes, but I mean we got Miss Dunstable."

"Thanks to me," I said, sounding cantankerous even to my own ears. "If I hadn't pushed her wretched motorcar over the ledge, she'd have got away."

"Christ," Ernie mumbled under his breath.

I couldn't help myself. I kicked him.

"Ow!" He looked daggers at me.

"Oh, be quiet."

"Stop it!"

I'd never heard Phil sound so angry, so I stopped it. So did Ernie, although his scowl didn't abate.

Phil went on, "Jacqueline Lloyd and Sylvia Dunstable—by the way, their real names are Pansy and Ida Flynt—were being blackmailed by Miss Hedda Heartwood because Miss Heartwood had learned that Pansy had acted in some scandalous pictures before she got famous."

"They were pretty bad pictures, too," Ernie said, his voice once again level. He only ever hollered at *me*, darn him.

"It's because they were very poor when they moved here from Tennessee, and she had to support the both of them somehow," I chimed in, just in case they didn't know that already. "Miss Dunstable said they'd had a miserable life back home with a wicked uncle, and they came to Los Angeles to escape."

Ernie looked as if he was going to explode again, but Phil said quickly, "Yes. Miss Lloyd told us that." He shot Ernie a quelling look and Ernie, to my surprise, was quelled. At least he didn't holler at me.

"Anyhow," Phil continued, "they both thought they'd put their past behind them when Miss Lloyd was discovered by Goldfish and started getting good-paying parts. By that time Miss Dunstable was working for Carstairs. Evidently she'd sought him out because he was known to work with picture people. That way, she'd have inside information on who was doing what and who was being sued, and who was trying to cover up things they didn't want anyone to know. She was the one who first realized Hedda Heartwood didn't earn her entire living by writing her gossip column."

I felt my eyes widen. "You mean she blackmailed other people, too?"

Nodding, Phil said, "I guess she had a thriving business going. I'm kind of surprised nobody'd murdered her before the Flynt sisters got to her."

"Gracious sakes." I pondered my meeting with Hedda Heartwood. "She did kind of look like a weasel. I guess she acted like one, too."

"Apparently she did."

"Are you going to release Rupert Mullins now?" I admit I sounded a trifle belligerent, but that's only because I'd known ever since they'd arrested Rupert that they'd incarcerated the wrong man.

"That's already done," said Phil in a soothing sort of voice.

"Good." I didn't feel like being soothed, darn it. "I hope Lulu knows he's out of the clink."

"She's the one who came and picked him up."

I lifted my chin and sniffed. "Good. And what a monumental miscarriage of justice *that* was."

"Justice wasn't bruised, Mercy." Ernie sounded bored. "You just don't understand tactics."

"Tactics, my foot! It was *wrong* to arrest him, and *I* knew it, even if *you* didn't! Why, that poor boy might be damaged for life from this experience."

"Oh, brother."

I'd probably have argued some more, but at that point James Carstairs entered the police station. He looked less dapper than usual. I suppose that was to be expected. After all, he'd not only lost a promising client in Miss Lloyd, who'd turned out to be a murderer, but he'd also lost his secretary, who was also one. A murderer, I mean. He seemed to brighten slightly when he saw me, and he removed his hat politely and said, "Good afternoon, Miss Allcutt."

"How do you do?" I said, also politely.

"Not so well," he muttered. Turning to Phil, he demanded, "Where's Jacqueline? Where's Sylvia? This has got to be some kind of terrible mistake."

"It's no mistake, I'm afraid," said Phil. He sounded as if he felt kind of sorry for Mr. Carstairs. "They both confessed to the murders of Mrs. Heartwood and Mr. Hartland."

"Oh, my God." Mr. Carstairs sank into one of the chairs near Phil's desk and slapped his hat into his lap. "This is just awful."

Ernie said, "And Dunstable would have killed Miss Allcutt if we hadn't found her in time."

"She would have killed me if I hadn't saved myself, you mean!" I glared daggers at Ernie, who scowled back.

"Good God," said Mr. Carstairs. "I had no idea. And here I thought she was such an efficient secretary and overall pleasant person."

I sniffed. "So did I until she pulled a gun on me."

Ernie grunted. I ignored him and gave Mr. Carstairs a sympathetic smile.

"I'm so sorry, Miss Allcutt."

"It wasn't you who pulled the gun," I told him, feeling rather noble.

"I guess not, but I'm still sorry about it." He offered me a weak smile, Mr. Carstairs said, "Say, Miss Allcutt, you wouldn't be interested in a change of employment, would you? I'm sure I can pay you more than he can." He hooked a thumb at Ernie.

Ernie said, "Hey!" He looked like he wanted to kill someone— undoubtedly me, although he probably wouldn't mind shooting Mr. Carstairs along with me.

As angry as I was at Ernie right then, I darned near took Mr. Carstairs up on the offer. Squinting at him and then at Ernie, and deciding they both were despicable creatures, I said, "Let me think about it."

Ernie said, "Hey!" again.

I said, "Hmph," and spent a few minutes thinking about all the movie stars I might meet if I worked for Mr. Carstairs while Phil continued to divulge information about the Hartland cases. He didn't tell me anything I hadn't already deduced on my own, thereby proving that I *was* a good detective, in spite of what Ernie thought of my deductive powers.

Naturally, I wasn't about to change employers. As irritating as Ernie Templeton could be a good deal of the time, I knew in my heart that I'd learn more about the human condition by working with him than by working for Mr. Carstairs. After all, Ernie dealt with *real* problems. Mr. Carstairs dealt with the fantasy world of the motion pictures. Although, as had just been demonstrated, sometimes the sordidness of the "real" world slopped over into the pictures. Or vice versa.

I must have sighed pretty heavily because Ernie startled me by rising to his feet and saying, "I've got to get Mercy home, Phil. It's been a long day, and her mother won't be happy with her condition." He gave me one of his insouciant grins, and I only barely restrained myself from kicking him again.

"That's probably a good idea," said Phil, and he, too, rose.

So did Mr. Carstairs. "Think about my offer, Miss Allcutt. You'd be privy to all sorts of inside information." He smiled a winning smile.

I didn't feel like smiling back. I was sore, scraped, achy, and, as our Irish cook used to say back in Boston, mad as a wet hen. Nevertheless I rose, trying to be graceful, from the hard wooden chair I'd been sitting in for what seemed like all eternity, and I *did* smile when I said, "Thank you, Mr. Carstairs." Then I stopped smiling, turned to Ernie and said, "I'll be fine, thank you. I don't need *you* to take me home."

"Nuts." Ernie grabbed my arm. "You're in no shape to go anywhere alone."

Rather than make a scene in the police department, I only hissed, "Curse you, Ernie Templeton! Release my arm!"

"Not until you're tucked safely away in my Studebaker, damn it."

And he hauled me across the floor and out the door and into the late-evening sunshine of that sultry August day. I didn't have the will or the energy to fight him. Curse me, too.

Mother hit the roof when I finally got home that day. Mrs. Biddle opened the door to Ernie and me—he wouldn't even let me walk to Chloe's door unaided, the fiend—and I tried to slither out of the way and up the stairs before anyone else saw me, but my maneuverings didn't work. I hadn't really expected them too. Mother's had a whole lot of experience in thwarting my intentions, and she'd become an expert at it over the years.

"Mercedes Louise Allcutt, look at you!"

I couldn't help myself. I glanced down at my filthy person. I was a mess, all right.

"What do you have to say for yourself, young lady?" Mother demanded.

"Um . . ."

"Mother," said Chloe, bless her heart, "Mercy's obviously had a very difficult day. Let her get cleaned up before you cross-examine her."

"*Cross-examine* her? What kind of language is that, Clovilla Allcutt Nash?" Mother turned her icy, infuriated eyes upon her older daughter. While her attention was off me, I fled. I know I was being cowardly, but I couldn't seem to help myself. It had been a really awful day, and all I wanted was Buttercup and a bath. Not together, naturally. I hurried up the stairs to my room as fast as my cuts and bruises would allow, listening to Chloe and Mother go at it in the entryway. Chloe was the best sister any girl could have, and I vowed I'd make this up to her somehow, someday.

Unfortunately, bathing, cuddling Buttercup, and using iodine and bandages on my various wounds didn't take the rest of my life. It only took about forty-five minutes, and then I knew it was my duty to go downstairs and confront my family. So I did, my poor knees throbbing with every step. I held Buttercup in my arms as a sort of buffer, although I knew I wasn't being kind to her, my precious poodle. Then again, what are dogs for if not to offer aid and comfort to the afflicted? And, darn it, I was afflicted. What's more, I knew I was going to suffer still more affliction once I hit the bottom of the staircase and had to go face the music. Or, rather, face my mother, which was infinitely worse.

Trying not to hobble and still holding Buttercup, I made my way toward the living room. I was surprised to hear a good deal of conversation therefrom. Was that Francis Easthope's cultured voice I discerned?

And—good Lord—was *Ernie* still there? Hadn't Mother tossed him out on his ear *yet?*

Thinking that perhaps all wasn't lost and that the evening might not be as hellishly miserable as I'd anticipated, I entered the room. I'd had to wash my hair, and it wasn't quite dry yet, but thanks to my shingled bob it fell neatly into place anyway. No matter what my mother thinks, short hair is ever so much more practical than long hair. I'd also clad myself in a neat dress of blue georgette that fell a little below my knees. I figured that although Chloe would disapprove, claiming I was looking dowdy, the length covered the worst of my knee scrapes. One of these days, I simply *had* to get myself a pair of those long Chinese pajama things that Chloe liked to wear indoors.

"So it was her intransigence that led to her being in danger?"

My mother. I couldn't tell whom she was talking to but knew darned well whom she was talking about. I decided I'd better hang back a bit while I figured who exactly was in the living room. She didn't sound as angry as she had when she'd met me at the door, but her tone was still awfully chilly.

"Well, I don't know that I'd call it intransigence exactly."

Ernie. And, by George, he sounded as if he was almost sticking up for me! Would wonders never cease?

"She's just got this idea that she wants to be a detective and she won't be dissuaded."

Ernie again, and I wasn't so pleased with him this time.

"She's always been a disobedient child. I don't know what will become of her."

"She only wants some independence, Mother," said Chloe, my heaven-sent sister.

"She helped me out a good deal."

It *was* Francis Easthope! Bless his heart, too.

Mother said, "Hmph."

"No, really," Mr. Easthope insisted. "She was a big help to me. She found me a houseboy, she knew exactly what to do when poor Mrs. Hartland dropped dead, and she really *did* figure out who had perpetrated the crimes, which I think was remarkably clever of her. You must admit that much, Mr. Templeton and Mrs. Allcutt."

My mother said, "Hmph" again.

Ernie joined her in the "Hmph."

Bother them both. I was about to stride manfully into the living room when the front doorbell rang. Deciding to buy myself another few minutes of peace before facing my mother, I opted to open the door. Mrs. Biddle was probably busy in the kitchen anyway.

I heard Chloe say, "I wonder who that can be?" but that's the last thing I remember hearing, because a great roaring in my head drowned out everything else.

"Father!"

CHAPTER EIGHTEEN

I very nearly dropped my beloved Buttercup. I think I didn't do so only because my fingers spasmed of their own volition.

Father looked grim. "Good evening, Mercedes. Is your mother here?"

"M-m-mother?"

"Yes." He frowned heavily down upon me.

My father, like my mother, is an imposing presence. He's tall—none of his offspring, even my obnoxious brother, had dared grow to his height—good-looking, and has steel-gray hair and a small moustache. I stared up at him, gaping and swallowing for I don't know how long until he restored me to my wits by a censorious, "Mercedes, what is the matter with you?"

I know I jumped. However, when I landed, I had come to what was left of my senses. "Yes! I mean, nothing is the matter with me. I was only surprised to see you." For all his stature and grim visage, my father doesn't frighten me nearly as much as my mother does, probably because he has shown himself to be human once or twice since I'd met him. Well, you know what I mean.

In fact, as if to prove his humanity, he smiled at last. "You look well, Mercedes. And is that a pup I see in your arms?"

"Yes. Yes, this is Buttercup, my toy poodle." I made a leap backward. "But please come in, Father! I'm sorry. I forgot my manners because I was so—"

"Yes," he said dryly. "I can tell."

He walked into the entryway. I glanced behind him and saw no luggage. What did this mean? Darned if I knew. All I knew was that here standing before me was the instrument of my mother's presence in Los Angeles, and I wanted to beg him to reform his wicked ways. In Boston, however, well-bred daughters of wealthy bankers didn't do such things, so I merely tried to catch my breath.

"Your mother is here?" he asked patiently.

"Oh! Oh, yes. Yes, she is. Um . . ." I felt *so* stupid. "Do you want to . . . um, see her?"

I knew he'd have rolled his eyes if he'd been a lesser man. He was Mr. Albert Monteith Allcutt, however, so he didn't. "Yes."

Oh, dear. Oh, dear. Oh, dear. I knew both of my parents were too stuffy to create a scene in Chloe's living room, but I wasn't looking forward to their meeting. Nevertheless, I knew where my duty lay. "Come right on this way, Father. I'll lead you to her. There are some other . . . er, guests here, too."

"Hmm."

He didn't seem particularly gratified to know that his reunion with his runaway spouse would take place in front of people who didn't belong to the family. I, on the other hand, felt a measure of security from the same set of circumstances.

I thought of something that might be nice. "Um, would you like to stay in the library while I fetch her? Perhaps you'd like to—"

"That sounds like a sensible notion, Mercy."

I knew he'd forgiven me for whatever sins he might have been holding against me when he called me Mercy. I heaved an enormous internal sigh—I'd never dare sigh openly in front of either of my parents. "It's right here, Father."

"Thank you, my dear."

"Sure."

After turning on the light and watching him walk into the

room—a very nice room, by the way, with lots of books and a big, old desk where Harvey did a lot of work having to do with the studio—I hesitated at the door for a moment. "Um . . . have you been well, Father?"

"Quite well, thank you." He peered at me through narrowed eyes. I held my breath. "I must say that your new hairstyle suits you, my dear."

"It does? I mean, thank you!"

"What have you been doing since you moved west, Mercy? Your mother and I were worried that you'd lose your way and begin to behave in the deplorably frivolous manner of so many people involved in the motion-picture business."

"Oh, I'm not at all frivolous, Father," I assured him. "In fact, I have a really good job." If you discounted an irritable employer who treated me as if I didn't have a brain in my head. And maybe a few bruises and scratches. And if you ignored my being shot at several times in the past month or two. I heaved another internal sigh.

"You have secured employment?"

He didn't sound nearly as disapproving as Mother had. I perked up minimally. "Yes, indeed. I'm confidential secretary to Mr. Ernest Templeton, who is a private investigator."

"Oh."

There it was. Now he disapproved of me.

Before he could say so, I said brightly, "I'll go get Mother." And I hared it out of there with my darling Buttercup before he could even open his mouth again.

"Oh, Lord, Buttercup, what's going to happen now?" I squeezed her hard, but she didn't seem to mind.

I must have looked a little pale or something when I walked into the living room, because Ernie stood up. So did Mr. East-hope and Harvey, but they *always* stand upon a lady's entry into a room. Ernie only stood up when females other than yours truly waltzed into his presence.

"What's the matter?" he demanded sharply.

Chloe said, "Who was that at the door, Mercy?" She appeared a trifle concerned, too.

I cleared my throat and looked at our mother. "Um . . . Mother?"

She scowled at me. "What is it, Mercedes Louise? Mr. Templeton has regaled us with your outlandish activities of this afternoon, and I can't believe even *you* would—"

Darn her, anyhow! "It's Father!" I spoke quite loudly in order to drown out her tirade. What's more, my words shut her right up. Good for me.

"Father?" Chloe's eyes went as big around as pie plates.

"Albert?" Mother, on the other hand, sounded weak for the first time ever. "Albert is *here?*"

"He's waiting for you in the library."

"I . . ." I saw Mother swallow. This evening she was clad in navy blue bombazine suitable for a dinner party in Boston, and totally inappropriate for a hot Los Angeles night among friends and family. "Very well. I shall go to the library."

She rose stiffly and just as stiffly made her way across the living room. We all watched her until she'd cleared the door, then Chloe and I exchanged a speaking glance. Chloe held her finger to her lips, but she needn't have worried. I wasn't about to say anything at all until I heard that library door close. To be on the safe side, I peeked. It was only when I saw for myself that Mother had entered the library that I dared speak again.

"Chloe!" I whispered. "Father!"

"Yes," she said, sounding every bit as stricken as I felt.

"Did we expect him?" Harvey asked pleasantly. Harvey was always pleasant. And his query wasn't odd, either, since he left the running of the household in Chloe's capable hands entirely and never knew who was going to show up when.

"No," said Chloe upon a difficult swallow. "No, we had no idea he'd be coming to Los Angeles."

"Oh," said Harvey. "Well, I supposed you'd best have Mrs. Biddle set another place at the table."

"Yes." Chloe rose and walked like an automaton toward the dining room.

"My goodness," said Mr. Easthope.

"Is he anything like your ma?" That, naturally, was Ernie, who was probably the only person in the known universe who would dare refer to my mother as anybody's "ma."

Harvey chuckled. "He's a little bit like her."

"Not nearly so bad, though." I was getting myself under control at last. The absence of my mother speeded up the calming process considerably. "He's stuffy, I guess, but he's more . . ." I couldn't think of a word or expression to describe my father that wouldn't make me sound like an undutiful daughter.

Fortunately, Harvey took the problem out of my hands. "Human," he said succinctly.

I nodded, feeling rather forlorn.

Ernie laughed. "Thank God for that."

"Yes. I fear your mother is a bit of a dragon, Miss Allcutt," said Francis Easthope.

"You have *no* idea," said I, and was instantly stricken with pangs of conscience.

Chloe rushed into the room just then. She, too, was over the initial shock of our father's arrival. She scurried over, sat next to me on the sofa, and started frantically petting Buttercup. "Oh, Mercy, what does this mean?"

I shook my head. "I don't know."

"What did Father say?"

"He only asked if Mother was here. And when I asked if he'd like to wait for her in the library, he said that was a good idea."

I gulped. "I was afraid of what might happen if I just hauled him in here, you see."

"Thank God!" Chloe's gaze visited the ceiling for an instant. Then she left off patting Buttercup and clutched my arm. "Oh, Mercy, do you think he's going to take her back home to Boston?" I could hear the fervent note of hope in her voice.

"I don't know. He didn't say."

"Oh, Lord. I guess he's not as bad as she is, but . . . oh, Mercy, what if he wants to stay here with us, too? In this house?"

Totally crestfallen, I could only whisper, "What an appalling thought."

Ernie, the rat, still chuckled. I glanced at him, but he didn't seem to be affected by my repressive expression.

"Oh, my," said Mr. Easthope. "One's parents can be so difficult, can't they?"

"They sure can," said Chloe.

"Well, I suppose it wouldn't matter so much if we had more room," said Harvey, who was one of the nicest people in the known universe. He and Chloe were such a special couple.

Chloe and I chorused, "Yes, it would!"

More chuckles from Ernie.

Mr. Easthope sighed. "Perhaps we should find a place for our combined parents. They could stay together and make each other miserable and leave us alone."

I'd never heard him say anything that so clearly expressed his distress over his mother and her feckless ways.

Chloe said, "Oh, Francis, I'm sorry. Is she still in thrall to those charlatans?"

"Actually," said he, "the O'Doyles are going back to Saint Louis, or wherever they came from, tomorrow. I think the atmosphere in Los Angeles was getting a little too hot for them."

"I think they were probably crooks," I said. "Will they take that spooky man with them? What was his name? Fernandez?"

"Yes, thank God, they're going to take Fernandez with them."

"He gave me the creeps," I admitted.

"He gave *me* the creeps," said Mr. Easthope.

"Well, that's one good thing, anyway. They'll soon be out of your hair and your mother won't be fleeced by them any longer."

"I suppose so. But now she's convinced she was born to be a horticulturist. She's pestering my gardener about planting peonies and rhododendrons and all sorts of things like that that don't grow well in Los Angeles. My gardener just gave notice, and he kept the grounds looking wonderful."

"Hmm," I said. "There's a huge section on plants and gardening at the public library. Perhaps you can take her there and set her loose. Surely she could learn which plants grow well here and which plants don't."

"I'm not so sure," said Francis glumly. "She doesn't take well to direction."

I think one of my teachers said something like that about me once, but I didn't mention it—not with Ernie there. And anyhow, it wasn't true. I just like to believe there's some good reason for me to learn things, is all, and I never did understand a particular need to learn algebra. "Parents can be *such* a problem," I said in deep sympathy.

Ernie laughed harder. Blast the man. I turned on him. "Don't you have any parents?"

"Sure, I have parents. They're in New Jersey, and they don't bother me."

"Never?"

He shook his head. "Nope. We get along great."

Chloe and I shared a glance, and Chloe said, "Mercy and I got along with our parents when they were in Boston and we were in Los Angeles."

"True," I said.

Chloe glanced at the cuckoo clock she and Harvey had picked

up in Germany when they took their honeymoon in Europe. "I had Mrs. Biddle set dinner back a half hour. I hope to heaven the parents are finished talking by then, or Mrs. Biddle might give her own notice."

"She'd never do that!" I cried, shocked. Mrs. Biddle seemed as much a part of the Nash household as did Chloe and Harvey.

"I don't know. You really scared her last month when you went in to ask her if you could help wash windows."

"I never did that! I only asked her what she recommended for cleaning windows so I could spruce up Ernie's office!"

Chloe grinned. "I guess you didn't tell her that part. She was worried for a while."

"Phooey. I only borrowed the Bon Ami for a day, and then I brought it right back again."

We didn't have time to pursue my habits of cleanliness, because Mother and Father entered the room. As if we were gathered for a royal visitation, we all rose to our feet. Even Buttercup stood to attention.

They didn't look as if they were still mad at each other. Chloe and I swapped yet another glance, this one questioning.

Mother and Father stood under the archway leading to the living room, and I noticed that Mother had her arm tucked under his. Was that a good sign? Who knew?

It was Father who broke the ice. "Well, well, well, I see you have some guests, Clovilla. Won't you please introduce them to me?"

Chloe jerked as if he'd pinched her, and then quickly made introductions. I noticed that Father's gaze remained on Ernie longer than it did anyone else. I held my breath.

"So you're the young man who's employing my daughter Mercedes?"

"Yes, sir," said Ernie, shaking Father's hand. He actually

comported himself with propriety and dignity for once in his life. Well, I don't know if that's the *only* time he's ever been polite, but it sure seemed like it to me.

"I trust she's pulling her weight in the business."

Ernie shot me a look, and I gave him a quick, meaningful scowl. "Yes, sir. She's a pistol all right."

"A pistol, is she?" Father sounded skeptical, but he left Ernie when Chloe introduced him to Mr. Easthope.

Francis Easthope was ever the gentleman, and he was suavity itself as he took Father's hand and shook it. He even gave a teensy bow. "Mr. Allcutt."

"Mr. Easthope."

And that was it for them.

Harvey and Father already knew each other, and exchanged all the proper greetings and expressions of pleasure. And that's another thing. Harvey had met our parents before he married Chloe, and he married her anyway. You have to honor a man like that.

Somehow, we all got through dinner. It was probably quite tasty, since it always is, but I can't even remember what was served.

After dinner, Mother regaled Father with my many sins, concluding with what she termed a "shootout" with a murderer that very afternoon. Father raised his eyebrows but didn't scold me. I must admit to being a trifle surprised. Perhaps, given his own foibles, he'd softened his attitude toward his children somewhat. Unlikely, but you never knew.

"And, Chloe and Mercedes, your father and I have decided to visit Pasadena and see if we can find a suitable winter home there. It's such a lovely community."

"A . . . a winter home?" Chloe stammered.

"Yes."

"In P-pasadena?" That was my shaky contribution.

"Yes."

And then Mother did something I'd never have anticipated if I'd been given all eternity to do so.

She admitted she'd been wrong.

"I fear I leapt to a rather tasteless conclusion, my dears."

Good God! She was even calling us her dears! I sneaked a peek at Chloe, who was doing likewise at me.

"Your father's secretary, Miss Jenkins, had just become engaged when I visited the office. Albert was wishing her the very best of luck." She took a deep breath and apologized. She *apologized*. The speaking looks whizzing between Chloe and me that evening could have filled the Grand Canyon. "I'm terribly sorry for my impulsiveness."

"That's perfectly all right, my dear. It's all forgotten now."

Not by Chloe and me. You could bet your life on that.

"I've always thought her a lovely girl," Mother said condescendingly.

"She's marrying my chief cashier, Robert Goodhugh," Father put in, looking almost happy. Boy, *that* didn't happen often. "I'm sure they'll make a most suitable couple."

Suitable. Hmm. I guess that was a good thing.

As if reacting to a cue given offstage, Mother and Father rose to their feet. Father said, "Well, my dears, I must thank you for a most delightful evening. Honoria and I will be repairing to the Melrose Hotel, where I've stashed my belongings. We'll be back tomorrow to pick up her traps."

And they left us there. I'm not sure about the others, because I could only stare at the retreating backs of my parents, but my mouth was hanging open.

As soon as the door opened, Chloe and I leaped to our feet and threw ourselves into each other's arms.

"It can't be true," I cried.

"It had better not be," cried Chloe back at me.

"What can't be true?" Ernie. "I thought you'd be happy that they'd reconciled."

We whirled as one to face the men. I said, "Of course, we're happy that they've reconciled."

"Naturally. Good God, I can't even *imagine* what life would be like if Mother decided to live with Harvey and me for all eternity," said Chloe.

"So what's the problem? Sounds like all your troubles have come to a satisfactory conclusion."

"Shows how much you know," I said bitterly.

Ernie lifted an ironical eyebrow.

Chloe and I exchanged one last speaking look. Actually, it was more a look of mutual horror. It was I who explained things to Ernie. "Our parents are going to be moving to California! That's the worst thing that's ever happened to us!"

Ernie only laughed.

"Bite him, Buttercup," I commanded.

But she didn't. I swear, sometimes you can't even rely on your best friend.

ABOUT THE AUTHOR

Award-winning author **Alice Duncan** lives with a herd of wild dachshunds (enriched from time to time with fosterees from New Mexico Dachshund Rescue) in Roswell, New Mexico. She's not a UFO enthusiast; she's in Roswell because her mother's family settled there fifty years before the aliens crashed. Since her two daughters live in California, where Alice was born, she aims to return there as soon as possible. Alice would love to hear from you at alice@aliceduncan.net. And be sure to visit her website at http://www.aliceduncan.net.